NIGHT VISION

Also By Frank King

THE ANONYMOUS PORNOGRAPHIC GENRE

DOWN AND DIRTY

NightVision

FRANK KING

RICHARD MAREK PUBLISHERS
NEW YORK

Library of Congress Cataloging in Publication Data

King, Frank, date.
  Night vision.

  I. Title.
PZ4.K52155Ni   [PS3561.I4755]   813'.5'4   78-24599
ISBN 0-399-90041-1

PRINTED IN THE UNITED STATES OF AMERICA

For Sandor Ferenczi

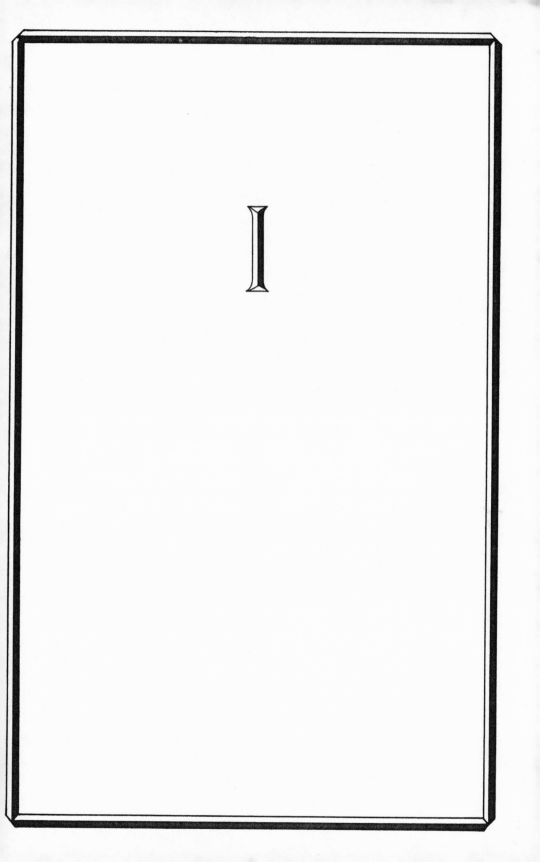

Between four and six P.M. Paul Stanislas saw no patients. He put on a record of Mahler's *Kindertotenlieder*, lay down on the couch his patients also used, and slept. He needed a nap each day because he rarely slept well in the evening.

When he napped on that cold Thursday in 1977, he had a dream. It was a simple dream. He was walking on a beach. It was night. He started to dig for a clam near the water's edge. From the hole came a gigantic, grotesque green man. The figure said nothing, but swiftly took his watch, his wallet, and his shoelaces. Then the green man fell back into the hole and vanished.

Paul awoke, mouth dry, head aching. He looked at the clock. It was five forty-five. The patient, Margaret Olsen, was due in twenty-five minutes.

Stanislas walked to the window, pulled back a simple brown curtain, and watched the river. The Hudson was ugly in late autumn, very ugly.

A movement in the park below, beside the river, caught his eye. Two figures were walking arm in arm. They stopped and embraced. The wind caught their hair and snaked it around their necks. The figures disentangled and continued their walk.

That sudden and brief passion in anonymous strangers brought forth an equally sudden and brief weakness in his body, as if something had been sucked out of him.

He walked into the small patients' bathroom and threw some cold water on his face. Then he patted his face, rather than wiping it.

He walked to his desk, sat down, opened the top drawer and

took out a small yellow pad. There were two sizes of pads in the drawer. One was large; he used this size for notes on patients. The other was small; he used this size for incidental jottings. On the small size pad he wrote: *green man—dream*. Then he put the pad back into the drawer and closed it.

Paul Stanislas was thirty-eight years old and a very successful practicing psychoanalyst. He was just under six feet tall and weighed just under one hundred and eighty pounds, well distributed on a frame that absorbed squash, sailing, and an ocassional jog through the park. He was dark, and some people called him ugly, though this was often the result of the perpetual scowl he seemed to wear on his face, rather than his physiognomy. He did have a cramped face. The eyes were too wide apart, the nose too small, the chin jutted too much.

He always dressed casually, and the same. A corduroy suit—either blue, black, or brown—and an open white shirt.

On his desk, framed, was a small crayon drawing. It was a picture of a dog next to a tree. The dog was yellow and the tree was black. A green sun was overhead.

Stanislas's nine-year-old daughter, Emily, had presented it to him on his thirty-eighth birthday. He reached over and moved it a bit with his hand, away from the ashtray.

He was suddenly very glad that he had decided to move his family out of New York City to the wooded North Shore of Long Island and keep the cavernous West Side apartment for his patients, and for himself to sleep in during the week. Emily was better off there. City kids, he had always reasoned, were tougher but not better off. No, never better off. City kids painted black suns.

As for his wife—well, Deirdre might have liked the city better, but it really didn't matter because she wouldn't be happy anywhere anymore, except, perhaps, in the grave. Except perhaps in the grave, he repeated to himself and wondered whether he had obtained the phrase from a poem.

A bell rang. It was Margaret Olsen. He reached down and buzzed her in. She would wait the remaining few minutes in what was once the dining room of the apartment but had been redone to approximate a sitting room.

Paul leaned back in his chair, remembering where they were

the last session. He usually made tapes of all sessions, with the patient's assent only, of course. But for this session, he hadn't played the previous session's tape over. It really didn't matter. He knew Margaret Olsen. She had been his patient for three years and she was getting better, much better. He stood up, walked to the door, opened it, and said softly: "Margaret."

None of the patients had shoes. And none of the patients had belts around their pajama bottoms. So they shuffled, hither and thither, holding up their pants with their hands.

Ward 25C housed only sixteen men. All were convicted criminals who had committed violent crimes. All were in varying states of psychosis. Their psychoses, however, were now blunted and made gentle with a regimen of sedative drugs.

Two attendants were in constant circulation on the ward, and another was at the enclosed desk. The attendants wore light blue jackets.

The patients had just finished shaving. Each one was accompanied into the bathroom by an attendant, given a safety razor, and carefully watched until the chore was complete.

This morning no activity was planned. Occupational therapy was held only three times a week, and this was not one of the days. It was raining outside, so there could be no exercise yard. The attendants laid out a series of chess and checker sets and turned on the television which was suspended high on one wall, out of the reach of all the inmates.

John Ligur stood in one corner of the ward. One hand held his pajamas up, the other moved in a slow pattern—from his genitals to his shoulder to his forehead. It was as if his right hand were playing a baseball game and running all the bases.

He was short, powerfully built, light complexioned, and while almost bald, a thin fuzz of red hair could still be seen. John Ligur was thirty-one years old and he would never see the light of freedom again. His career had progressed from shoplifting and car theft to armed robbery to rape and child molestation to murder.

"Watch that sonofabitch," said one of the attendants to a colleague as they both set the chess and checker pieces up.

"Who?"

"There," came the reply, and a finger pointed out Ligur.

"Why?"

"Roth has him on minimum dosage."

The patients began to walk. This walking was almost an infection, an epidemic. It would start suddenly, silent bodies walking the length of the ward, then turning and walking back—and it would stop as suddenly as it started.

Ligur didn't walk. As each walking patient passed him, however, he did stare at him and blink his eyes once—while the movement of his right hand never stopped.

Ligur walked to a spot under the television set, watched the screen for a moment, and then squatted down. A minute later he was up, walking to one of the tables which held the checker sets.

He sat down and stared straight ahead. An attendant sat down and asked him:

"Want to play, John?"

"What is your name?" Ligur responded.

"You know my name, John."

"Who moves first?" asked Ligur.

"You."

Ligur reached out, gently lifted a checker and moved it one space.

The attendant made his move. Ligur sat back and stared at the board. A minute passed. Five minutes passed.

"Your move again, John," the attendant finally said.

Ligur picked up one of his opponent's pieces and moved that. The attendant just placed the checker back on its original square and shook his head.

"You move black, John."

Ligur smiled. Then he picked up another white piece and moved it—backward.

The attendant patiently put the piece back where it had been.

"You move black," he said again.

Ligur's right hand began to make the triangular path from genitals to shoulder to forehead. He stared at the board.

"Do you want to play?" the attendant asked.

Ligur didn't respond. Instead he began to pick up all the white checkers and stack them neatly on one side. Then he picked up all the black checkers and stacked them on the other side. Then he folded the board.

Then he picked up the board, grasped it by one end, and slammed it over the attendant's right eye.

The blood spurted and the screams commenced at the same time. Ligur didn't move. The other two attendants came running. One of them grabbed a towel and pressed it over the bleeding eye.

"That stupid cunt, that stupid fucking Roth," he kept saying as he pushed the towel tighter and tighter against the spurting eye.

When the bleeding had stopped, they trussed Ligur in a restraining jacket, shoved three pills down his throat, and threw him in a room that was completely devoid of objects—but which had a window.

The session had been neither good nor bad. And when it was "neither," Margaret always walked home. South on Broadway until Columbus Circle and then east until she reached the small residence hotel that she had been living in for the past five years. It was expensive, but it was necessary. Three times a week, when she came back from work, the room would be cleaned, the bedding and towels changed, the ashtrays emptied and washed. And the rug was vacuumed. She took care of the small kitchenette herself. Yes, it was worth it.

She opened the door of her apartment, kept the lights off, and made herself a cup of tea. It was already dark out. She wrapped her palms around the thick cup. It felt good. She lit a cigarette, flicked on the kitchen light, and made a small slash mark on a pad which rested on the edge of the kitchen table. It was the seventh slash, which meant it was her seventh cigarette of the day.

Margaret Olsen was a beautiful woman. Tall, heavily built, with broad shoulders. She had been born and raised in Maryland, came to New York when she left college after her junior year, and after a series of job debacles, now held a responsible position with a New York City planning agency.

But Margaret Olsen was neither well, nor happy, nor in con-

trol of anything—except perhaps for the teacup which she cradled in her palms. She could not understand people and people
could not really understand her. The most mundane conversation was a struggle, and often ended in a battle, or weeks upon
weeks of reflection by Margaret on what was said, who said it,
what was really meant.

As for men, there were none. Twice in her twenty-nine years
she had slept with a man. And twice it had been disastrous. The
penis elicited horror, fright, and ultimately nausea in her. When
the men had entered her, she had felt that she was being murdered, literally; that she was being torn apart; that she was being
violated in a fashion that was so bizarre and obscene it had never
been captured in a book, on a film, on a record.

And then there were her lists. Her infernal lists. Lists of fruit.
Lists of places she would like to go. Lists of attributes in a male
that she supposed would lessen or hide or transform the reality
of the penis. Lists of people she had known in Maryland. Lists of
books she would like to read and lists of books she had read.

Lists of cigarettes she had smoked and money she had spent—
and sometimes lists of symbols that she herself didn't know the
meanings of.

She finished the tea and lay down on the bed. In the past after
a session, she would often go home, lie down, and masturbate,
the face and hands of Paul Stanislas in front of her.

She remembered the slight smile about Paul's face when she
had told him, after those first few sessions three years ago, that
she loved him.

Margaret had never heard then of transference. And for a long
time she had truly believed that it didn't exist in fact. That it
was all theory, bullshit, all without empirical proof. That she
loved him—isolated from the analysis, isolated from Freud, isolated from everything.

Things were much better now. Paul said so. She believed it.
She was calmer, much calmer. There were no problems at work.
There was none of that immense exhaustion which used to follow each working day. She could walk a lot, and last week she
had even rented a bicycle—and that was good. Margaret fell
asleep.

The clock read midnight when she awoke. She jumped off the

bed. She felt very good, happy, alive. She decided to go to a bar. She would put on a nice dress, nice shoes, go to a bar and listen to some music as she got pleasantly high. And perhaps there would even be a man. Why not? Why not a man? She was better now.

Margaret slipped into a dress, her favorite: the pale brown one that emphasized her shoulders and angled her body. She put on brown Italian shoes that she had purchased more than five years ago and worn only two or three times.

She walked to the mirror and brushed her hair. It was short, thick, and brown, cut in a pageboy. She smiled at herself; her teeth were still good, and white.

Margaret lit a cigarette and made another slash mark on the pad. It was her eighth cigarette of the day. She put on her fall coat and walked to the door. Her hand felt the brass knob and started to turn. Nausea came suddenly, and then weakness. If there was a bar and music and whiskey, there would be a man. And if there was a man, there would be a penis. And suddenly she flung the small pocketbook across the room.

No, she would not go out tonight. Perhaps not any night. Perhaps there was nothing at all for her. Nothing, never, nowhere.

When Helene Roth was younger, she used to make a joke: "I'm feeling so good I feel five feet tall."

She had stopped making that joke many years ago. In fact, her height—or lack of it—didn't bother her at all anymore.

But as she sat on the leather chair in the director's office, which was the jewel of the hospital's administrative wing, she did notice that her shoes barely touched the carpet.

She hadn't any idea why she was summoned there. Then she heard the door open and a waspish voice said: "I'm sorry I'm late, Dr. Roth. Thank you for waiting."

The director walked softly to his desk and sat down. She had never seen a man walk so softly, as if the very placing of his feet would somehow disturb the physical nature of the universe.

He smiled at her. Helene smiled back at him.

"How have you been?" he asked.

"Well," she said, smiling, "and you?"

"Excellent. Just excellent."

She knew he was, like her, a few years past forty-five. But he looked twenty years older and he looked ill.

"I have bad news for you," he said.

"Are you dispensing with my services?"

"No." He smiled because he had said the "no" too quickly. Then he rearranged the desk so that the stapling machine was closer to the telephone.

"John Ligur attacked an attendant."

"When?"

"Yesterday morning. Rather, yesterday noon."

Helene crossed her legs. She opened a button of her brown tweed jacket. She would have to be careful now, she knew that. She would have to be very careful.

"Was anyone hurt?"

"The attendant—ten stitches in the eye."

"And . . ." She caught herself as she was about to say "John," and then said, ". . . Ligur?"

"Not hurt at all. He's in a room."

She knew what he meant. Ligur was alone, lying stretched out, dazed, his eyes going from window to wall, from wall to window. His body encased in the newest jacket, unable to make that motion with his hand. That motion from genitals to shoulder to forehead.

Helene spoke now in a formal voice. "What were the circumstances surrounding the assault?"   ⸱

The director waved a hand.

"Nothing at all. A game of checkers. Just a game of checkers."

Helene leaned forward and placed both hands in her lap. There would be more, she knew, much more.

"I understand," said the director, "that Ligur was on minimum dosage at the time." He stopped and waited for a response. But there was none, so he continued.

"I assume you are responsible for that."

"Yes," she said quietly.

"Ligur is a very dangerous man. Very dangerous. His record is readily available to the staff. Though I'm sure you're familiar with it."

"I am."

"Why, Dr. Roth, did you place him on minimum dosage?"

He asked the question in such a low voice she could barely hear him, but she knew what he was saying.

She leaned back. It would have to be a good lie, one that was medically sound, and one that would scratch the director's rather overt Christian conscience.

She lied well: "He had some bad drug reactions. Diarrhea, flaking skin, and what seemed to be the beginnings of bursitis."

"Was it reported? Recorded?"

"They were not yet that bad. I thought a lessening of the dosage was warranted on my own responsibility—and besides, he had seemed to be making some improvement."

She leaned forward again, to watch his response.

The director shook his head sadly. "Ligur is a very dangerous man. And a very unfortunate man."

"So I understand," she replied.

There was a long silence. The windows of the director's office looked down on the rolling hills of Dutchess County in upstate New York. When Helene had arrived at the hospital eight years ago, she could look out those windows and see the last remaining dairy farms in the area. Now they were gone. There were no more cows. But there were still rolling hills.

"Well," said the director wearily, "it was an unfortunate incident, from beginning to end. Let's hope it doesn't happen again. I know that the European tradition in psychiatry is much looser. I understand that. But with men like Ligur—well, one must be careful, and very formal."

Helene smiled at him. "I was born in Germany," she responded, "but I was raised in Canada, and all my medical training was in this country."

He bowed his head gently and smiled at the correction. The interview was over.

Helene closed the door behind her and walked to the end of the corridor. There was a window at the end with a screen mesh on the outside, even though no patients were housed in the administrative wing.

She was very frightened. Things had been going well, and now a mistake. At least the mistake had been tactical and not strategic. She looked at the mesh. Her mesh was better. The mesh she was creating was infinitely stronger, and more powerful, and more beautiful. She was interlocking minds—and perhaps what used to be called souls. What were they called now? She laughed out loud. She didn't really know.

They call the place Cold Spring Harbor. And each Friday afternoon as Paul Stanislas boarded the Long Island Railroad to rejoin his family there, he longed for it. The moment, however, he was picked up at the station by his wife and driven home—and on the drive could see the waters of Long Island Sound and the circling gulls and could smell the trees and the gravel and the water—he wished he were elsewhere.

This Friday was not different. Deirdre, however, looked well. She even smiled when he entered the car. And Emily was bouncing about in the back seat, chattering about everything.

There were lamb chops for supper. Lamb chops and fresh broccoli, and ice cream and coffee for dessert. Emily stopped chattering at the table and morosely forked her chop. Deirdre smoked constantly, eating a piece of meat, putting the fork down, taking a puff of the cigarette, then putting it down to take another bit of meat. He was always astonished at the brilliance of her choreography, though he wondered if one day she would become confused and cut the cigarette and attempt to smoke the chop.

"Do you like collages?"

He looked up at Deirdre. "Yes," he replied.

"What's a collage?" asked Emily.

Deirdre laughed, reached over to her daughter's plate and rearranged the lamb chop and what was left of the broccoli. Then she folded a paper napkin and placed it on an edge of the plate.

"That's a collage," she said.

Emily stared at the plate, perplexed. Finally her face lit up and she picked up the napkin, tore a hole in the center, hung it on her nose, and asked in a muffled voice if she was now a collage.

Her father laughed, and said yes emphatically. He finished trimming a piece of gristle from the meat, then decided to eat the gristle anyway.

"Why do you like collages?" Deirdre asked him.

He thought as he chewed, and then answered: "Disparate elements made coherent."

"Spoken like a true shrink," she said, laughing.

"Are you making a collage?"

"I am," she replied. "I have decided to make a collage out of our room."

He looked at her, wondering whether she was making a simple statement, or making a joke, or trying to tell him something in her elliptical style.

"Look at this," interjected Emily.

The girl had removed the napkin from her nose, rearranged the plate collage, and wrapped the paper around the shank of the chop.

"Well," said Paul, "she wasn't going to eat it anyway."

He looked at his daughter. He was glad he had never gone into child work. Children were too complex; too unformed. He knew what they were, theoretically. He knew that he loved one—his own daughter—but he had the intuition that in spite of her health, and energy, and humor, there was mystery and violence in her—and God knows what else that no one had ever elucidated, or ever would.

Emily was smiling at him. He smiled back. She cocked her head to one side and stuck out her tongue. He cocked his head to one side and made a face. And then the dinner dishes were cleared.

After dinner they walked down to the water. Bunches of mussels clung to the outcropping of rocks. The summer season was long over, but a few autumn sailors were still out, meandering around the coverts which dot that part of the Sound.

Deirdre took his arm as they walked, and once she reached over and kissed him gently on the neck. Emily was throwing stones in the water, trying to make them skip, unsuccessfully.

Paul disengaged himself from his wife, searched for and found a flat stone, and showed his daughter how to do it. The stone skipped four times. Deirdre and Emily both applauded.

They both sat down on a rock. Emily wandered off. Deirdre lit another cigarette. It was becoming chilly. He put his jacket collar up and thrust his hands into his pocket.

His fingers closed around something metallic in his right-
hand jacket pocket. He pulled it out. It was a long, thin cigarette
lighter, either of real gold or imitation gold. He had never seen it
before in his life. He turned it over and over, trying to place it.

"So, you finally bought me a present," Deirdre said.

"No, I didn't buy this. I don't know where I got it. Or how."

Deirdre took the lighter and looked at it. She flicked the top. It
sparked but didn't light.

"Brand-new," she said. "It has to be filled."

"I don't know where I got it."

"Did someone give it to you?"

"No."

In Pennsylvania Station he had wandered into a few stores
while waiting for the train. In the cutlery shop. In the card shop.
In the bookstore. But he had purchased nothing but a newspaper.
He didn't even remember seeing lighters. He didn't smoke. He
hadn't smoked for five years.

Stanislas retrieved the object from his wife. It had grown dark,
with only a few slivers of light filtering onto the dirty sand. He
rubbed the side of the lighter with his fingers. The golden color
expanded and retracted in the dim light, from pure gold to dross
and back to gold again.

Cheap, he thought, cheap. And the moment after he formulated those words, something clicked in his head, as if he was
thinking about the cheapness of lives. His life. About a human
being changing from gold to dross and then back again.

"Well," Deirdre said, laughing, "why don't you giftwrap it and
give it to me?"

"Take it," he said quickly. He got up and walked to the house.
He was feeling very uncomfortable. Deirdre and Emily followed
soon afterward.

Helene Roth stood outside the door which held Ligur. She was
waiting for an attendant to arrive with the keys. The staff had
been hostile, as she knew they would be, for one of their colleagues had been hurt and she was, in their scheme of things, the
cause. It was Sunday afternoon, and she had waited until Sunday
to visit Ligur because most of the regular staff would be off.

A young man approached, nodding deferentially to her white coat. He selected a key, tried it, then selected another one, which worked.

"Lock us in; I don't wish to be disturbed. Come back in fifteen minutes."

The attendant looked at her quizzically and then nodded. Helene Roth walked inside and heard the door shut behind her.

The room was bathed in sunlight. Ligur sat in a corner of the room. The restraining jacket had been removed. He was calmly staring up at the window.

She walked swiftly to his side and knelt. "Oh, God, I'm sorry," she said, her hand resting gently on his cheek. He didn't register the touch with his body. He just shook his head up and down, once.

Helene stood up, agitated, and walked to the far side of the room. She turned and looked at him. They had made sure he would not bother an attendant for some time. He looked so calm. There was a slight smile at the corners of his mouth. The powerful body was totally relaxed.

She walked back and knelt beside him again. Her hand went into the top of his pajama bottoms and moved downward until it touched his penis. She stroked him gently. She felt herself shaking.

There was no response. None at all. The penis lay limp. She brought her hand along the inside of the thighs, feeling the sinews. Then down under his scrotum, and returning to the penis. She moved away from him, and with a nervous gesture brushed the hair away from her eyes.

She stood up and walked beneath the window, trying to capture his line of vision. It was no use now. It would take a day or two.

The attendant came and finally let her out, locking the door again.

The grounds of the hospital were crowded with visitors. Helene Roth walked quickly toward the parking lot, entered her Buick, started the car, and drove out. Ten minutes later she was in the house she rented, which stood a few hundred feet off the main highway. It had once been the gatehouse of an estate, but the estate had vanished. It was stone, with good wood floors and a large fireplace. The stable, attached to the gatehouse, was now a garage. The house was warm in the winter and cool in the summer, and she loved it dearly. The grounds around it were overrun. One summer she had made an attempt to clear a small segment. She had gone so far as to plant tomatoes, eggplant, and lettuce, but the experiment died with the bugs.

It was a small house: living room, large kitchen, two bedrooms. One of the bedrooms she had converted into a study and it was lined with books and periodicals.

There was a pot of breakfast coffee on the stove. She heated it, poured a cup, and walked into the study. The study was dim; it received only morning light. She walked over to one bookcase. A bottom shelf was cleared of books; in their place were cassette tapes, each one labeled with a date, in order from left to right.

She picked out the earliest tape, the one on the far left, and inserted it into the tape deck which rested in front of the shelf on a sturdy wicker table. She sat on the chair and sipped her coffee as her own words, now almost seven years old, moved off the tape.

"Today I have been on the staff of Moorland Hospital for a year. I knew it was a year at three o'clock this afternoon when I was summoned to the director's office and there was greeted by the staff, and champagne and strawberries. It was a surprise party for me and I accepted the honor, if it can be considered an honor, as graciously and as mannerly as possible.

"But what do they think of me, or I of them? Perhaps the year was a trial period, to see if I really had purged myself of all allegiance to Freud and had embraced their chemical creed. In fact, I now disown both creeds, and all of them.

"Yet, Moorland is a fine hospital. I am often regaled with horror stories about what happens in other institutions for the criminally insane, and I believe the stories. Yes, Moorland is a fine hospital and perhaps I have found a home among the drugged rapists and killers and perverts, where I couldn't find a home among those witty anal compulsives in the city.

"I must begin to talk to my colleagues. I must begin to be more social. Surely they have something to say to me and I to them."

* * *

Helene stopped the tape abruptly. She had remembered what came next. She walked back to the chair, sipped the coffee, and watched the tape deck. Its mystery and potency had never ceased to fascinate her. Her own words had never ceased to frighten her. She walked back and flicked the switch.

"As for Paul Stanislas. As for him . . . more than a year has passed . . . more than a year. What is there to say? Love? Perhaps. And the most crushing hate. Hate that suffocates. There are still hours and days when I feel like a balloon that was once filled with precious metals and is now filled with dirt. Six months ago I thought of writing him a letter . . ."

This time Helene shut off the machine and pulled the tape out, replacing it quickly on the shelf. She walked over to another machine, the record player, and switched it on.

A record was already in place. She put the needle on the disc. It was *Kindertotenlieder*. She sat and listened and finished the cold coffee.

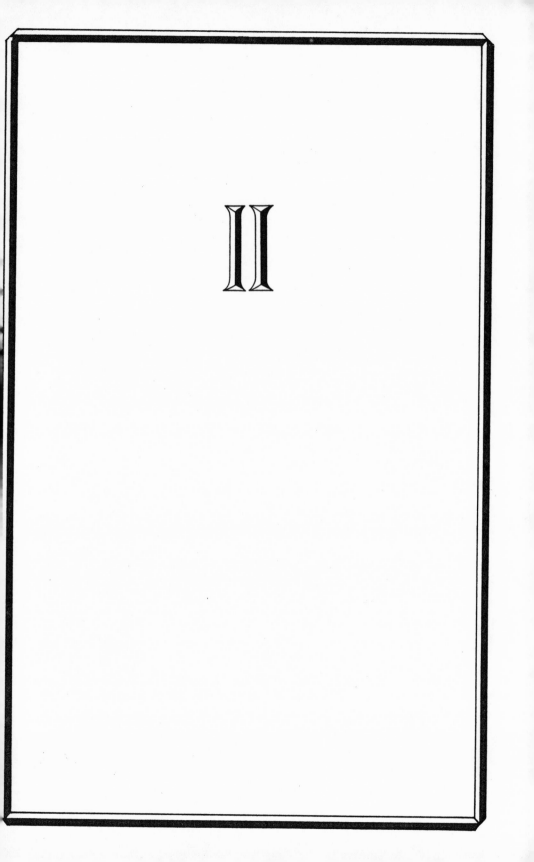

In the late afternoon, Margaret Olsen stared out the window of her cubicle. She could see the Statue of Liberty. She swiveled in her chair back to the desk. A sheaf of papers was piled neatly on the desk, and next to the sheaf were two magic markers, a black one and a red one. The walls of her cubicle were bare but for a single print of a Degas drawing of a horse which was hung over the desk.

Margaret was disgusted with herself because she had neglected to note the number of cigarettes already smoked during the day. Now she lit one. Was this her fifth, her eighth, or her tenth? She suspected it was more than five and less than ten.

She took up a small piece of memo paper from a tray and the red magic marker. She began to list those blocks on the Lower West Side on which she would like to live: "20th Street, 16th Street, 13th Street, 10th Street."

Then she realized what she was doing and ripped the memo to shreds.

Since arriving at work that Thursday morning, Margaret had been of the opinion that she was emitting a strange and not too pleasant body odor. On days that she saw Stanislas—and there was a session after work this day—strange things often beset her. But this, she thought, had nothing to do with the forthcoming session. There *was* an odor about her. But she couldn't determine the source, nor even give a precise description of it. The odor was similar to what she had encountered while growing up in Maryland, in the small inlets which were choked with weeds and scraps of wood and metal which had been washed or dumped there over the years.

Margaret had decided to avoid all her co-workers that day. She didn't want to break the uneasy truce which had been so laboriously constructed. She didn't want any of them to have the opportunity to say, "Did you get a whiff of Olsen today?" So she stayed alone in her cubicle and worked.

Now, as always on days she had a session, Margaret left work half an hour early and took the train uptown. There was still fifteen minutes to wait, so she ordered a cup of coffee at a small luncheonette on Broadway. The counterman was leering at her. She looked away. Sometimes she wanted a gun in her pocketbook so those leers could be blasted to eternity. She lit a cigarette, then realized abruptly that she had already lit one. Now there were two burning. She stared at the cigarettes, one in her hand and one in the ashtray, perplexed. What should be done? Which cigarette should be put out? The coffee was terrible. Probably it had been in the urn since morning. She poured more milk into it, then more sugar. Finally she put both cigarettes out at once.

She looked at the clock on the far wall of the luncheonette. It was time. Margaret didn't move. She watched the second hand travel around the clock. It was nice to see an old-fashioned clock with a visible second hand. She felt almost friendly toward the leering counterman.

She bent forward to take another sip of coffee. Her breasts brushed the counter and she felt a tingling in one nipple. I am tired of being on time for his sessions, she thought. I am going to be *late.*

Margaret waited in the luncheonette until five minutes past the hour and eventually arrived at her doctor's office ten minutes late.

"I'm late," she said, standing in the office. She was holding her coat and purse, which she usually left in the anteroom.

Stanislas nodded.

"I'm late because I *chose* to be late."

He nodded again and straightened a paper on his desk.

"Don't you have a response?"

He looked at her. "I'm sorry you're late," he said finally.

"Tell me, since I've never been late before," she said icily, "do I get a reduction in the fee?"

"No."

"I have something to tell you," she said.

"What, Margaret?"

"Don't call me Margaret! It's so goddamn pedagogical."

"But Margaret is your name."

She felt herself flushing. She felt terribly uncomfortable, as if about to succumb to a fever. She kept her eyes away from Stanislas, focusing on the spot just above his head.

"I prefer to stand for this session," she blurted out.

"It would be better to sit."

"I prefer to stand. Is that all right with you? Each session you give me an option: the couch or the chair. For three years you've given me that option. To lie down or sit. But this evening I prefer to stand."

He did not assent and he did not dissent. He said nothing and he waited. He always waited. Margaret lit a cigarette and expected to hear his protestation. She knew he would protest because he had once explained that she could not smoke during analytic sessions. Why? She never understood the explanation, but it had something to do with the dilution of a certain type of energy.

Margaret drew deeply on the cigarette. No, she would not be the first to speak.

The room was losing its air. She unbuttoned her coat. Then she looked at him directly for the first time.

"Are you feeling ill?" he asked. "Would you like a glass of water?"

Margaret didn't want any water. She knew what she wanted. She wanted to be out of there—forever. She wanted the dreams of health, of life, of love, to fade radically. She didn't want ever again to suppose that things might be different, that her life might be changed. There she was, and there she would always be until she died. No more lies. No more health and normalcy fantasies. No more Paul Stanislas.

She started to speak, but tears choked her. She closed her eyes, clenched her fists, and waited. When she opened her eyes, she stared into the eyes behind the desk.

"I will never set foot in this office again," she said.

Margaret turned and walked slowly out of the room. She felt as though she were executing a dance to unnaturally slowed down music. She felt as though the light were shifting from one exquisite pastel tone to another. When she reached the street, however, she saw that it was cold and colorless.

John Ligur watched the morning sun. He was sitting against one wall of the ward, beside his bed. No patients were allowed on their beds during the day; their mattresses were rolled up.

Ligur held an unlit cigarette in one hand. Patients were allowed to keep their own cigarettes, but not matches. Attendants kept the matches, and Ligur had not yet asked for a light.

He liked the sun best just as it was now, strong and direct. He played a game with the sun, staring, unblinking, at the round golden mass until his eyes burned and teared. Then he would grin, close his eyes and wipe the tears away, and then start all over again.

Sometimes, if he stared long enough, he could see the face of Ann Favori. She had been six years old when he raped her, slit her throat, then eased her down into a shallow pond. Ligur missed her. She was very nice. They had a long discussion about the sun.

An attendant walked by, noticed the unlit cigarette and proffered a match. When his cigarette was lit, Ligur waited patiently for the attendant to move away so that he could resume his dialogue with the sun.

As he sat there against the wall, one hand made the circular motion which characterized him: from genitals to shoulder to forehead. Inexorable it was; always at the same speed; always touching precise points; inexorable and exact.

No one knew why he made that motion. Ligur would never tell them. Never. He would never tell even the woman doctor. Many people had tried to find out. Ligur knew they had tried. Ligur knew that was why he had been tortured so frequently. Horrible things had been done to his body; hot pokers had been inserted in his rectum; pieces of silk and sandpaper had been moved up his penis; horrible stews of feces and insects had been shoved into his mouth. But Ligur had never talked. He had never told them a thing.

"Ligur, you're wanted."

It was the voice of the attendant who had lit his cigarette. Ligur didn't move. His eyes were just beginning to tear.

"In the consultation room. Now. Dr. Roth doesn't like to be kept waiting. And put your cigarette out in an ashtray."

Ligur did as he was ordered to do. Then he walked past the other patients into the long hall. He stopped in front of a room, the door of which was ajar.

The woman was sitting behind a small desk. John Ligur walked past her and leaped lightly onto the high, leather-covered examining table along one wall of the room. Next to this table was a battery of testing equipment: an EKG machine, a blood pressure surcingle, a scale, a fluoroscope.

No morning sun penetrated the consultation room. There was no window. No window at all. Ligur looked at his doctor and sniffed. He smelled something strange. Perhaps it was the scent of a leopard.

She had a folder with many papers in front of her, and she was writing something. It did not occur to him to wonder what she was writing.

"Well, John, how are you feeling?" she asked without looking up.

"My feet are much better," he replied.

"I didn't know there was anything wrong with your feet."

"Yes, they were burned."

"When?"

Ligur didn't answer. He climbed off the table, walked to one wall, touched it with a finger, then climbed back onto the table.

The woman closed the folder, stood and walked to the door, locked it. Consultation rooms could be locked from the inside (although a master key was always available to the staff), but restraining rooms could only be locked from the outside.

"I've brought you a picture, John."

She moved closer to him, holding a photograph at arm's length. "It's the same picture. Do you like it?"

John Ligur looked at the photograph. Then he looked at the woman's face. He watched her eyes.

"John look what I'm wearing today."

She opened her long white coat. Under it was a green sweater. Dark, thoroughly green. She put the photograph down on the desk, beside the folder. She walked closer to him. Her hand touched his knee.

"My brother William used to have a sweater like that."

"I didn't know you had a brother, John."

"He's dead."

"When did he die?"

"I don't remember."

"How did he die?"

"I don't know."

"Did he die in the war?"

"Yes," said Ligur, reaching out and touching the sleeve of the green sweater, "he died in the Great War."

The sweater felt strange to his hand. He let his fingers crawl up and down the sleeve.

The woman moved between his legs. No, she didn't smell like a leopard. She smelled like a sweater. Maybe that was why she was a doctor. They put sweaters on sick people. They saved them from death. Now she was going to save him from death.

She pulled off the sweater.

"John, do you like my breasts?"

"They're round."

"Do you want my breasts?"

He looked across the room. He wished there were a window.

She placed her hand on the back of his neck and gently drew him to her. His face dropped onto her flesh. Her breast was very soft. It made him feel good.

He tasted her nipple. It was sweet. He sucked gently on the nipple to get the sweetness into him.

Her hands were around his head. She was making strange little noises that he couldn't understand.

"Now, lay back, John," she whispered.

But he didn't want to relinquish it.

"Lay back," she said more firmly.

He let the nipple slide out of his mouth and lay back on the table. Her hand cradled him just beneath the back of his neck. Her other hand went down inside his loose pajamas and grasped his penis. She bared it. He stared at the white erect thing which seemed to have leaped from nowhere.

Her hand moved along its length, drawing on the flesh like a glove. She was smiling. The breast he had sucked was wet.

Abruptly, his whole body shook and there was this wonderful feeling in his neck, his bowels, his legs. In this moment the wall opposite him seemed to have a window. Then it was gone.

Ligur's body was quiet, and he was tired.

Paul Stanislas awoke with a start. He looked around. Today was Saturday. He was in Cold Spring Harbor. And that was his wife seated in an upholstered chair across the spacious room from his bed. She was smoking a cigarette and drinking coffee.

He looked at the clock. Ten after ten.

"So, you've finally decided to get up."

He grinned at her and lay back again.

"Would you like some coffee?"

He waved a hand, signaling no.

The sun was streaming into the room. From the window he could see the trees near the water's edge. He knew that just a few feet beyond the trees was the Long Island Sound, but he could not see it. He closed his eyes and heard the tinkling of Deirdre's cup against its saucer.

That sound brought forth a silent question: where is the gold cigarette lighter? And then another question: why had the lighter appeared? And then another: where had it come from? And then a final one, which, in its absurdity, aborted further questions: had it been sent?

He sat up again and looked at his wife. She was dressed in a light blue wool suit, her light brown hair pulled back.

"You look ready for a football game," he said.

"No, we're going for an outing."

"Where? Where are we going?"

"We'll walk into town."

Paul groaned. He picked up the pillow and bounced it on his face.

"Where's Emily?" he asked suddenly.

"Outside. Feeding the birds."

"What does she feed them?"

"Libido," said Deirdre.

"I suppose I ought to get up."

"*Ought*? How very British, Paul."

He stiffened. She had given him the clue as to why she was sitting in the room like that, watching him. She was mad at him. She wanted one of her "conversations."

"Deirdre, I had a difficult week."

"So did I. On Thursday I began to speculate on the big bang theory. You're familiar with that, aren't you? Of course, you're basically a scientist. Anyway, the theory states that the universe started a few billion years ago with one enormous explosion. We are merely the flying parts. There's a parallel theory which states that the universe will one day reach maximum expansion, and then contract back to the original ball, like a rubber band. Isn't it a depressing theory—very depressing, Paul?"

He did not answer. Because, as usual, he couldn't understand her tone of voice. Was she angry? Was she truly curious about his view of the theory? Or was this just a prelude. . . .

"Well, isn't it? Depressing, Paul?"

"Not really."

"Not really, not really," she mocked his tone.

"What did you do on Wednesday?"

Deirdre carefully put her coffee cup down on the bureau.

"I thought about why you don't make love to me anymore."

"And what was your answer?"

"I had none."

Her face had suddenly shifted from the hard conversational mask to one of gentleness, of incredible gentleness. And, just underneath, was longing.

Paul moved his feet over the side of the bed. He looked down at his feet. Then he stood up. He did not have an answer to that question either. He walked to his wife and put a hand on her shoulder. There was no answer. Sometimes he seemed close to one; it had to do with cycles, or the clocks of eros. But could he prove it empirically? Ridiculous. But he and Deirdre had intimacy, they always had intimacy, whether or not they made love.

"Could we be cowardly and change the subject?" he asked.

She looked at him once, then quickly gathered coffee cup and ashtray.

"Let's have a formal breakfast," she said at the door of the bedroom, "when Emily gets back."

Paul showered and shaved and went downstairs. Emily was already seated at the table, her face between her hands.

"There was only one bird. One bird," she noted.

"Did you feed it?"

"That bird does not eat bread. All I had was bread." Emily looked accusingly at her mother.

"What does that bird eat?"

"Raw turkey," said Emily.

They breakfasted together and Paul felt good. This was a family. Nothing important said but everything important felt. Yes, they were a family.

Paul Stanislas spent the next two hours reading in the autumn sun on the small veranda in back of the house. He was reading a memoir of a naturalist's trip to the Amazon basin. Stanislas never read in his field anymore. He felt guilty about this. He believed that a practicing psychoanalyst should know what his colleagues were up to, but he found this impossible. He read for escape—for escape from patients like Margaret Olsen, whose analysis was painful and exhausting, and always problematical. And he read for joy, to feel once again, no matter how faintly, those spasms of intellectual ecstasy which had characterized his first reading of *The Interpretation of Dreams,* and Sandor Ferenczi's *Thalassa,* and that small, obscure monograph by Helene Roth, *Notes on the Transference.*

But these spasms never returned to shake him. He had only approximations, only hints and whispers.

Now he arrived at the following passage:

> Contrary to popular belief, I have never found the Amazon Basin to be a "green hell." It has always appeared to me as almost Wordsworthian: a green glade.

Stanislas closed the book. He could hear Deirdre humming a tune he could not place. Green hell. Green glade. Green man.

He remembered now. Just before waking this morning he had dreamed once again of a green man. He stared out toward the sound. A green man. Who was he? A large green man, fully bearded, an immense gargoyle of a man with a beard made of foliage, of seaweed or weeds or vines.

Stanislas recalled no scene, conversation, or action. He closed his eyes and tried to associate to the dream, to green, to a green man. Nothing.

He remembered the first green-man dream—on a beach, when

the figure had appeared suddenly and taken his wallet and his shoelaces—or was it his keys and watch? He couldn't precisely recall. How long ago had it been? A day? Three days? Was it the same man in both dreams? Or were they different men who shared the same color on the spectrum?

Emily appeared, sulking, from the house. He held out his hand. She just looked at it.

"When are we going?" she asked, now petulant.

"Where? When are we going where?"

"Into *town*."

Stanislas groaned again. He had forgotten the outing. The family gathered, made preparations, and started out. The path was one that Deirdre had discovered shortly after their move to Cold Spring Harbor. It followed the water through several wooded acres which were part of a bird sanctuary, then skirted a small marina, and led one into town through the back alley of the drugstore.

All three were silent as they walked. They changed positions often; sometimes Emily led the way, then her mother, and occasionally Stanislas moved to the front. At one moment Deirdre turned and smiled at her husband. The smile upset him, though he didn't know why. She did not smile at him again.

They reached the town. Cold Spring Harbor consisted of three blocks of stores. There was a bank, a luncheonette, two real estate offices, a gourmet food and candy shop, a bookstore, three art galleries which opened only in summer, and a small parking lot.

"Well, here we are," said Paul with little enthusiasm.

Deirdre took her daughter's hand. "We'll be in the candy shop. I promised this child a handful of wretched candy. Gooey stuff."

"I'll be in the bookstore," replied Paul.

"Give us half an hour."

Deirdre waited until Paul had crossed the street and then took Emily into the candy store. The child was sophisticated in these matters. She went from bin to bin without exclamations of joy. She merely made selections and dropped them into a plastic baggie provided by the store.

Deirdre went to the coffee corner and sniffed at the beans. Then to jams and preserves, where she reached for a jar of quince jelly. As she held it in her hand, she felt an indescribable sadness: her mother used to make quince jelly. She had always loved the strange, ambiguous color of the quince. She had loved her mother.

Deirdre looked around. Emily was still making choices. So she moved to the gourmet housewares section and inspected spoons, strainers, crepe and omelette pans.

"I'm ready," a small but definitive voice articulated.

There was Emily, her plastic baggie bulging. Deirdre examined everything and weeded out the overdone, such as four different kinds of licorice. They walked to the cash register, then left the store, poorer by three dollars and seventy-seven cents.

Stanislas was not outside the candy store.

"Where's Daddy?" asked Emily, beginning her first assault on the purchase.

"He always gets lost in bookstores. We'll wait a few minutes and then go look for him."

A Mercedes pulled up to the curb in front of the candy store. Deirdre moved a few feet away from the car, which obstructed her view of the bookstore across the street.

The car's driver honked three times. Then more. It became an incessant noise. Dierdre finally looked at the driver.

It was Paul behind the wheel.

"Paul! Whose car is this? Where did you get it?" Deirdre leaned toward him through the window.

Stanislas didn't answer. He switched off the ignition. Emily approached and stared at her father through the open window.

"What's going on, Paul?" Deirdre asked.

Stanislas opened the door and slid out of the car. He walked around the front of the car to the curb and simply stood there, looking at his wife and daughter.

"Whose car is this?" Deirdre repeated.

The flat of his hand smashed against Deirdre's face and sent her reeling backward into the window of the candy store. Emily screamed and dropped her candy.

Paul Stanislas turned and walked slowly away from them.

Helene Roth selected a tape cassette from the shelf, inserted it in the machine, pressed the switch, then sat down to listen to her own voice.

"I have fallen into a benign and not unpleasant routine. Three days a week in the ward, one day set aside for staff meetings, and another day spent in a variety of meaningless tasks.

"This is now the start of my third year at Moorland. Strangely, a sense of exile still haunts me. But from what have I been exiled? Where shall I return?

"As for my patients, their exile is eternal. Little can be done for them. We vary the drugs, we vary the dosage, and they, in turn, vary the configurations of their psychoses. Some of them suddenly become sane. Those we watch carefully, and when remission is deemed authentic, they are sent back to jail, or to the courtroom, or God knows where—until one day they come back here again.

"At first my lingering psychoanalytic conscience was disturbed. I reasoned that if I could not help them, I was not a physician. Now I know I can't help them. It doesn't bother me at all.

"I miss nothing in the city: not the theater, nor the concerts, not the conversation, not the shops. More and more I appreciate this solitude. More and more I am content to stroll about, pausing to watch a solitary hawk in flight, or a rock at the side of the road.

"And more and more I am at ease with the face and form of madness which is all around me. Now, it seems as natural as the countryside. When I leave the hospital at the end of a day, I find no discontinuity. The countryside is not mad, no; but I have simply stopped thinking in terms of a beginning and an end.

"As for me, as for Helene Roth, of her I know very little. She appears to be a nice, middle-aged woman, with a liking for certain music, a fairly incisive mind, and a desire to be quiet—quiet and modest.

"This woman, I think, will never love again. She no longer cares to.

"Sometimes, when I'm unable to sleep, I think of Doctor Freud. I think of his definition of normalcy: *Leben, Lieben, Arbeiten.* To live, to love, to work.

"On the face of it, such an impossible definition! Perhaps he was joshing us all."

Helene quickly shut off the machine. She walked to the other end of the bookshelf, her hand running along the row of bindings. It was late, but sleep would be difficult. She moved to the window. A wind was circling the house, rustling the trees, whirling above the roof and making music with the old, loose tiles.

She reached inside her dressing gown and felt her breast, still slightly bruised. Helene shivered. Sitting down in the chair, she wrapped a large woolen shawl about her neck and shoulders.

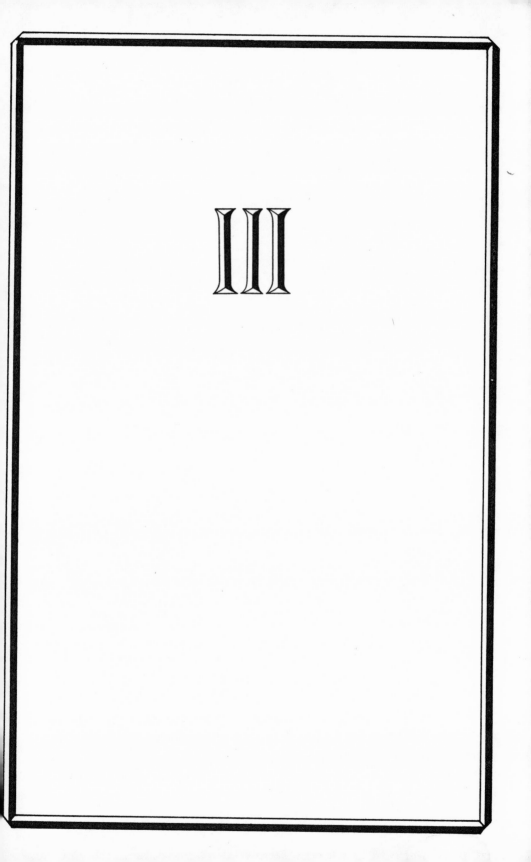

III

Deirdre stared at her face in the mirror. Her lower jaw was now a bluish black. She turned toward Paul, who was sitting, fully dressed, on the edge of the bed. The bedroom door was half-open and she caught a glimpse of her daughter standing just outside the room, trying to remain unnoticed. Deirdre shut the door.

"Tell me precisely what happened," said Paul.

"You drove up in a Mercedes-Benz. You stopped the car. You honked the horn. I spoke to you. You walked out of the car and slapped me."

Deirdre turned back to the mirror. She could hear her husband make a clucking sound with his tongue, a sound of astonishment. Her finger traced the line of the bruise. The slap had been so sudden that there had been no pain—until after. Until she had reeled against the store window, which, luckily, had not broken.

"What did you do with the car?" he asked.

"We left it there, and walked home. You had already walked away."

"I don't remember a thing. Not a single thing."

Deirdre smiled at her image. In retrospect, the blow had been pleasurable. She had once read Buddhist books about the achievement of *sunyatta,* of nothingness. His slap was the same. It was a violent blank. A jolt into nothing. The world: colors, forms . . . then there was a shock and darkness. Yes, it was good. She pouted at herself in the mirror. Perhaps Paul was going mad. Many of them went mad. Many of those shrinks went crazy.

Behind her in the mirror she saw Paul's face. Calm. He was always calm, always analytical, always supportive. In that instant she knew she would like to see him go mad. She would like to see him crumble.

And then she was ashamed. This man was hers, as she was his—in the most profound sense possible. Something had vanished between them, but it could not be made to reappear by his crucifixion.

Deirdre turned and faced him. He smiled at her.

"Are you worried about me?" he asked softly.

"Not really."

"Once, as a child, I found myself in a classroom with a pen in my pocket. It wasn't my pen. The teacher was saying that a student had lost her pen. I listened, and knew that the stolen pen was the one in my pocket. I didn't know how it got there. But it was there. I never remembered taking it."

Paul smiled as he finished speaking. Then he stood up and began to undress. It was necessary, he realized, to let the thing alone, to throw the event away, right now. Tomorrow or the next day or the next week, one could deal with it. But not now. He believed what Deirdre was saying. He believed that he had stolen a car and slapped her. What color had the car been? What kind of shift did it have? Where had it been stolen from? Nothing connected. Nothing became apparent. So, he believed but did not know. It was necessary to drop it. He could feel the fabric of his garments against his fingertips as he removed them, item by item. That was real.

"Are you sure that's all?" Deirdre asked.

"I don't know what happened, or why it happened. Something happened. But it's really nothing to worry about."

"I'm not worried." Deirdre's response was emphatic.

Paul looked at her, perplexed.

"However, Emily was worried," she said.

Paul laughed and leaned under the bed to search for his bedroom slippers. The most errant surface factor in the life of Paul Stanislas was that he could never find his bedroom slippers. Now he located one and held it up in triumph.

Deirdre found the other one under the bureau. She walked toward Paul and held out the slipper. He reached for it.

She swung her arm with all the strength she could muster against the lower part of his face.

She felt his teeth graze her hand and then felt a terrible pain in one finger. Paul did not move or make a sound when the blow struck him.

Deirdre sat down on the bed, shaking. Stanislas leaned over and kissed her on the forehead.

It was Crafts Sunday. Once a year the community was invited to the hospital to view and purchase the various items made by patients in their occupational therapy sessions. All money received went to the patients' accounts and could be used for canteen privileges.

The director considered it essential that all staff attend. Notices were placed in local papers and special bulletins of church groups. Over the years it had taken a hold upon the community's conscience as a worthwhile cause, so when Helene Roth pulled into the hospital's parking lot, she was not at all surprised to see that the lot was almost full.

The fair was held in the director's wing—along the walls, in the administrative rooms, in any space possible. A ladies' auxiliary society contributed coffee, cookies, and a few other edibles, the proceeds also to go to the patients.

It was two in the afternoon when Helene crossed the threshold of the administrative wing, and the fair had been in progress for an hour. The halls were packed. She could see familiar faces interspersed among faces she did not recognize at all. Yet she knew that the man who fixed her electrical wiring was probably there, and the grocer, and the woman who owned the greenhouse, and dozens of people she had met, if only briefly, during the past few years.

She passed a long low table with a white linen tablecloth on it. Coffee was being sold here. She put down a quarter and a smiling woman handed her a cup. She sipped the coffee as she walked slowly around the exhibit. There were baskets, quilts, dolls, clay pots—every conceivable crafts item. Directly in front of each piece was a small white card with the name of the patient-creator and the price.

Helene stopped in front of a shawl that had been woven in bright pinks and reds. The name on the card meant nothing to her; the patient was not in her ward.

"Is it true that love exists to help us survive Sunday afternoons?"

Helene turned quickly. It was William Bunche. He was grinning.

"Are you propositioning me, Dr. Bunche?"

"Not at all, Dr. Roth, not at all."

Over the years a distant friendship had developed between them. They liked each other. They respected each other. But they rarely met, and when they did, they chose to indulge in humor.

"And how do you survive—when not in love? What do you usually do on Sunday afternoons?" Helene asked.

"Same thing you do."

"Which is?"

"Plot."

Helene stiffened. The word made her uncomfortable. He picked up her discomfort.

"I scheme. That's the difference. You plot and I scheme," he said with a grin.

She sipped her coffee and moved on. William Bunche followed, making comments—some funny, some lewd—on every item she picked up to inspect.

"You missed something," he said.

She turned and read the small card he was holding up to her. It said: *John Ligur, $3.00*

Helene picked up John Ligur's creation.

"What hath your patient wrought?" asked Bunche.

She bounced it gently in the palm of her hand.

"It's a beanbag," she said, "a green beanbag."

Bunche took the beanbag from her and threw it up and down several times.

"I'm glad that lunatic is keeping himself busy," he said, chuckling.

One of the reasons she liked William Bunche was because he used archaic terms like *lunatic*.

"Dr. Roth, correct me if I'm wrong, but didn't the Master say there were two kinds of neuroses? The transference neurosis and the narcissistic neurosis. And the latter was really psychosis. The difference between them is that, in the former, the libido is outside the ego, fixing on objects, while in the latter, the libido is all within the ego."

Bunche paused and held up the beanbag until it looked like a hanging man. Then he continued, "If you listen carefully, you can hear his libido jangling around."

"That was early Freud," Helene said.

"Are you sure it's just a beanbag? It looks like a green man."

"It's a beanbag," she said, taking Ligur's creation from him. Helene looked around, saw the check-out table, and walked over to pay for the beanbag.

Bunche followed. "Why are you buying it?" he queried.

"I've always loved beanbags," she said.

A woman put the beanbag in a white paper bag, took Helene's three dollars and thanked her profusely. Helene began to walk toward the exit.

"Where are you off to?" said Bunche.

"Home. Just home."

"I want to talk to you."

"About what?"

"I think we should get to know each other better."

Helene smiled up at him. He was so much taller than she was. Although past fifty, he wore his hair brushed back like a teenager's. A dark tweed jacket enclosed his thick chest like armor. Helene was very fond of him.

"Why should we know each other better?" she wondered.

"Because life is brutish and short, particularly for us."

"Us?"

His hands gestured, capturing with a movement the milieu.

"I am otherwise engaged, Dr. Bunche."

"With what? Or with whom?"

"A project."

"A book?"

"A project."

"And this project leaves you no time for other projects?"

She reached out and placed one hand gently on his brown tweed arm. "This project leaves me no time for anything. This project is me."

He moved back a step, inclined his head as if to bow, turned and walked back to the crowd. Helene watched him for a moment, then walked swiftly to her car.

There was always a small light burning in Emily's bedroom. Her father had bought her the lamp, and around its ceramic base a bevy of strange creatures cavorted, one animal holding the next one's tail and so on following the circle. Some of the animals looked like elephants and some looked like seals. There was even one that resembled an underweight walrus with tusks that curved every which way. An animal that used to look like a giraffe now appeared to Emily as a swan.

The lamp was turned off. Emily had turned it off the minute she began to hear *those* sounds from her parents' bedroom. It had been a long time since she heard those sounds: the moaning, the murmuring, the movement of the bed. She usually hated those sounds. But now they were good, she knew. Very good.

She sat on her bed with the quilt pulled up around her head like a tent. She wished she was in a tent in the desert. One hand was pulling the toes of one foot. She had seen what had happened. Her father had slapped her mother. Right out in the open.

She reached down by the side of her bed and pulled up a paper bag. Almost all of the candy was gone. She extracted a piece of salt water taffy, unwrapped it, popped it into her mouth, and sucked on it loudly.

Now the other room was quiet. Emily could hear no more sounds. She finished her taffy and secreted the paper bag under the pillow. Then she jumped out of bed, put on the little lamp, jumped back into bed, and arranged the quilt for sleeping.

But she felt too sad to sleep. She felt very sad. Across the room on her dresser sat Blackie, Emily's moth-eaten bear. A long time ago she had told her mother to throw him away, she was too old for stuffed bears like that. Now she was glad that Blackie was still around. Once more she jumped out of bed and returned with Blackie in her arms. Poor Blackie. There were moth holes all over him. He looked sad. Emily kissed the bear and propped him up on the pillow, next to her face. In two minutes they were both asleep.

"Maybe we ought to strike each other more often," said Deirdre.

"You think that's why we made love?"

"The circumstantial evidence is there, isn't it."

"I remember a saying of Thoreau's about circumstantial evidence—something to the effect that it's like finding a trout in the milk."

Deirdre turned on her side and faced him. Paul was sweating. No matter the time of year, he was always drenched after making love. The perspiration stood out in dots up and down his whole body. She remembered how, just after they were married, she used to take a towel and gently dry him. It had been a long time since she had done that, and an even longer time since she had wanted to.

Deirdre felt tired. She did not feel good. Even orgasm was now trivial.

"Tell me, Paul, did I have a clitoral or vaginal orgasm?"

Again, he didn't know if she was making a joke or asking a question. He didn't answer.

"Don't you know? Aren't you supposed to know? Don't you think both kinds exist?"

"I think," he said finally, "that there are clitoral orgasms and vaginal orgasms and anal orgasms and orgasms of the toes and of the ears and of the mouth—and even, occasionally, of the heart."

"Praise be to heaven," she said sarcastically, touching his limp penis with one hand, "for the liberality, the essential humanity of shrinks."

Why, she suddenly thought to herself, am I speaking in a way that does not reflect my feelings? He did that to her. His coolness forced her to lie. And she was lying. It *had* been nice—making love. For a moment it had even felt like it used to feel—that roller coaster blocking out the world.

He turned away from her. Deirdre reached over to the night table and lit a cigarette. There was a rising wind outside that made tentative forays against the shutters.

"What will you do, Paul, if it happens again?"

"If what happens?"

"What happened in the village."

"It won't happen again."

"But what will you do, *if?*"

"I don't know."

"You could see a colleague."

He turned on his back and stretched. "I probably would."

"Would you see that woman?"

"Which woman?"

"Your training analyst. Helene Roth."

Stanislas felt something grow rigid within him, within his musculature. Helene Roth was a name he had extirpated from his existence. She was now only a series of letters and sounds in an archaic and lost language. He could not speak about her truthfully. But he had to speak—and he would lie, dissemble, formalize. A meaningless sentence would come out. And it came out.

"You still haven't forgiven me for that, have you? It was the *only* time, you know, I was unfaithful to you. And I did it for professional reasons. You know all that."

No, Deirdre thought, I don't know anything. She was sorry she had brought up the name. Memory was radical, it always broke through. She remembered precisely the way she felt when he had told her. Was it two years after the marriage or three? She couldn't remember that—but the feeling as if someone had slammed something hard and pointed deep inside of her, the feeling that what was good was extinguished forever, the feeling that her marriage was ultimately a filthy, adulterous lie—that she remembered and would never forget.

"Would you see her?" Deirdre asked, carefully.

"She's no longer practicing. I don't know where she is."

He sat up and ran a finger along his stomach, reassuring himself that the muscles were still there, and hard.

"It won't happen again," he reiterated, "and if it did, and if I saw a colleague, it would not be Dr. Roth even if I could find her."

"Do you want to make love again?" she asked him suddenly.

"No," was the reply, with equal suddenness.

She ground out her cigarette, hesitated, then lit another. Tears were coming to her eyes. She fought them, and won.

"Paul, I have been unfaithful to you five times."

"And how many times have you been unfaithful to yourself?" he asked bitterly.

Then he moved closer to her, as if to apologize. But Deirdre was already staring at the smoke, at the ceiling, her mind on the expanding universe.

Stanislas followed her gaze through the smoke to the ceiling. A face was forming in the smoke. He blinked it away. It came back—small and dark and lovely. It moved from section to section in the ceiling. The face did not accuse him. It was just there—almost wistful in its smoke wreath. He turned on his side and brought his hands together between his legs, like a child. I had to throw Helene Roth away, he thought, clasping his hands tightly, and I must keep her thrown away.

In Emily's room, Blackie the bear had been knocked off the bed by a sudden movement of the dreaming girl. He lay on the floor, upended, moth-eaten.

Margaret Olsen stood in front of the movie house. It was a re-run theater just off Fifty-seventh Street. Behind glass, the placard announced the original *Hunchback of Notre Dame* with Charles Laughton. The timetable said that the next performance would start at four-twenty. It was four o'clock now.

Quasimodo. She had always loved the name. An uncle of hers, now dead, used to ask her, "Who am I?" Then before she could answer, he would scrunch up his body, affect a swinging gait, and screwing up his face in a horrible way, would say, "I am *Quasimodo*."

And Margaret had always been frightened. The charade never lost its power. Now it was windy and growing colder. She could go back to the hotel, but that was no option at all. That was simply waiting for sleep, waiting for the morning and work.

She paid her three dollars and walked inside.

A few people were waiting in the lobby. Margaret walked to the candy counter, covertly studying the faces. She wanted chocolate. It was always chocolate she wanted when the cold weather came. This selection was minimal: plain chocolate bars or chocolate bars with nuts. She bought one of each and slipped them in her bag. Then, as an afterthought, she bought a bar of coconut and almonds, covered with chocolate.

She lit a cigarette. Margaret always smoked before or after a movie, never during a movie. She could not tolerate sitting in the smoking section, which usually was the balcony. The balcony brought back too many uncomfortable childhood memories of balconies where she had heard injudicious necking, where the seats had been prey to sticky substances . . . She realized this was Manhattan, that there was no making out in Manhattan balconies—but she couldn't bring herself to sit in one.

From time to time, as Margaret smoked, she watched the others who came into the lobby. This was a precautionary step she always took. If someone appeared who might be a problem, who might be dangerous, someone who would uncomfortably distract her from the movie, she noted the person and sat far away.

Holding hands in a desultory manner, a young couple entered. No problem. A short fat man about sixty, clutching a rolled up newspaper in his hand. Occasionally he looked at Margaret, or rather, at her legs. No problem. A young Hispanic man with an umbrella and a felt hat. Margaret didn't like him. Keep away.

She surveyed those waiting.

The doors opened. A few people came out, and those waiting walked in. Margaret sat down in the aisle seat about halfway between front and rear. She put her purse on the seat beside her but left her coat on, still feeling chilled. Her eyes caught the movement of the young Hispanic taking a seat on the other side of the theater. That was good.

Margaret ate a chocolate bar, methodically, breaking off one square at a time. As the movie began she ate another chocolate bar. Her eyes were now accustomed to the dark and she checked out those who had been in the lobby with her. None had moved from their original seats. That was good.

Up on the screen, there was Charles Laughton masquerading as Quasimodo. Masquerading as her uncle. But she couldn't focus on the screen. She felt ill at ease. She unwrapped the last candy bar and consumed it. Now she was suddenly sick to her stomach. Too much sugar, too quickly. There was pronounced tension in her calf muscles. Margaret stretched out her legs and then brought them in, stretched them out and in again.

Now they were flogging Quasimodo as he lay chained to a wooden platform which turned and turned. Quasimodo called out, "Water, water!" The mutilated hunchback kept spinning, slowly, like the globe itself, and with each turn his plea for water became more primitive, more pathetic, softer. Suddenly, from the crowd, Esmeralda bounded and skipped. She let cool water trickle down into the hunchback's obscene mouth.

Margaret could watch no more. She walked quickly out of the theater, her fist full of candy wrappers. It was pitch dark.

Where to go? Where to put the candy wrappers? How to avoid the hotel room? She knew what she was waiting for: *someone*, an unnamed, unmet someone to take her by the hand, to take her home. Home was not Maryland. Home was not the hotel. Home was home. However, no one arrived. She crumpled the candy wrappers and let them fall to the sidewalk, where they separated. The wind rolled one into the gutter.

Margaret was hungry, as always after eating chocolate. She walked slowly toward the hotel, looking for a suitable place to have dinner. She peered inside the window of a bar and grill. It looked safe, and was crowded enough to insure that the food would be fresh. She walked inside, took a tray, and moved to a hot table presided over by a man in a white chef's coat.

The roast beef was a bit too rare. The brisket looked old. The corned beef was fatty. As the man waited, his knife beat a slow tattoo on the wooden carving board in front of him.

"London broil," Margaret said finally.

He plucked the meat out of its case with a long fork, then expertly sliced it, trimming the sides. Carefully, he placed the London broil on a plate which he then held up, as though inquiring. He was waiting for the vegetable order.

"Cabbage," said Margaret.

"Gravy?"

She shook her head, took the plate, paid at the register, and walked toward the rear of the dining room. One could sit at the bar or at a table. Choosing the bar, she ordered a glass of white wine. Margaret ate slowly, relishing each bite. From time to

time she sipped the wine. Except for the movement of chairs and
the low murmur of voices, the bar was quiet. Those who patron-
ized it were serious eaters and serious drinkers.

Margaret's plate was finally clean, clean and round in front of
her. She lit a cigarette and finished the glass of wine. There was
time for another glass, for five or six more. The bartender filled
her glass. Margaret nodded thank you. She flicked a last shred of
cabbage off the empty plate with her fork. Now the plate was
truly empty. She stared down at it and saw that it resembled the
movie's wooden platform.

She turned the plate, slowly, as the platform had turned.
Through the chocolate bars and white wine a vision came to
Margaret: Quasimodo was lying on the plate. In the role, not
Charles Laughton, but Stanislas. The body of her doctor was being twisted and flogged. And as the wheel turned, Quasimodo
cried out for water. And a woman rushed out of the crowd—a
brave and tall and beautiful woman—and she poured water into
the parched lips of Stanislas . . .

The plate dropped onto the bar with a clatter. As the bartender
quickly glanced toward her, Margaret pushed it away, drank her
second glass of wine in four gulps, then left.

Reaching her apartment, she paused and breathed deeply, as
though she had finished a one-mile run. Her body was lathered
with sweat and she was trembling.

Cradling the beanbag in the palm of one hand, Helene Roth
ran her other hand along the row of tape cassettes. She stopped
at one, plucked it out, and set it into the machine. Then she
flicked the switch and turned to face the window.

"Received file on new patient, arriving tomorrow. Name: John
Ligur. Diagnosis: paranoid schizophrenia. Age: 29. Father: Edward, deceased. Mother: Laura, age 53, Harrisburg, Pa. Occupa-
tion: retail clerk.

"Ligur was arrested at age fifteen for shoplifting. Sentence
suspended. Arrested again at age sixteen for shoplifting. Convicted. Eight months in reformatory. Arrested again at age nine-
teen for car theft. Convicted. Spent two years in state peniten-

tiary and six months in hospital. Early diagnosis: paranoid schizophrenic. Released and then worked two years in federal work programs.

"Arrested at age twenty-five for robbery, assault, and assault with intent to kill. Sentenced to seven and a half to fifteen years. Served four years. Released. Arrested five months ago for murder and rape of young girl. Court ruling: incompetent to stand trial. Remanded to Moorland.

According to the file, Ligur is an only child, left school during the ninth grade, possesses a borderline I.Q. The file recommends extreme caution in dealing with this man.

"So, they keep coming in—the killers, the rapists, the mutilators. They keep coming in. And we look at them and speak to them and drug them. They no longer affect us and we no longer affect them.

"Next week I shall see this Ligur for the first time. And next week I shall also repair the hem of my coat."

Helene switched off the machine and replaced the cassette carefully on the shelf. Looking out the window, she saw shadows across the countryside. There were degrees of darkness in the night air. Winter must be approaching, because the windowpane in front of her clouded as she breathed on it. She erased the cloud with a finger. Then she blew on the pane and it clouded again. She traced the outline of a head and shoulders, then made sticks for the legs.

"It's happening to you, isn't it, Paul." Helene whispered almost casually to the design. She felt odd, strange; both depressed and triumphant at once.

"I know it's happening," she whispered again. She erased the figure with the beanbag. Tomorrow was a day in the wards. She walked toward the bedroom, slowly unbuttoning her blouse.

IV

Deirdre stared at her daughter, who was sitting up very straight in front of her toast. The toast had long been cold.

"Why don't you put some jam on it?" asked Deirdre.

Emily shook her head. No.

Taking up a small butter knife, Deirdre spread jam on the toast. Then she sipped her coffee, smoked, and ate an English muffin without enthusiasm. The wall clock read seven-thirty. There was plenty of time before Emily must be delivered to school. There was plenty of time for everything.

Next to the clock, the wallpaper was peeling. The wallpaper would have to be redone. Deirdre was pleased. The wallpaper had been Paul's selection. Endless repetition of ships, sailing ships, each on its own breaking wave. The ships were black, the waves were red, and only the foaming tip of each wave was blue. A dizzying maritime spectacle, almost nauseating. But she had grown accustomed to it. One gets used to anything.

Emily finally took a bite of her cold toast.

"Want some hot cocoa?" asked Deirdre.

Emily nodded her head. Yes. Deirdre went to the stove, poured a glass of milk into a pot, stirred in two large teaspoons of cocoa, two teaspoons of sugar, and turned on the flame. The trick was to remove the pot just before the mixture boiled. Deirdre did so, expertly, then poured the steaming cocoa into a mug, which she placed in front of Emily. She bent over and kissed the girl on the top of her head.

Mornings are always ugly, thought Deirdre, as she slipped back into her chair. No matter the season, no matter the weath-

59

er, mornings were always ugly. Why had she suddenly kissed Emily?

"You know, Emily, I love you."

Emily chewed the piece of cold toast and stared at her mother.

"But that, I agree, is neither here nor there," Deirdre noted.

Emily picked up a spoon and added more jam to her toast.

"Do you want more cocoa?"

Emily tipped her mug to show that it was still three quarters full.

At what point in her life did mornings become ugly? Deirdre tried to reconstruct. They were not ugly when she was a child like Emily. Then they had no content whatsoever. They were not ugly when she was adolescent. The furies drove her from hour to hour. They were not ugly when she was in college or working at her first few jobs. Deirdre's cigarette smoke crossed the table and Emily waved it away furiously. Emily didn't like smoke.

Deirdre suddenly isolated the moment: mornings became ugly in the time just prior to meeting Paul Stanislas. She was surprised at her ability to recall this. She thought, now, that she had fallen in love with Paul Stanislas and married Paul Stanislas in the hope that mornings would stop being ugly. And if that were truly the case, then their marriage was a failure. Because Paul had not made the morning beautiful. And, perhaps, Paul had married her because he had a problem with his mornings, or his afternoons, or his evenings.

Futile, futile speculations, she thought, and ground out the cigarette. She looked across the table, but Emily was gone. She had probably gone to get her school books. Deirdre rose from the table and slipped on a plain cloth coat that had hung from a hook on the kitchen door. She stood near the door and waited for her daughter. Emily arrived, looking dour.

"You're not going to an execution, it's only school."

Emily ignored her mother and stomped out of the house. They walked down the gravel driveway toward the car. A cold, clear, still morning.

Suddenly Emily stopped—and pointed. Deirdre followed the direction of her finger. Something lay on the ground near the car.

It was alive. A bluejay. One of its wings seemed to be bent, awkwardly.

They moved closer. The bird let out a raucous cry, like a crow. Emily was almost crying.

"There's nothing wrong with it, Emily. Nothing. It's feinting a broken wing to keep us from her nest."

But now the child was weeping. Deirdre pulled her close.

"We'll just walk around the jay, just walk around it," she said softly.

They climbed into the car from the other side. Emily was rubbing her thumb into a wet eye.

Deirdre felt a quick and almost overwhelming rush of love for her. She wanted to smother her with it; to exhalt her with it; to wrap her into a cocoon of love so that her mornings would never be bad.

But all she did was turn the key in the ignition. The bluejay was gone as they drove off.

Helene Roth entered the coffee room in the administrative wing. It was a refuge from the wards that all the staff used from time to time. A long oak table in the center of the room was surrounded by an odd assortment of chairs. In one corner of the room was a small folding table that supported a coffee machine. Helene poured herself a cup and sat down.

The madmen were all doing well. Ligur had just now stared at her and popped his pills. It was always difficult passing him in the ward; there was always the desire to say something profound, to acknowledge him, to touch him, to place a priority on their haphazard meeting.

The coffee room was colder than the ward. Helene reminded herself that she needed a wool scarf for the winter. Yes, she would have to buy a scarf. Maybe a green one. The thought made her happy.

William Bunche walked into the room. He filled a cup with coffee and sat down at the far end of the table. He was carrying several folders but let them drop every which way onto the table.

"Well. Sometimes I don't run into you for weeks on end, and now I've met you two days running."

Not knowing what else to do, Helene smiled.

"Would you like to read my files?" said Bunche.

"For what reason?"

"To see whether my murderers, rapists, assassins, and arsonists are as delightful as yours."

"I'll take it they are. I'll take it on faith alone."

Bunche sipped his coffee and stared at Helene. His gaze made her uncomfortable, so she looked out the window.

"May I make a confession?" said Bunche.

"By all means. I love confessions. They're so therapeutic."

"Well. How does one say this? Look—about two years ago I developed an inordinate affection for you. Since I'm a married man, and a pillar, albeit rotted, of the psychiatric community, I restrained myself. About six months ago I decided to lift all restraints. And yesterday, at the crafts fair, I think I made my position quite clear."

"And I made my position equally clear," said Helene.

"So you did, so you did." He sipped the coffee, made a face, sipped again. "Are you curious as to why I decided no longer to restrain myself?"

"Obviously, you fell under the spell of my raw eros."

Bunche laughed, pulled his scattered files together, and drummed his fingers on them.

"Something is happening to you."

Helene looked at him. He was still smiling, but his statement had not had the tone of a joke.

"I don't understand what you mean."

"In other words: I decided to become your lover in order to save myself, and to save you."

"Save us from what?"

"To save me from my life—which, to be quite honest, I can no longer tolerate—and to save you from . . . I don't know what. Something."

Helene folded her hands together. There was a calmness about the man which made him difficult to read.

"Do I have any symptoms?" she asked.

"Symptoms?"

"Yes, of this strange malady, this unnamed malaise, from which, according to you, I now suffer."

"A thousand symptoms, Dr. Roth."

She stiffened. The conversation was moving in directions she did not like, approaching grounds she could not afford to traverse.

"Among the staff, Dr. Bunche, you are noted for your frankness. So why don't you just say you want to sleep with me?"

"Because it is more complex. Are you trying to fool a colleague? Something has happened to you."

For a brief moment she was seized with a desire to tell him. To tell him that she was wandering through places that he never even thought might exist; that she was using madness as one uses a rifle; that she had been swept into a phenomenon that neither he nor his colleagues could even describe, much less believe.

"Freudians are very wise," Bunche continued, "because Freud was correct in every area save one."

"And that is?"

"Treatment. He should have stopped with description. He knew the strings, but his program for retwisting those strings was wrong. He should have stopped, like Darwin, who neglected to offer a program for curing evolution."

"I am no longer a Freudian."

"The only point of that little speech was to let you know that I think you are a wise woman. You know that you have changed. You know that you are now on shaky ground. You know it."

"Dr. Bunche, are you saying that I am going mad?"

He pushed the folders away from him again, almost savagely. He stood up and walked to the window, one hand still holding his empty coffee cup. He turned to her.

"Is it that you don't trust me?"

"Trust is a funny word."

He put the coffee cup down on the table and held out his hands, palms up. For a long time he stared at his hands, rotating them slightly.

"Dr. Roth. I am fifty-six years old. I am virile. I am literate. I am gentle."

He paused, suddenly embarrassed. Then he waited.

Helene did not speak. She looked at him with pity. It was too late. Years too late. Years too cold. Too banal. Too simple.

Slowly, he said, "I believe I have made a fool of myself."

Helene walked to the far end of the table, gathered his folders and brought them to him. She placed his arm around them.

"If I'm going mad," she said, "I'm glad that you know."

She felt his hand on her cheek. A large, rough hand. It rested against her skin, fingers brushing lightly. Then he was gone.

He was the kind of man, she thought, with whom one could be in equilibrium. He was the kind of man with whom one could take a walk, and look at things and name those things. He was the kind of man with whom one could lie in bed and feel nothing or everything as the desire fell. He was the kind of man who synthesized Stanislas and Ligur. Synthesis. Synthesis. The word entranced her. Was she the synthesis? Was she the dialectic? Was she the first to truly use madness? She felt a springiness in her feet. She knew what Nietzsche meant now—what her father had spoken of—what she'd tried for years to comprehend: living on the tightrope. Living on the taut, taut rope which gives yet never gives out. This was the tightrope. At one end of the rope was Stanislas: educated, urbane, healthy. As the other end was Ligur: demented, visionary, receptacle of thoughts and acts that no one could approach. And there she was, Helene Roth, moving from one to the other. Moving, dancing, pirouetting on the slender rope. When this is over, she thought, it will be good to be dead. Dead.

She lifted her head, just a bit, in the empty room. The memory of an odor came to her. Like a wild animal, she sniffed. It came for a moment and then it was gone. It was the odor of Stanislas. The way he smelled when they had made love. Strange, powdery scent, unmistakable. Sour. Sour was the memory now.

She moved up on her toes. Every movement she made brought Stanislas closer to his dissolution. That was what she wanted more than his death. Dissolution. Unraveling. Stanislas was a ball of twine. Stanislas was unraveling. See Stanislas unravel. See the man shed his feigned humanity.

If I am going mad, she thought, it consists only in the possibility that nothing is happening to Paul Stanislas, while I believe that something is happening. If I think I am destroying him and am not, in fact, doing so, then I am mad. If I think I am destroying Paul Stanislas, and he is, in fact, being destroyed, then I am merely evil. But I am not evil. I am paying a debt of destruction. I am paying like with like.

Poor Dr. Bunche. She smiled wanly. He was of them: the drug doctors, the apothecaries, the surgeons, the masters of the electrode. They wanted to be healers. She walked over to the coffee table and poured a bit of hot coffee into her cup. The liquid swirled. All healers were dissolved in liquid, like that. Dissolved. She had found something else. Helene Roth closed her eyes for a moment. Then she opened them and raised her coffee cup in a toast. She had seen him, large and massive and green, with a beard torn from the sea. From times past and in chaos. She had toasted the green man.

"Margaret, could I see you for a minute?"

Margaret looked up from her desk. Edward Lupica was standing in the doorway, a sheaf of papers in his hand and his face covered with that expression of profound professionalism she despised.

"It's about your memo . . ."

On the organization chart, Edward Lupica was her equal. The same salary, the same responsibilities, the same everything. But somehow, in some unknown ascent, he was now above her. She had to submit memos and all other work to him for approval. She did not know how this condition of servitude to an equal had developed.

". . . on that area south of SoHo," he reminded her.

He was always impeccably dressed and he always wore a vest. Today he wore a dark blue pin-striped suit. His face was thin, almost ascetic, and when Margaret looked at him she thought of a starving bird that had landed in the wrong place. The memo he spoke of concerned an area of the city which had once been a center of light manufacturing and was filled with massive nineteenth-century loft buildings. Now the artists were moving in, spilling over from SoHo and other areas, and the artists wanted zoning variances so that they could live in the lofts.

Margaret had spent weeks in the area, making surveys of the

buildings, meeting with the residents and the remaining manu-
facturers. Her conclusion was simple: keep the artists out. Or let
very few in. The city, Margaret reasoned, needs manufacturing
more than it needs another bohemian watering hole, so keep the
facilities available for the time being.

"I'll be there in a moment," she said. Edward Lupica nodded as
though she had made a very profound remark and then vanished.

Margaret sat quietly at her desk. It was ten-thirty in the morning. The coffee wagon was due in another fifteen minutes. She
longed for a cigarette but decided to delay this particular grati-
fication until the coffee arrived.

She waited six minutes before going to see Edward Lupica.
The time span was deliberate. It was the only way she could ex-
ert that sliver of independence left her vis-à-vis Lupica. Ten
minutes would have provoked him. Four minutes would have
been capitulation. Four minutes would have confirmed the fact
that he was, indeed, above her in the agency's structure.

A chair was already waiting for her by his right hand. Edward
smiled. Margaret sat down. On the wall behind his desk were
pictures of architectural interest: cathedral naves, sports pal-
aces, several vanguard structures which seemed to leap from the
ground. Lupica believed that architects should be the city plan-
ners.

"Well," Lupica began, "I think it's an excellent survey of the
problems. An excellent survey."

Margaret said nothing. She looked at the sheaf of papers in his
hand—her work—and noted that he had smudged several of the
corners.

"And I'm sending it on. I just want you to know that I'm adding a note to the effect that I don't agree with you. The only way
to revive that area is through a careful, planned, SoHo-type de-
velopment."

He waited, as though sure she was about to see the light and
would acknowledge that light.

Again she said nothing.

"Do you want to discuss it?" he asked.

She had rarely been this close to him. She noticed a slight discoloration near the corner of his mouth. The skin was smudged,
just like her memo was smudged. A birthmark, she thought.

"Do you mean, should we argue the point?" she said.

"Explore it," he corrected.

Explore. Abhor. She tried to think of other words with the same sound endings.

"I mean, Margaret, do you know of any area in the city which recovered industry or light manufacturing once they moved out?"

"No," she replied.

"So, in a sense, your position is Utopian."

"Hopeful," she corrected.

They were too close. Much too close. Margaret was getting uncomfortable. She pushed her chair back just a bit. When would the coffee wagon come?

"I'm not trying to change your memo. I just want to understand it."

"It was clearly written, I thought."

"I mean the reasoning behind it."

"There are facilities for manufacturing. These are now empty. If artists take them over, they'll never be available again. Simple."

"Yes, I know that. But you don't take into consideration the changing reality of the city."

Margaret noticed that in the center of his desk were three piles of paper. On top of each pile was a heavy object, used as a paperweight. On the first pile was a stapler. On the second, a brass letter opener. On the third, a potted plant.

"The changing reality of the city," she said, quietly repeating his phrase.

"Excuse me?" he said, leaning toward her.

"I was just thinking of what you said. About the changing reality of the city."

He sat back, a pleased expression on his face. He took her repetition as concurrence with his views.

"Well, I just wanted you to know," he said.

"Know?"

"Know that I'm adding my comment to your memo."

"Yes, I know that," she said, rising.

"Thank you, Margaret."

"Actually, Edward, I have another memo in my desk. I have

very carefully worked out a program for that area. A program to turn it into an indoor dairy farm. A neighborhood of cows."

Lupica put on his professional mask and then wiped it off. He didn't know if she was joking with him, or teasing him, or making fun of him. Neither did Margaret. She turned and walked out.

Margaret bought a container of coffee from the roving wagon and returned to her office. She sipped the hot coffee and savored a cigarette. The brief encounter with Lupica had been less painful than it could have been.

Her "in" box had a new envelope, one not there when she'd left the office. While she had been with Lupica, the mail boy must have delivered it. Margaret opened the manila interoffice envelope. Personnel wanted her vacation schedule for the year.

She took a piece of scrap paper and reached for her fine-point black magic marker. She would choose a few weeks in May. It didn't really matter what dates she put down now, as vacation time could always be changed or traded.

The pen wasn't there. She looked carefully over the top of her desk, then on the floor. She must have left it in Lupica's office. Margaret walked down the hall and knocked. Lupica looked up, smiling.

"I think I left my pen here."

He went on smiling and looked over his desk, moving the papers loudly to show he was trying.

"Not here," he said finally.

Margaret nodded and returned to her office. She lit another cigarette. She opened the desk drawer which contained her supplies. There were many other black pens, but they all had thick points. Margaret only used a fine-point pen. The one she was missing was perfectly balanced, perfectly inked, perfectly shaped. She opened all her desk drawers one at a time. The pen wasn't there. She searched the wastepaper basket. She turned out her coat pockets.

Lupica didn't look carefully enough, she realized. She walked back down the hall and knocked. He looked up, smiling.

"Could you look again?"

Once again he went through the same motions, even standing up and checking his own pockets.

"Not here. Are you out? I have a whole drawer full."

Margaret shook her head and returned to her office. The coffee was cold, but she sipped it anyway. Clearly, something was happening. Lupica had taken her pen. But why? Perhaps it was another of his power plays. Perhaps he would use the pen to write . . . a memo. Perhaps he was . . . Margaret stood up.

Fury was building in her. She lit another cigarette. The match trembled in her hand. No, she had to make a stand here. It was more than just a fine-point pen. It was a matter of priorities; of dealing with people; of will; and, yes, of survival.

Holding the coffee container in one hand and the cigarette in the other, Margaret walked back down the hall. This time she didn't knock. She stood in Lupica's doorway and said, "The joke's over, Edward."

He looked up at her, head cocked to one side.

"What are you talking about?"

"I want my pen back."

"Margaret, I didn't take your pen."

"Give it back to me, Edward. Now."

"Margaret, calm down. I didn't take your pen. But let me get you another one."

He began to rummage through his top drawer.

"Stop that," said Margaret sharply. He glanced at her, then closed the drawer.

"It's always been this way with you. It's always been the way you operate. Theft. Theft of ideas, theft of responsibilities. But now it stops, Edward. It stops now."

"What in the world are you talking about?"

"I'm talking about this, Edward."

Margaret threw her half container of cold coffee into his face. It stained the discoloration near his lip. It dripped down his chin and onto his shirt.

Neither Margaret nor Edward spoke. Margaret gazed for a moment into the empty coffee container. Then she returned to her office, slammed the door, sat down at her desk.

She trembled. She felt nauseous. It seemed that she would vomit. Margaret picked up the phone and called Paul Stanislas for an appointment.

Paul Stanislas began to chew the car incident halfway through his morning jog. Dressed in sweat pants, a sweat shirt, and a plasticized parka, he took the incident from beginning to end as he ran.

Stanislas liked to think while running. It was a process that seemed philosophically elegant. After all, thinking was motion, movement, act. Why should not the most cerebral of all movements be combined with the most physical of all movements—why not?

Besides, there was a rhythm in the feet, the pound-pound-pound of one foot after another that worked itself up into the body. One heard one's feet pounding with the body, not with the ears. And therefore the head would ape the feet—and one would think with a rhythm. And that was really what one needed for a solution, a right rhythm.

He was not running well. The beginning of the run was always a struggle, but halfway through the five or so miles there would usually be a breakthrough into smoothness, into the feeling that one could go on forever.

Stanislas pulled up short and stood facing the river. Today was not his day. He ran another fifty yards and pulled up once more. Everything about him was sluggish. Nothing about the car incident made sense. He walked to the rail, picked up a stone, and flung it into the river, recalling the number of skips he had made with a stone in Long Island Sound. The stone did not skip this time because the walkway was high over the river and one needed to be at the same level with the water to accomplish that trick.

He leaned over the rail and stared into the swirling current. There was a distorted reflection of his face that could be made out in the water. It was humorous. He looked like a gargoyle. Stanislas laughed and turned around, his back against the rail, his eyes scanning the high-rise skyline.

Suddenly the pieces of the car puzzle fell into place and he laughed louder. He understood everything. It was one of those funny incidents, one of those inexplicable absurdities which everyone undergoes. An absurd rite of passage.

He remembered a previous one. Not more than a few weeks ago. He had crumpled up a piece of paper and at the same time picked up a pair of dirty socks. The socks were to go into the laundry hamper in the bathroom. The scrap paper into the garbage pail in the kitchen. He had calmly walked into the kitchen, put the dirty socks into the pail, and then walked into the bathroom where he threw the piece of paper into the hamper. Eight hours later he realized what he had done.

The more he thought about it, the more absurd and the more similar the car incident seemed. Dangerous holdup man Paul Stanislas loose on the North Shore of Long Island with a souped-up Mercedes. Violent lover Paul Stanislas abuses young wife in village.

He turned quickly back to the water, laughing, picked up another small stone and flung it as far as he could.

Stanislas turned and started to jog toward his office.

A face stopped him. A face was right in front of him. He stopped short. The face belonged to a body and it was blocking the path.

The old woman had appeared so quickly, seemingly from nowhere, that Stanislas felt a sense of obligation after the surprise was over.

He knew who she was—one of the old shopping bag ladies who inhabited the neighborhood, going from street to street and park to park, long lost in a psychotic world of their own choosing, homeless, treasuring the bag of bizarre and useless items so laboriously collected.

He had seen her often over the years, either standing or sitting in the park and mouthing deprecations against one and all, the exact phrases of which were always unintelligible.

Scraps of cloth were wrapped around her face and head to protect her from the cold; and her long woolen coat seemed stuffed with objects. The visible parts of her hands and neck and face were filthy and rubbed raw.

The woman grunted and then started to tap her finger into the palm of the opposite hand. Stanislas couldn't understand. She tapped some more, and the grunt took off and became a screech. Stanislas understood. She was asking for money. It was the first time he had ever seen a shopping bag lady beg. He dug into the pocket of his parka. There were a few bills and some coins. He took a dollar bill, folded it, and pressed it into the woman's hand.

A wide, fertile, toothless grin creased her face.

"Good man, good man," she muttered.

Savagely his hand shot out, knocking the dollar bill out of her hand, and equally savage was his retort: "Good man? Ask Helene Roth. Ask her about my goodness."

The old woman bent down and retrieved the bill, clucking her tongue against the roof of her mouth.

Stanislas stepped to one side. The words had emerged without thinking. The hand had struck without volition.

He was cold, and trembling slightly. I'm frightened. I'm frightened. I'm frightened. It wasn't like the laundry incident at all.

Helene Roth was tired. But she had to review, to continually review. She had to know at every moment what was happening, what *had* happened. So she blinked the tiredness away, walked into her study, and placed a tape on the machine. Feeling cold, she draped an old wool blanket across her knees as she sat.

"First interview with Ligur confirms prior diagnosis: paranoid schizophrenic. Patient was virtually mute during entire interview except for occasional outbursts in clearly nonequivocal schizophrenic speech patterns. Patient exhibits obsessive repetitive behavior with one hand. Carriage is ramrod straight, almost tilting backward as in some catatonic posture. Patient hallucinates that he once had a brother, 'William.'"

There was a long pause on the tape. Background noises could be heard: shuffling of papers, movement of feet. Helene lifted the blanket higher so that it covered her whole body and draped over the sides of the chair.

"Now I know what they mean when they talk of the back wards. What can be done with this man, Ligur? Nothing. What can be learned from him? Nothing. What can be the purpose of his continued existence? Nothing. He stole, murdered, raped. Now he is judged insane. One might say that Ligur is the finest living monument to the death penalty. Ligur is the end. The steel door at the end."

Helene moved quickly from her chair to the machine and pressed the fast forward lever. She stopped the tape once, listened, then ran it forward again, stopped it, returned to her chair.

"A strange occurrence today. Stood by the fence and watched the ward in their exercise period. Ligur was standing off to one side, as usual, his hand moving in that ritualized pattern. He saw me and turned away, turned completely around so that his back was to me. Suddenly, he turned again to face me, and he was holding a green leaf in front of his face, like a mask. Then he pulled the leaf away and there was his face again, sodden, insane, unapproachable, unfathomable."

Helene was off her chair again, moving the tape forward. Finding the place she wanted, she stood near the window, listening, the blanket still wrapped about her.

"Again, Ligur. Something strange. I visited the wards this morning. Ligur was squatting in his usual place, near his bed, his back against the wall. An attendant was speaking to me. Ligur was not more than fifteen feet away and nothing blocked our sight of each other. I looked at him all the while the attendant spoke. Something was wrong. Then I isolated it. He had stopped that motion of his hand. He was looking at me.

"The attendant glanced at Ligur and the motion began. He looked away and Ligur's hand stopped moving. All the while his eyes were on me.

"The attendant left. I looked at Ligur, trying to get some clue from his gaze. As I started to walk toward him, his hand began again to move. I stopped. It stopped. His eyes were riveted on my face. They were not the eyes of a madman and they were not the eyes of a normal man. And I could not meet his gaze."

Helene stopped the machine, removed the cassette, and quickly inserted another. She pulled the blanket more closely around her.

"I have made a mistake. I don't know who Ligur is. But he is not merely a paranoid schizophrenic. He is not merely a retarded psychopathic murderer. The more I watch him, the more I intuit something else.

"A thousand small events: a movement of the hand, a placing

of the feet, a twist of the head, the way he suddenly stares at the sunlight.

"But what do I intuit? And why should I be anxious to intuit, to study him, to watch for the smallest clue?

"Perhaps it is something that is happening to me. Perhaps Ligur is an immovable, unchangeable psychotic rock and I am using him to reflect changes within myself. What changes? It is too late for me to change either for better or for worse. The sutures of my brain have closed. The sutures of my heart. The game is played out. There is nothing more."

Helene leaned over and rushed the tape forward.

"Ligur was standing still by his bed, facing the window. I asked him how he was feeling. He didn't respond. I reached out and touched him on the shoulder with just my finger. Why, I don't know. I pulled my hand back. He didn't move or speak. I touched him on the shoulder again. It was strange, touching a psychotic. Shrinks don't touch. They talk. They shrink. They analyze. They prescribe. I touched his very muscular shoulder. I wanted to say something to him, something to the effect that I was watching him. I wanted it to be a compliment, to say something complimentary.

"Another patient walked toward us, looking for something on the floor. I knew him, so I greeted him. When I turned back to Ligur, he was squatting by his bed, eyes staring forward, refusing to recognize me. His hand was moving relentlessly in that circle.

"I left the ward. My hands were shaking. I felt stupid and weak and without purpose. Oh, God."

There was a long, shrill, nervous laugh on the tape, and then a silence, and then her words came again.

"I am becoming infatuated with a psychotic. Yes. The world won't end with a bang or a whimper. It will end with Thorazine."

Helene stopped the tape. She listened to the silence.

V

John Ligur sat quietly beside his bed. No one in the ward knew he was suffering indescribable pain. They were torturing him again. This time they were concentrating on his penis. From time to time he crossed his legs and squeezed very hard, to allay the pain. Also, from time to time, he smiled, because he knew his own strength and he knew he would not talk. An attendant passed and greeted him. Ligur did not return the greeting. When the attendant was out of sight, he opened his pajama fly and looked at his penis. One day, he realized, one day soon, he would have to cut it off.

It didn't matter; he could grow another one whenever he wanted. It was easy. He would communicate with his lord and master, who would then command the sun. The sun would focus on the wound and a new penis would sprout.

He shook his head violently. The torturers had also sent someone into his ear during the night. But that was his own fault. Usually he slept with both his ears covered, as he knew that was absolutely necessary. Last night, however, he had grown lax, and they sent someone inside. There was little pain in his ears. They were concentrating the pain on his penis. Just what was going on inside his head? It was an assault on his brain. A sort of worm boring through his cerebrum in an attempt to reach his primitive brain. Ligur was not too worried about the enemy within. He had outfoxed the enemy before. The way to do it was to keep shaking his head so that the visitor kept losing his balance and sense of direction. Ligur knew that the ear borer had a life span of only twelve hours. The ear borer would then be absorbed by brain tissue.

A tiny drop of sweat formed on Ligur's forehead. This was the worst it had ever been. Now they were working on his testicles. Leather thongs treated with sandpaper and soaked in water had been wrapped around his testicles. As the thongs dried, they crushed. An electrical machine pulled the thongs so that they both crushed and lacerated. Another drop of sweat. He crossed his legs again.

Ligur looked up. An attendant was standing at the foot of his bed.

"Let's go, John, it's time for your session."

Ligur did not move or respond, or in any way show that he had heard. The attendant repeated his request. Again, Ligur did not acknowledge him. The attendant walked down the hall and knocked on a closed door. Helene Roth opened the door.

"Ligur won't come," said the attendant.

She stared at him. It was the first time Ligur had ever refused. It wasn't like him.

"You want me to bring him?" the attendant asked.

The inference was clear: Ligur would be dragged to the session.

"No, I'll talk to him," she said.

The attendant shrugged and followed Helene into the ward.

"Why won't you visit me, John?"

Ligur looked at the woman. He only shook his head from side to side.

"What's bothering you?"

Ligur closed his eyes. Then he opened them and pointed to his penis.

"John, what's the matter?" She moved closer to him, and her hand touched the fabric of his pajama top.

"Watch yourself, Dr. Roth, watch yourself," said the attendant.

She could see the sweat on Ligur's forehead. The attendant hovered around her, watching carefully, his body tense and ready.

Helene reached under Ligur's arm.

"I want to talk to you, John. I think we should talk."

The other inmates of the ward began to move away. They turned toward the wall. They picked up pillows. They sat down in front of checkerboards.

Ligur pointed to his penis.

"John, tell me what the trouble is."

Suddenly the pain subsided. It was always this way. The torturers left the premises when other people were near. The torturers did not wish to be identified.

Ligur stood up. The attendant touched Helene's arm in a silent warning to move away. She stood her ground, grasped the loose sleeve of his pajamas, and side by side they walked slowly to the consultation room.

Ligur climbed up on the table and lay there. She watched him for a long time without saying a word. She tried to comprehend his mood, to catch precisely what was happening to him. His hand made its circle but in slow motion.

"I've brought you a picture of William again," she finally said, holding a photograph next to his face. Ligur stared straight ahead for a few moments, then turned his eyes to the photograph.

Looking at Helene, he said, "I am hungry."

Helene walked to the desk, and from the top drawer removed a chocolate bar. She unwrapped it, broke off a piece, and gave it to Ligur. Ligur put the chocolate in his mouth. She broke off another piece. He ate with no enthusiasm. Soon the bar was finished.

"I am hungry," said Ligur.

The ritual was repeated with another chocolate bar. Then repeated two more times. Melted chocolate dripped from the sides of Ligur's mouth.

Opening his pajama top, she placed a hand on his bare chest. With the other hand she wiped the chocolate from the sides of his mouth and fed it back to him on her finger. Then she put both hands on his chest and slowly massaged him. The muscle, bone, and sinew didn't give. An impenetrable wall, his chest. She could feel his heartbeat through her fingers—steady, relentless, a dull throb that never changed pace.

"Why wouldn't you come into the room, John?"

Ligur shook his head slowly.

"Is there anything you want to tell me?"

No response.

"Or show me?"

No response.

"John, look at William again."

She held the photograph directly in front of his eyes. He stared at it, unblinking. Then his eyes darted to the left. She moved it closer, two inches away.

Ligur's arm lashed out and knocked the photograph from her hand. Helene stifled a cry. Composing herself, she picked up the photograph and returned to Ligur.

She slid a hand inside his pajama top, under his armpit. He was sweating. He was scared. She massaged his shoulders, then his neck. She quietly hummed a song.

Ligur's hand was making its circle. Helene watched it, and when his body felt relaxed under her hands, she reached out and broke its continuity, catching it like a bird on the wing. The hand resisted for a moment, then lay still in her grasp. She guided Ligur's hand under her sweater. Passive at first, it soon began to grope. Then it found her breast and encircled it. His fingers were cold. Cold. They began to knead her breast. They were strong and they were soft. And cold.

Helene started to tremble. She felt fear and longing. It was the beginning and the end. His hand was reaching out from an invisible land, from a region she could never visit, could never know. His hand's gentleness held a thousand knives. It held thoughts she would never perceive. His hand was on her nipple. Death and wisdom. She closed her eyes. Death and wisdom.

"Stand up, John, stand up."

She moved back to let him stand. His hand slid from her flesh. Another step back and she was against the wall. Ligur swung his legs over the side of the examining table. She made a motion with her hands. He didn't understand. She made the motion again. He pushed at his pajamas. She slipped the bottoms off him and they fell onto the floor.

"John, stand up. Stand up."

He stood. She stepped out of her shoes, then reached under her dress and removed her panties. She held them out and Ligur took them. He stretched the fabric with both hands. He rolled it into a ball. He placed it over his eyes. Then he let the garment flutter to the floor.

Ligur moved closer to Helene and put his hands under her dress. She felt his fingers around her bottom and then slipping between her legs. She felt an odd passion composed of engagement and abstraction.

Ligur lifted her as though she were a child and placed her on the examining table.

This is better than love, she thought. Better than all the sighing and meandering, better than the dumb sequential tale that ended with penis in vagina. It would end the same way here, but there were other factors.

Ligur looked at her as he stood by the table, but his eyes were light years away.

She was glad her life had resolved itself in this way: sex with a psychotic. This was a fitting end to her desire to draw something vital and horrible from her profession. Too long she had played around the edges of madness. Now she was in it. And it was in her.

She spread her legs. He lay his cheek on her stomach. I need you, she thought. You revolt me, she thought.

"Come," she said.

Ligur vaulted onto the table, his hands on either side of her, his body hovering inches above her. Although he did not touch her, she felt a great weight, as if he had blotted out the sun. His face seemed carved out of prehistoric stone. She looked away, at her panties on the floor.

She pulled up her knees. He kneeled in the space between her legs. He doesn't know what he is doing, she thought. He is not doing sex. He's doing something else. He's participating in another ritual. She caressed his face.

He entered her suddenly. Helene arched her back. He pushed in deeper and she felt herself crushed into the table. He thrust into her like a nail driving her to the table. Then he was still. Then he thrust again. She reached up and circled his neck with her arms, but his neck was hard and aloof. Again he thrust, and again and again. He began to move faster and faster. She tried to rise to meet him, but the force was overwhelming and she let herself be carried along.

Now it was beginning to feel good. Now it was beginning to make some sense. Her breath came out in little sobs. Her insides were churning and something was growing inside her. It was expanding, moving outward toward the walls. It was rising and falling. It was gathering moss and leaves and all the dross of her. It was a ball, a balloon, a bubble. It was stretching and squirming. It was too big now, too delicate. It burst. Her body shuddered and fell. She lay still.

Ligur looked at her as though she were dead. He touched her chin with a finger. She smiled at him. He vaulted off the table and stood quietly, facing a wall.

In a few minutes she rose and picked up his pajama bottoms from the floor. She handed them to Ligur and he dressed like an automaton. Helene put on her panties and sat down at the desk. She doodled on a scratch pad.

"Are you ready to go back?"

He said nothing. She opened the door. He walked out. He did not look at her.

Helene sat down at the desk again. I'm exhausted, she thought. Her face was pale and drained. Her body ached, her mind ached. There had been only one thought at the moment of orgasm: *Die, Paul.* And that was why he was going to die. Because even at that moment of what the world calls ecstasy, her thoughts were fatally on him. Thus he had killed her freedom, and now she was killing his. She drew two lines on the pad. One she continued until it was off the page. There was a non-Euclidean geometry in which parallel lines met in space. That had made her feel good when she first learned it in school. She drew the other line off the pad. Dimly, she could hear the sounds of the ward outside the door. The clatter of wagons, the shuffling of feet, an attendant's reprimand. It was her only world now. There were other patients to see. Were there really? She opened a desk drawer and pulled out some files, only to leaf through them with no interest. Ligur was her only patient. She smiled. She was Ligur's only patient. They had both eschewed sanity. For different motives, but so what. She returned the files to the desk drawer, her eyes falling on an old copy of *The Interpretation of Dreams.* It was the only gospel she had kept after leaving New York. Freud. Her fingers ran over the book's cover. He would have approved, she thought. He was radical. Always ready to take a dream a step further. But he wanted evidence. Evidence. Evidence. The word clattered in her head. Stanislas would give him her evidence.

Helene walked briskly down the ward. Ligur was back in his usual place. Attendants nodded as she passed. She headed toward the administrative wing. I need, she thought, a cup of coffee.

Margaret sat quietly, her hands folded on her lap. Stanislas was in his usual place behind the desk.

"I'm sorry about the way I behaved the last time I was here."

He nodded, smiled briefly in acknowledgment of the apology, and said, "You're not here to apologize. You're here to understand." She straightened her back, crossed and then uncrossed her legs. She told Stanislas what had taken place in the office between herself and Edward Lupica.

"Is that all?" asked Stanislas.

"I threw coffee at him. Then I called you."

"Did you see him again before coming here?"

"No."

Stanislas moved just a bit in his chair as though a sudden cramp had come upon him. Margaret caught the move and wondered. She always caught every move he made.

"Do you think, now, that he stole your pen?"

"I don't know."

"Refresh my memory about this man, Edward Lupica."

"To put it bluntly, I hate him."

"What do you hate about him?"

"Everything. Him. The way he dresses. His subterfuges. His ambition which he cloaks with intellectual interest."

"Do you think he stole your pen?"

"You asked me that before," she retorted angrily.

"Do you?"

"Yes! Yes." Margaret stood and walked to the couch, stared at it, walked back to the chair and sat down. God, I wish I could smoke, she thought.

"Why would he steal it?"

Lost in reverie, Margaret didn't answer. She was running her hands along his cheekbones. She was touching his shoulder. He was talking to her about music.

"Why would he steal it?" Stanislas repeated.

"I don't know."

"Surely he has his own pen."

"I don't know why he would steal it. I don't know why people steal, or kill, or maim. But they do."

"Do you often get attached to pens?"

"No."

"Then why this one?"

"It had a good point." Margaret suddenly felt ridiculous. "You don't understand," she continued. "It's a question of finding a point that's the right width—a point that can be used both for drawing and writing."

She felt her breath coming with difficulty.

"What color was the pen?"

"I don't remember."

"And you had not one pen to replace it?"

Why was he asking these stupid questions? She wasn't here to discuss the theft. She was here to be calmed, to be put back on the right track again.

"How long have you had the pen?"

"I don't know," she said wearily, "maybe a week, maybe a month."

"Have you ever been friendly with this man, Edward?"

"Never."

"Didn't you even have a cup of coffee with him?"

"No. I hated him from the beginning."

"Why?"

"You asked me that before!"

"And what did you say?"

"I forget now. But I told you why I hated him."

"Ah, yes. His dress."

"And him. *Him.*"

"Does he remind you of anyone?"

"No."

"Have you ever poured coffee on anyone else?"

"I don't remember."

Stanislas was silent. She felt a bead of sweat trickling down her leg. It made her uncomfortable.

"You once poured coffee on someone. I recall your telling me about it, some time ago."

"It wasn't coffee!" Margaret responded violently. "It was buttermilk. And not on a person. On a *rug*."

"And your father struck you, then, I believe. It was the first time he ever hit you."

"And the last time. The last."

It had been a large glass, filled with buttermilk to the brim. Sometimes she loved buttermilk and sometimes she hated it. She walked into the living room where her parents were talking together. The glass was suddenly very heavy. She didn't pour the buttermilk out—the glass just dropped, straight down. Buttermilk spread all over the rug. She was astonished to see the white buttermilk darken as it seeped into the rug. Her mother screamed. Her father said, *"Why?"* She did not answer. Her father hit her across the shoulder. Not hard. As though he was hitting a dog, a cur. It was a slap, really. A slurring slap. A hit off the shoulder. And then she ran out of the room.

"Edward Lupica," said Margaret sarcastically, "is just like my father, isn't he. Lupica has nothing to do with my father!"

"Everything has to do with one's father, I would say."

"Lupica has nothing to do with my father or my mother or me! I hate him. He's a thief."

Realizing how childish this sounded, her cheeks flushed.

"Anyway, I wanted to talk to you about something else."

"What something else?" said Stanislas.

"A dream I had a few nights ago."

"Tell me again about the pen. I don't recall what color it was. Or didn't you tell me?"

"It was pink, with mauve polka dots around the point," she said furiously.

Stanislas rummaged through his desk, finally found a pen and held it up. "Was it like this one?"

Why doesn't he leave it alone, she thought. Why is he going on and on? She shook her head.

"My questions about the pen seem to bother you."

"They bother me."

"Why?"

"I don't know why they bother me. I came back here because I was bothered."

She suddenly remembered something else about the buttermilk episode. Before walking into the living room, she had dipped one finger into the milk and sucked it. Yes. She was sure of it.

"Did you carry that pen around when you weren't at work?"

"I don't remember."

"Do you have a pen in your purse now?"

"No," she lied. There was a pen in her purse, but she wanted to stop this dialogue. She wanted something else to happen.

Suddenly she laughed. His line of thinking dawned on her: pen, penis; inordinate attraction to cylindrical object; inordinate fear of fleshy cylindrical object; Lupica the villain; her father the villain. Margaret couldn't stop laughing. Stanislas watched her playing with the pen.

"It's the wrong tree," she said at last.

"What is the wrong tree?"

"The pen."

"I don't understand what you're saying."

"Yes, you do. The pen and the penis. The penis and the pen."

"Did I say that?" he wondered abstractedly.

"You didn't say it, of course. You never say anything."

Another buttermilk memory intruded itself. God, she thought, after so many years. But the memory was there, vividly. She had fallen asleep and woken up hours later feeling nauseous. In the bathroom she was overwhelmed and crouched to the floor, retching. When she looked up her parents were there. Carefully and lovingly they helped her to bed, wrapped the coverlet securely around her. Then they cleaned up the mess. She could see them from her bed, kneeling together on the bathroom floor with paper towels. She saw their hips touch as they cleaned. Safe under the coverlet, she was happy that she had vomited.

"Did you ever find Edward Lupica sexually attractive?"

Margaret laughed out loud.

"Why do you find the possibility amusing?"

"I told you I hated him."

"Yes, you did."

"Do you ever find someone you hate sexually attractive?"

"It's not impossible."

"But do you?" Margaret persisted.

He didn't answer. He was holding the pen in front of him on the desk, turning it slowly from tip to end.

Margaret wanted to say that she hated him, Stanislas, but found him sexually attractive.

"I shall have to apologize," she said.

"Do you feel you ought to?"

"I'll tell him that I mistook him for the coffee disposal unit."

Stanislas laughed. Margaret felt good. He so rarely laughed.

"Or maybe I'll tell him that I accused him of taking my pen because I was really in a turmoil about his penis, which is really my father's penis . . ."

Stanislas wasn't listening. He was shuffling some papers and straightening his desk. Margaret knew what this meant: the session was over. She didn't want it to end.

"Will you be coming regularly now?"

"Yes," said Margaret softly.

"Well, I will see you later on in the week."

He stood. The ritual was always the same. He rose and walked to a place halfway between his desk and the door. She opened the door and let herself out, then closed the door behind her. The last thing she saw of each session was Stanislas, standing in the center of the room, looking as though he could stand between desk and door forever without discomfort.

It was dark outside. Margaret took the bus downtown. She huddled in her seat, letting her body bounce easily with the movement of the bus. The larger the bumps the better. After Stanislas, the more she felt like a rag doll the better. She was Raggedy Ann. The bus swayed and lurched and stopped. A cold wind blew through the doors when they opened.

Nice, here in the bus. But tomorrow there was Lupica and her job. And the day after that and the day after that. And in five years—what? More Raggedy Ann. I am the last of the rag dolls, she thought. It seemed funny and profound. She smiled.

The bus lurched violently and threw Margaret halfway off her seat. She grasped the chrome rail and slid back into place. Her stop was approaching. No, she didn't want to get off. What was the point of getting off? There was no point whatsoever. Better to keep moving in the bus. She closed her eyes. Like a whale, the bus moved through the city. No, she thought, like a centipede. No, a crippled bird. She was the heart of the beast. She controlled it.

Margaret moved to the back of the bus, to a seat right over the engine. She lit a cigarette and cupped it, feeling wicked and good.

The cigarette was finished. Her stop was passed. She lit another cigarette as the bus moved on. A passenger lurched against a seat and she heard a jangling sound, like a glass of buttermilk dropping . . . Why had Stanislas dredged that up? But no, *she* had brought it up. No—who? Just who? She closed her eyes and saw Stanislas leaning over her neck, pressing his lips against her collarbone. In pinstriped malevolence, Lupica hovered in the background.

The bus stopped and Margaret looked out the window. Where was she? The bus moved on and she recognized a few landmarks. Not bad, not too far. Soon she would get off and take another bus back. Maybe she would spend all night driving up and back, back and down, east and west. What did the bus driver think of her? Did he wonder who the tall, handsome woman was, breaking the smoking laws?

No one else was left on the bus. It's time to get off, she said aloud. She walked to the front of the bus and pulled the signal cord. The bus edged up to the curb and opened its doors. Margaret stepped down, avoiding the driver's glance. For a brief moment she had the feeling that her father was at the wheel. But her father was dead, long dead. She crossed the street and boarded the uptown bus.

Paul Stanislas took an egg from the egg carton. He held it gingerly and rolled it between his fingers. Eggs had never ceased to fascinate him. They were so much simpler than the human brain. They were elegantly primitive. Yes. That was it. He was glad he'd finally come upon a term to describe his fascination. Elegantly primitive. Yes. He placed the egg on the counter and put the carton back in the refrigerator. Then he half-filled a pot with water and sat it on top of the stove to boil.

When the first blurps appeared in the water, he took a large spoon, placed the egg on it, and lowered the egg into the boiling water. He checked his watch. It was seven-thirty in the evening. At seven-thirty-five he would remove the egg.

He walked to one of the windows facing the river and stared out. But for the lights on the Jersey side, there was nothing to see. Timing eggs always made him apprehensive. He always wondered why this should be so, but over the years had reached no solution. Three minutes to go. He walked to the bookcase and leafed through a stack of periodicals. Two minutes to go. He walked back into the kitchen and stood over the pot. The water was boiling furiously now. No crack appeared in the egg. Everything was going well.

He remembered an analogy a colleague had made between eggs and psychoanalysis. If one pierced an egg with a pin, the innards slowly ran out, leaving the structure and shape of the egg untouched. Of course, the baby chick ran out in the fluid. So it was with the patient. The analyst must draw out the baby, let it trickle out, so that the baby vanishes and the egg remains. No. He hadn't remembered correctly. An element was missing in the analogy. He looked at his watch. It was time.

He began to peel off the shell. A failure. The shell adhered to the flesh of the egg. The more he peeled the more the egg's body was lost. He threw it into the garbage. He consoled himself with two apples. He suddenly remembered the missing element, the person who had made the analogy. Helene Roth. She had used it with her usual effectiveness. Finishing the second apple, he returned to the living room and sat down on the sofa. That woman was returning, constantly, ever since Deirdre had so cavalierly brought the name up as if it were merely a name attached to a body. It was like trying to hold water in the palm of one's hand— some would always seep through. A closure here, an opening there—the map of one's hand could not hold the substance checked. Nor could he, Stanislas realized, hold the substance called Helene Roth in check. She was dripping through, seeping out and in.

He stretched out his feet, massaged an aching shoulder for a moment, and then dozed.

Ten minutes later he awoke very quickly. He shook his head. there was sweat on his chest beneath the shirt. He had dreamed. He remembered only that an egg had been offered him. When he reached out to grasp the egg, it splintered and the fluid ran over his hand. The horror of the running fluid had awoken him.

He looked at his watch: not yet eight o'clock. The watch suddenly transformed itself into an egg, and the egg splintered again, and he almost gagged at the running yolk.

He felt a tightness in his chest, and the sides of his temples seemed to be pushing out against his skull.

For a moment, for just a brief moment, he felt a total loss of control—as if his life was running out like the yolk—and the only thing which kept him in a human shell was fear. A filthy sheet of fear which covered his body and would not identify itself.

Breathe, Stanislas thought, breathe. He pulled the air in and expelled it, in and out, until he was in control once again. And once in control, he realized he was hungry.

He put on a heavy jacket, perched a wool cap on his head, and went downstairs. He passed a Chinese restaurant and studied the menu. Nothing struck his fancy. He kept walking, getting hungrier and hungrier. A Japanese restaurant featured raw tuna. Stanislas had never eaten raw tuna. He studied the entire menu. Yes, raw tuna was the thing for him to eat.

He went into the restaurant and sat down. A couple at the next table was speaking in hushed tones. He ordered the fish and a glass of plum wine. The wine arrived first and he sipped it contentedly. Ten minutes later came the food. A dish of rice in a lacquered bowl. Strips of raw tuna in another bowl. A glob of green paste at the edge of the bowl.

Stanislas studied the fish. Intelligent, he thought, to eat raw fish. Like an egg, it was elegantly primitive. He spurned the chopsticks, and taking a forkfull of fish, dabbed it in the green paste and put it into his mouth. He chewed thoughtfully, in the same way that he lived thoughtfully.

The taste was excellent. He had expected raw fish to be slimy. But it was thick and dry. He could feel the give of the flesh, and the green paste was delightfully tart. He swallowed, ate some rice and sipped the plum wine. The couple next to him raised their voices for a brief moment, then resumed the low murmur. He studied them; lovers obviously. Their presence made Stanislas feel good. He speared another strip of raw fish. The couple joined hands across the table. He hoped the man wouldn't drop his sleeve in the sauce.

Stanislas had one more glass of plum wine, finished the rice, and asked for a check. Usually he lingered after a meal, but now the lovers were making him uncomfortable. He'd been a shrink too long. Normalcy made him nervous after the first fifteen minutes.

The street was cold and clear. He decided to walk, keeping to the curb side of the sidewalk, pacing himself so that he wouldn't be stopped by red lights. The plum wine had made him a little lightheaded. He walked on, hoping to walk it off.

By the time Stanislas let himself into the apartment he was tired. He pulled off his clothes and folded them carefully. The small alarm clock by his bed read eleven-fifteen. That can't be right, he thought. I wasn't out more than an hour. He checked his watch. Eleven-fifteen.

He sat down on the bed. The time business was peculiar. Suddenly he whipped his head around as if someone was behind him. A strong but vacant panic seemed to grasp him. He had lost *time!*

It had vanished to somewhere. It had converted to something else, something that he couldn't recognize. A three-minute egg requires three minutes to boil. Time is the test of truth. Stanislas reached out in a jerky, pathetic motion as if he could retrieve what had vanished. Then the panic subsided.

He remembered that he had taken off his pants without emptying his pockets. He walked to the pants, neatly folded on a chair, and emptied the pockets onto the night table. Wallet, keys, wad of bills, change. There seemed to be a bit too much money. He counted the bills. Three hundred dollars. He never carried that kind of cash. Maybe Deirdre had given him some money before he came back to the city. He couldn't remember. But why would she give him money?

Feeling leaden now, Stanislas climbed into bed. Just before dropping off to sleep, he remembered the beginning of the egg dream which had woken him up from his nap hours ago. A green man had offered him the egg. A massive, corrupt green man, wearing a tunic he could not place historically. A massive, leaf-wreathed green man, holding a small white egg in his hand. Stanislas fell asleep.

A drawing in one hand, Helene Roth sat in her study. The drawing was made on simple notebook paper. She stared at it from many angles, then smiled and selected a tape cassette.

"Fellatio. Fellatio. What a strange name for a sexual act. Where does it come from? The Latin? The verb, to fellate?

"How does one fellate a psychotic? Place one's mouth around the penis of the psychotic, slowly move one's mouth in a certain rigid pattern. Take care not to use one's teeth.

"What does a psychotic do while being fellated? A psychotic does not moan. A psychotic does not tremble. A psychotic accedes to fellatio with a steady thrusting of his penis.

"What type of women fellate psychotics? Only women psychiatrists. What am I? What have I fellated?

"Do I love Ligur? How can that be? He is psychotic. Have I totally despaired of any experience that approximates normal love?

"It was bound to happen. These past weeks have been filled with Ligur. Filled to my fingertips with his presence, with the realization that I've been dealing with something beyond my experience. It is a sobering fact that whenever I see him, every move he makes is a new clue to his equality. Radical equality. I am the psychiatrist, he is the psychotic. But something else is transpiring.

"I will be scientific. I will be accurate. I will be descriptive. As for analysis of events, that is now beyond me.

"Today is Wednesday. Last Friday I had another interview with Ligur. I spoke. He listened or seemed to listen. I asked questions. He replied, but of course the replies were not comprehensible nor did they have anything to do with the questions. He was sitting on the examining table; I was sitting at my desk.

"I was looking at him, and stopped talking. Suddenly I perceived this massiveness, this awesome connection of flesh and bone and neuron, and it made me profoundly sad. Sad for me. For the hospital. For humanity and God knows what else. I walked to him and opened his pajama fly, bent over and kissed his penis until it was erect, and then made love to him—fellatio. I stood back then, opened the door, and bid him good morning.

"There it was. That was it. That was last Friday. For hours after I thought nothing of it. Then it landed. Hard. I was in a form of shock. I could not explain my actions. I felt no shame or love or excitement or perversity, after the fact. Even worse, I did not feel I had done anything counter to professional ethics.

"On Monday we had another interview. What happened was a foregone conclusion. We spoke, or rather, I spoke and he made sounds. Then, fellatio. It is my need now. Why? Who cares. Who can care?

"Then, afterward, the most astonishing thing of all. He stared at me for the longest time. For once it was a look I could recognize. It was a stare of evaluation. I was being evaluated. At first I thought he was evaluating my skill as a lover.

"There were note pads on my desk and pens, pencils, magic markers of all colors. He chose a green pen, and standing stiffly by my side, began to execute a drawing. An astonishing performance. In a few moments he completed a drawing, a magnificent drawing. It was the massive face of a demonic man.

"I opened the door and Ligur left me. I sat down and stared at the drawing. It was brilliant. A green, demonic, brilliant face. But I had seen that man before. I had looked upon that drawing somewhere in the past, in another context. Where?

"I folded the drawing and put it in my pocket. This was Monday and I proceeded with the day. Monday night, at home, I studied the drawing once again. I couldn't remember where I had seen it before. Yesterday, Tuesday, while walking from the ward to my car after a staff meeting, I remembered.

"I had seen it carved in two fifteenth-century British churches in north Lancashire. Ligur's face, but for a missing horn, was the same. And I'd seen it at Fountain's Abbey, and at a dozen other medieval monasteries scattered throughout northern and western Europe.

"Ligur drew the face of the leaf mask—a motif stemming from Mesopotamia, through Dionysian Greece, through Roman and into the Christian West. A mask in the form of a head, in which facial hair takes the form of vines and trees. Art historians call him the Green Man. In the thirteenth century the mask of the Green Man takes on a more demonic existence. He grows horns and snakes. But the shape and form of the face is always the same. For some he stands for regeneration. For others, he stands for the absolute evil of the natural world.

"Ligur drew the mask. How, how could Ligur draw him? Why would he draw him?

"Today is Wednesday. Ligur and I were in the consultation room. I showed him his drawing. I asked the name. I asked the origin. I asked a thousand questions and all I received was a stare.

"So, fellatio. Fellatio. Only this time there was something else. There was a certain connection. I could feel something other than his penis. I could taste something other than flesh. Ligur was not alone. Ligur was with the past.

"Today is Wednesday. It had been so many years since I felt any kind of sexual joy. So many years. That single feeling, gone. A feeling you never forget and rarely recoup. But it came back to me this morning, from Ligur's body. I let myself go. It was different. I let myself go."

Helene Roth turned off the machine. She walked into the kitchen and lay the drawing on the breakfast table. She put her face down on the drawing, sideways, like a child, and began to hum a tune. Everything felt fine. Everything felt warm and a bit fuzzy.

Enid Williamson always waited until midnight to walk her two dogs in Riverside Park. She had walked in the park at midnight for the past ten years. She had walked a whole series of dogs. Now she had two: the old male, Igor, a malevolent German shepherd, and a five-year-old mixed breed bitch with lots of terrier showing.

No matter how many times her friends and neighbors warned her, no matter how often the doorman cautioned her, Enid went her own way. Igor looked ferocious. What rapist would tangle with Igor? In ten years no rapist had.

Enid attached leashes to the dogs and took the elevator down at midnight. She crossed Riverside Drive and entered the park. Enid never let the dogs off the leash until she was deep in the park. She'd done it once, and a policeman had given her a summons. Enid was furious and argued forcefully. The policeman advised her to shut up or be taken to the station house. Enid shut up. She was fifty-five, a successful personnel consultant, and wary of arrest.

Several hundred yards into the park, Igor began to pull. She slipped the leash and Igor sprinted away. Then she released the bitch, who followed after Igor at a steadier pace. Enid walked after the dogs, swinging their leashes and admiring the night.

The park was empty at this hour. In late autumn, everyone deserted the park, the good folk and the bad folk. She arrived at her favorite spot, from which she had a clear view of the river, and behind her the great facade of massive buildings that line Riverside Drive. She thrust her hands into the pockets of her beaver coat and rose to the tips of her toes. Enid felt good at night in the park.

Igor was returning, his tongue hanging out, having made, she supposed, his first successful reconnaissance. Igor collapsed in the apartment after these walks. The old dog now considered half the park his territory and thus was forced, genetically, to mark every other tree with his urine. An exhausting procedure.

The shepherd sidled up to Enid, took a playful nip at the bottom of her coat, and ran off again. The bitch came back and then U-turned after Igor.

Enid stared at the buildings along the Drive. Astonishing, she thought, the number of people who lived, anonymously, on her block. Astonishing. She heard Igor's growl. Oh, God, she thought, he's met the setter again. A week ago, Igor and an Irish setter had nearly torn each other apart. The growl came again, truly ferocious, and then she heard the bitch yipping and yapping.

Enid walked quickly, almost trotting toward the sound. Igor was pulling at something. The bitch was circling. Igor pulled and growled and pulled and growled.

"Igor, *heel*," she shouted. The shepherd didn't know what heel meant, because Enid never trained any of her dogs. But he did recognize a persuasive shout. He growled twice more and then sauntered back to his mistress. Enid grabbed him by the collar and looked back at what he'd been pulling at. On the ground was a well-dressed Hispanic man. One of his trouser legs was in shreds. Igor. Something was wrong. Half the man's face was obliterated with blood. It had caked and resembled a mask. Spurts of fresh blood occasionally surfaced.

The man was alive. His chest moved up and down slowly. A wallet lay on the ground beside him, and his pockets were turned out. He'd been beaten and robbed. Enid's foot came against something on the ground. A steel fence spike, like many that littered the park. She felt weak. God, what animals. To smash a steel spike into a living being. It was beyond her comprehension.

Should she cover the man? But with what? Should she speak to him, to give him courage? Should she administer artificial respiration? But he was breathing.

Igor was sitting, exhausted, on his haunches, his tongue lolling out the side of his mouth. Enid felt grateful to Igor. True, he had torn the man's clothing, but if not for Igor, the man might have lain there all night and died from exposure.

She kneeled beside the man and patted him on the head. Then she rose and walked to the nearest park exit, the dogs following. Once she looked back and saw that the bitch had something white in her mouth. Enid paused and took it away from the dog. It was only a white paper napkin, stained with blood. There was a figure in one corner that told her it came from a Japanese restaurant.

"Now's not the time to play," she advised the bitch, crumpling the bloodied napkin and tossing it into a trash can.

VI

Stanislas took the folded bills from his pocket and spread them on the desk. He picked up one—it was a ten dollar bill—and felt the grain of the paper carefully.

It was the first time he had ever inspected money. One earned it and one spent it, but one rarely felt it, consciously. The paper was subtle, almost a fabric. There was a portrait of Alexander Hamilton in the center. He tried to remember what he knew of the life of Hamilton—very little. There were all kinds of numbers on the front and back of the bill and signatures.

A sentence in the upper left hand corner of the front of the bill caught his eye: "This note is legal tender for all debts, public and private."

He pulled the bills together and counted them: three hundred dollars in all, a potpourri of various denominations.

Stanislas pressed his back against the chair. His hand held one corner of the wad, and he flicked the bills with violent jerks of his wrist, creating fanlike gusts of air.

Then he leaned forward again and counted the number of bills in the stack, regardless of the denominations.

There were thirty bills in all. Thirty.

His free hand slammed down hard on the table. He didn't know where the money came from. He didn't know at all. Just like time had vanished for him, now money had accrued for him. The money in his hand was his, but he had no inkling whatsoever of the source.

The color drained from Stanislas's face. A slight tremor started on one corner of his mouth, traveled a short distance, and then firmed.

Thirty pieces of silver. Thirty pieces of green, grained paper. *Judas Stanislas.* Stanislas Judas. But whom did I kiss? Whom did I betray? From whom did I take the tainted money?

He left the bills on the desk and walked swiftly to a large bureau which stood in one corner of the room. He opened the cabinet-type doors and plunged into a sea of papers and envelopes. His fingers unclasped each envelope and leafed through the contents. There were old books and magazines scattered throughout, and he shook the pages of each, waiting for something to drop.

He stepped back, puzzled. He didn't know what he was looking for. His hands slowly pushed the now protruding papers back to safety and struggled to close the bureau. When it was closed, he just stood there for a while trying to get a fix on his orientation.

He walked back to the table and shuffled the bills with the same force as he had shuffled the papers. He watched his own hands in astonishment.

A litany came to him. A clear, unequivocal confession came to him. I betrayed her. I betrayed my profession. I used the only sacred process in psychoanalysis—the transference—to debase the only sacred relationship in psychoanalysis—training analyst and neophyte analyst.

They were his own words and they were said silently, but they seemed to be spoken by someone else and to be spoken loudly.

I betrayed in order to understand.

He scooped the bills up and shoved them back into his pocket. Melodrama, he thought. He was being afflicted with bizarre turns of melodrama. Judas. And betrayal. And thirty pieces of silver.

His thoughts embarrassed him. That was not the way to proceed. That was not the way to get to the bottom of a very simple problem. That was not the way to proceed at all.

The tension, he knew, was in his own mind; the sudden intrusion of Helene Roth, he knew, had nothing to do with the reality of his or her world today. She was undoubtedly a matronly woman now, languishing from nothing, performing her tasks as she had always performed them—with competence and a . . .

The phone rang. He let it ring twice and then reached for it. The caller had hung up. Stanislas grinned. He had learned that a long time ago. Pick up the phone on the third ring. Many patients call from a hallucination of danger, but that danger often vanished after the second ring. Between the second ring of the phone and the third ring, fifty percent of his patients realized the call was neither necessary nor wise.

Between the second ring and the third ring—the formulation intrigued him. It was like the rungs of hell in the medieval manuscripts. Or perhaps the rungs of heaven.

History, he thought, is conservative. Rungs are changed to rings. Gospels to telephones. Nothing else changes. The wad of bills became lighter in his pocket.

When Humberto Palma opened his eyes he saw a ceiling. Sounds were all around him, frightening sounds, sounds of machines purring. As pain seared his face from ear to chin, he closed his eyes. Move your toes, move your toes, he thought. Fifty years ago, when he was thrown from a horse on the outskirts of Havana, his father had told him, "Move your toes." Humberto tried to move his toes, but he couldn't tell whether or not they moved.

Enid Williamson stood quietly beside his bed. It was the first time she had ever been in an intensive-care unit and the first time she had ever been in St. Luke's Hospital. She didn't know the man stretched out in front of her. But her dogs had rescued him. She felt obliged to follow through. She had called the office and said that she would be in after lunch.

This was a very bad place to die, she thought. Tied to all these machines. She turned away from the bed and sat down on a chair that was shoved against the far wall. From where she sat she could see the bandage covering the left side of the man's face which had been mutilated by the spike. A nurse entered the room, nodded to Enid, and studied the purple and white lights dancing on one machine.

Enid checked her watch. It was eleven-fifteen. She would wait until noon and then go to work. The room was warm and she opened the top button of her suit jacket. She could see the man's chest rising and falling in an even tempo.

One of the machines had a moving graph in a window. Enid watched the line move from left to right, varying in height as it traveled. It must be measuring something, she thought. It must be measuring pulse or blood cells or kidney function. She didn't know. When it is time for me, she thought, I won't be tied to a machine. She would refuse to be measured. She would reject a twentieth-century death. Recently, Enid Williamson had been thinking of death a great deal. So it was only fitting that she had come upon this man. Three weeks ago, in the Metropolitan Museum, in an out-of-the-way corridor, in a glass case, Enid had seen a horsehair brush. The card informed her that it was used by a noblewoman in fourteenth century Italy. It seemed to Enid the most beautiful thing she had seen in her life. So she had begun to think profound thoughts about death and the twentieth century.

The man stirred. Enid emerged from her reverie and leaned forward in her chair. It came to her that if she had that brush in her hand she would simply brush him and all would be well. She looked at her watch; there wasn't much time left.

A young woman with rumpled clothes entered the room. She stared at Enid for a moment, then walked to the bed, looked closely at the man, turned back to Enid.

"He will be fine," she said.

Enid could think of no response.

"I am his daughter," the young woman explained.

Enid rose to her feet.

"I found your father in the park. I'm very glad he's going to pull through."

The daughter nodded, absentmindedly smoothing the blanket.

"I have to go to work," said Enid.

The young woman smiled her thanks.

Humberto Palma opened his eyes again and saw his daughter. Then he realized she was touching his hand. Then clarity came. He was Humberto Palma. He was lying in a hospital. Something terrible had happened to him. He closed his eyes and slept.

When he awoke some minutes later there were two men standing beside his daughter.

"They are police. They want to know what happened," she said.

He formulated words: the man who attacked me was not as tall as me. Those were the words that came to him. The man was not as tall as he was. But no sounds left his mouth.

"We can't hear you," his daughter said.

He tried again. Nothing. One of the policemen made a sign with his hand and they both left the room. His daughter leaned over and said, "They will be back tomorrow, when you're feeling stronger." Then she walked to the chair and sat down.

The side of his face was throbbing, but otherwise he felt well, almost lightheaded. He could remember everything now.

He had left the apartment to buy a newpaper from the all-night paper stand that was eight blocks north. He had decided to walk uptown through the park, buy the paper, and walk back on Broadway. As he entered the park, he saw a man sitting on a bench a hundred feet ahead of him. It was odd, he thought, for a man just to be sitting there in such cold weather. He was sitting as though it were spring. He looked as though he were thinking pleasant thoughts. Humberto Palma passed the man and twenty paces later turned around, cued by nothing he could name. The man was right behind him. The man was not as tall as he was.

They faced each other. The man smiled at him. It was a charming, gentle smile. Then the man held out a hand, in the palm of which lay an iron spike. With his other hand he pointed to the spike. Humberto Palma didn't know what the man was trying to tell him or show him. Guess he don't know English, thought Palma. He remembered when he hadn't known English either. All he could do was nod encouragingly. The man nodded back and smiled his charming smile.

Then the slow motion sequence began. Everything happened in slow motion. Humberto Palma watched it happen to him. The man raised both his hands high in the air, the iron spike between them. Humberto Palma had seen the motion many times before in the bull ring. He saw the hands slowly begin to descend. He was not afraid in the ordinary way. His terror aborted his flight. He did nothing. The spike was for him, but he could do nothing. He stood quite still and waited. He watched the charming smile.

Finally he screamed as the spike punctured his cheek and sent him to the ground. His tongue tasted the iron inside his mouth and he choked on blood. His own blood choked him.

"You must stay still," someone said. Humberto looked up and saw his daughter standing by the bed.

"The doctors said you will be well soon, but you must lie quietly now. Do you understand?"

Humberto obediently closed his eyes. He had felt the man's fingers in his pockets. He remembered something else, but he couldn't be sure. The man might have bent over him and kissed his forehead. He could not be sure. But it was possible.

Dr. William Bunche reluctantly opened his eyes. It was six-ten in the morning, it was the time he always opened his eyes. The room was still pitch dark. His wife lay next to him in a long flannel nightgown. The door of the unused barn was swinging back and forth on its hinges, whining. The radio alarm, set for six-twenty, was about to go off. Dr. Bunche sat up and switched the radio alarm to OFF. He got out of bed and dressed.

For more than twenty years he had followed the same morning regimen, and this autumn morning was no different. He went into the kitchen, opened the refrigerator, and drank some orange juice out of the container. Then he left the house and began to walk the farm. In his father's day it really was a farm, and this walking was what remained of his tie to childhood, for his father each morning had walked the farm. He had walked, looking for nothing and for everything. So William Bunche still walked the farm that was no longer a farm, looking for nothing and everything.

After the walk he returned to the kitchen and made a bowl of oatmeal. After the oatmeal, coffee. Then he carefully sponged the kitchen table, opened a seldom used silver chest, and brought forth two books and a pad which he placed on the table.

One book was a very old edition of *The Iliad*, in Greek. The other was a Greek-English lexicon. He opened *The Iliad* to a page marked with the remnant of a paper napkin, copied a single line of the Greek epic onto the pad, then proceeded to look up each word in the lexicon.

He worked steadily, and when an hour had passed, the single line was translated. He sat back in his chair, read the line in English, then closed the books and put them away.

He had often tried to break himself of this habit. The attempts were always unsuccessful. He translated because he was still alive and he wanted that sense of disclosure. He would fight for that sense of disclosure, for that moment when something is revealed through work, through intuition. Singular, fragile moment. Nowhere else did he find it. So he translated a line a morning. Never more, never less.

Bunche sat down at the table again and contemplated the coffee cup. Will you have another cup, Dr. Bunche? It was too early to leave for the hospital, but he would leave soon anyway. The alternative was talking to his wife. He did not wish to speak to his wife. He wished only to speak to Helene Roth.

Looking down at the circular ring of fat that buttressed his still formidable stomach muscles and was clearly visible through his shirt, Bunche thought: An aging man, going to fat, is in love. Although the picture was absurd, he would hardly fight it.

He heard his wife moving about upstairs. Quickly, he scribbled a note on a napkin, left it under the coffee cup, walked out of the house to his car.

Ten minutes later he parked the car on a level gravel strip abutting the highway. He could look across the road and see Helene Roth's house. Was she up yet? He didn't know. What did she have for breakfast? He didn't know. What did she wear in bed? What did she look like naked? Were her breasts large or small? Did she ever cough? He didn't know.

He grimaced. It was bizarre, all this tenderness he felt for her. Bizarre. He felt no tenderness for his patients, none for his wife. For them he felt the need to be honest, to be, perhaps, just. But here was something different.

The sky was beginning to lighten. He turned on the car radio, listened to the news, turned it off. A light went on inside Helene's house. He leaned forward, pressing against the steering wheel. Another light. He rolled down the window and felt the cold morning air on his face.

He thought he saw a shadow cross the light. His watch read seven-twenty. It was still too early for the hospital, but getting too light to stay parked where he was. He started the engine and drove to a small diner half a mile from the hospital.

Sitting at the counter, he ordered coffee and stared at the salt shaker. He had seen them all come and go, white grains against a psychotic curtain. He had seen the patients and he had seen the doctors. He had watched the academics, suddenly faced with the real thing, crumble and lose their reserve. He had watched the humanitarians, suddenly faced with violence, cry out for restraints without a thought to their avowed positions. He had seen doctors go crazy and psychotics get better, but he had never seen anyone like Helene Roth. She was different. She was wise. And she was in trouble. Bunche sipped his coffee and moved the salt shaker behind the pepper shaker. Yes, she was in trouble. And he was in love. Indisputably.

He would make another effort, and another if that failed, and another after that. He had to be with her. It was as simple as that. And after he was with her, he would translate her, line by line. The lexicon would be his life, with all that he had learned and all that he had forgotten. He would translate her, because he loved her.

Deirdre lay fully clothed on the well-made bed. Behind closed eyes she counted the rings of the telephone. She counted to seventeen and then the phone stopped ringing. It had to be Paul, she thought, opening her eyes, even though he rarely called in the morning. There was no one else it could be. Tradesmen ring only five or six times and give up. Friends, maybe eight. Even breathers don't hang on for seventeen.

If it really was Paul, he would call again in an hour. She looked at the clock on the night table and noted the time, then closed her eyes again. It was not sleep. It was a sort of comatose state now endemic to her mid-mornings. Emily was out of the house.

There was little to be done and less to be thought. This sleeplike procedure was a kind of wifely hibernation.

In an hour the phone rang. She let it ring four times and then picked up the receiver. It was Paul.

He was using his between-patients voice—quiet and steady. Over the years there were other voices she had come to recognize: the end of the day voice; the family voice; the strong father voice. The differences between them were subtle but unmistakable. She always knew which voice was talking and responded accordingly. The between-patients voice required direct response. He was calling for something quite specific and had neither the time nor inclination for conversation.

"Did you put any money in my pocket?"

The question was so peculiar that she didn't answer for a full ten seconds. Then she laughed.

"No, Paul. I didn't put any money in your pocket."

"I found three hundred dollars."

"Where?"

"In my pocket."

Deirdre reached over to the night table and lit a cigarette with the new gold lighter.

"Congratulations." Her husband made a lot of money. She couldn't understand why he would get excited over three hundred dollars. And he was excited.

"How are you doing?" He had altered the conversation.

"Fine, just fine."

"Well, I might as well spend the three hundred. Is there anything you want?"

"Want?"

"A gift. A dinner. Anything."

"I can't think of anything I want right now."

There was a long pause, a long silence. She let the ash of her cigarette roll along the ashtray's edge. She did want something, she knew, and only her husband could provide it. But it could not be articulated—it was too banal. And even if articulated it could not be comprehended—it was too subtle. She wanted him.

He said good-bye then, briskly, professionally. He hung up.

The call had broken her lassitude. She went into the kitchen and made a cup of coffee. It was bitter, just as the morning was bitter. She quickly put on a coat and left the house.

A few minutes later she was standing near the water, worrying a small rock with her shoe. A cold wind came in off the Sound. She kicked the rock toward the water. Fifty yards away a gull hovered in the air, buffeted at times by the wind.

She moved a ways back from the water and sat on the trunk of a gale-mangled tree. It had been there when they bought the house. No doubt it would be there in a century. The gull was moving along the shore line.

This is the way it would always be, always be, always be. Unless she made a move. But what move was there? And why should it be made?

The gull was out of sight now. It vanished after passing the roadhouse which jutted into the Sound a few hundred yards to the east. Deirdre wondered if the roadhouse was open. In the summer it was a popular place and she'd gone with Paul many times. She rose to her feet. She wanted to find out. She would follow the water and reach the roadhouse from the Sound side, climbing the steps of the extended pier.

She reached the pier a little breathless, her face wet with salt spray, her shoes soggy and speckled with seaweed. The steps of the pier were slippery. Indeed, the roadhouse was open. Even the bar was open. She knocked on a window. A man who was wielding a large mop over the lounge floor looked up. She waved and he walked to the waterside door and unbolted it.

"We don't get many visitors this way," he said.

She stamped her wet shoes against the doorframe and walked in. The bar stools were covered in leather and they swirled easily. She swiveled on one and started to laugh, suddenly, loudly. The bartender, who was washing glasses at the far end, looked up at her once, then returned to his task.

Deirdre felt astonishingly good. She had just emerged from the sea. A sea nymph.

"Do you want to drink or you want to dry out?" The bartender was addressing her.

"I would like a glass of dry white wine. Dry," she said.

He brought her a glass of white wine and she sipped it and lit a cigarette. It would be intelligent, she thought. Nymphing. To follow the water for mile after mile, suddenly emerging in a house, a roadhouse, a marina, all the establishments that lined the southern shore of the Long Island Sound. People would get to know her. She would be known as the wife of the shrink who emerges from the sea. And soon she would grow webbed feet . . .

What rot, she thought. Romantic rot. The bartender looked at her questioningly. She didn't want any more wine and covered her glass with her hand. Then she reached into her coat pocket and turned it inside out. No miraculous money. She didn't, obviously, have Paul's magic. But he didn't have her wisdom. Wifery's wisdom: only the living corrode; the dead rot.

The exercise yard was formidably fenced. Inmates of the ward filed out of the main building and took up stations at various points inside the yard. Attendants brought out the equipment: two basketballs for the two hoops situated on the far side of the yard, a volleyball for the tattered net on the opposite side, and a set of quoits. Years ago there had been horseshoes, but steel had proved dangerous on several occasions, and rope quoits were substituted.

Quoits were the only items supervised by the attendants. One stood hovering about the two pegs which had been set into the ground. Another held the five quoits on an arm, and when an inmate stepped up to the line, would hand over one quoit at a time. The thrown quoits were then retrieved, and the two attendants changed places.

Most of the men participated in nothing. They walked about, or stood quite still, or ran their fingers along the chain-link fence. Once in a while someone threw a basketball toward the hoop or kicked a volleyball from one end of the yard to the other.

Ligur stood at the furthest end of the yard. He was doing what he always did here—absolutely nothing. His arm made its eternal circle. Facing the fence, his nose was six inches from the wire. Every five or ten minutes he turned forty-five degrees, so that by the end of the exercise period he had usually made a complete circle and was once again facing the fence.

One of the attendants, growing restless, began to throw the

quoits. He threw all five. One landed on the peg. The other attendant retrieved the quoits and walked back to the line.

Helene Roth was standing beside a large tree on the lawn, some hundred feet from the yard. She was watching Ligur. He stood, motionless but for his arm, staring from the enclosure in her general direction. She had no way of knowing if he actually saw her. She jangled the car keys in her hand. It was cold just standing there. She felt she ought to drive home.

The fences between them were insurmountable. This chain-link fence and the other. She was, in the end, a psychiatrist. He was, in the end, psychotic. We have a language, she thought, of color and sound and inference. She laughed. This was the language of psychosis. Who was the real practitioner? Thrusting the keys into her pocket, she began to walk to her car. Ligur suddenly wheeled and jogged to the middle of the yard.

He stopped beside the attendant who held the quoits. The attendant, grinning, offered Ligur a quoit. Ligur closed his hand around it. The attendant pointed to the peg, then mimicked a throw.

Ligur threw the quoit. He didn't throw in the correct manner, from the opposite side of his body with a flick of the wrist. He threw with a great sweep of his arm behind him and then over his head.

The quoit sailed high in the air, elevating, slowly spiraling through the frigid morning. It seemed to hover endlessly over the dreary yard. Then it fell. It fell like a bomb, fell squarely on the peg.

The two attendants were staring at each other in astonishment. Ligur stood motionless once again, his arm making its circular pattern.

The attendant offered him another quoit. Ligur took it passionlessly. Again he swept his whole arm behind him, then over his head and up through the winter sunlight. The quoit rose high in the air and fell slowly. It landed, unerringly, on the peg.

An inmate passed the peg, glanced at the quoit and cursed it. He moved off as the attendants grinned at each other. Another quoit was handed to Ligur.

He felt the rope against his fingers. Rope was good. Rope belonged to the gods. With rope you could hang someone. You could tie a man to another man, a table to a chair.

He held the quoit up to the sky and looked at the sun through its circumference. His arm swung back. He proceeded to throw. The quoit was launched high in the air. It did not land on the peg. It did not even move toward the peg.

The quoit rose over the yard, over the lawn, and slowly settled five feet away from Helene Roth.

She had not seen it coming. She had been watching Ligur as he made the throw, and then, suddenly, there had been a change in the light around her. The quoit had landed on the hard ground, bounced an inch, then landed again.

She walked to the quoit and nudged it with her foot. A love letter? A threat? A sign from his gods that retribution was at hand! Or, perhaps, a reward?

The attendant was walking slowly but purposefully toward her. He stopped in front of the quoit.

"If it'd hit you, it would've hurt," he said. He seemed to be grinning on one side of his mouth. There was a scar under his left eye. Helene suddenly recalled that this was the man Ligur had attacked with a checkerboard.

"But it didn't hit me," she said.

He bent down and picked up the quoit, holding it gingerly in his hand. He wanted to impart a sense of its danger. Helene looked past him into the yard. Ligur was standing near the fence, staring out at things, visions, memories unknown to her. She wanted to keep the quoit because Ligur had given it to her. But what could she say? She said nothing.

The attendant smirked, then turned and trotted back to the yard. Once inside he flung the quoit toward the peg. It landed a long way from the mark.

"Did you enjoy the performance?"

The voice startled her and she turned. William Bunche stood on the lawn.

"For a large man you make an appearance very silently," Helene said.

"Would you prefer that I banged into things?"

She laughed, at the same time watching the inmates file out of the yard and back into the ward.

"Your patient appears to be an excellent quoit thrower."

"Yes, so it seems," she agreed, and started to walk toward her car.

"Are you in a hurry?"

"It's cold," she said.

"Give me just a minute."

Helene paused and waited.

"I'd like to tell you a joke about two Russian psychiatrists."

"But I thought you had given up," she said mildly.

"So did I. We were both wrong. Let me tell you this joke. I tell so few. Two Russian psychiatrists meet on a road. The first asks the second where he's going. The second replies that he's going to the Minsk Psychiatric Clinic. The first one says, 'You tell me that you are going to the Minsk Psychiatric Clinic so that I will think you're going to the Pinsk Psychiatric Clinic—but I know, anyway, that you're really going to the Minsk Psychiatric Clinic.'"

Helene suddenly laughed out loud with pleasure.

"Well, Dr. Bunche, you've successfully corrupted Freud's favorite joke!"

"I thought you might appreciate it."

They watched each other, both of them jangling their car keys.

"Do you know the north fork of the highway?" he asked.

"Yes."

"Well. If you take the north fork north about twenty miles, you come to an old barn that's been converted to a French restaurant. Perhaps you might find the time to join me for dinner there. Tomorrow night. We can go straight from the hospital."

"I don't think so."

"You don't like French cuisine?"

"I love French cuisine, but I don't see the point."

"The point, Dr. Roth, is *coquille St. Jacques.* They make the finest *coquille St. Jacques* in Dutchess County. Maybe the world. That is the point."

Helene stared down at the place on the ground where the quoit had fallen. It had not made a mark. The ground was frozen. The only mark was in her mind's eye. Why not, she thought. Why not have a nice dinner in a good French restaurant with an intelligent man. Why not?

She looked directly at Bunche and smiled. "I accept your invitation. Bring a lot of money. I eat voraciously when I'm hungry."

She turned and began once more to walk to her car. His hand closed around her elbow, stopping her.

"Just one other thing. You shouldn't be impressed with a psychotic's ability with quoits. If they chose to, psychotics could break every athletic record in the world. They don't have—or rather, they have lost—the innate restraints that stop you and me from going to the limit, automatically."

"Are you going to lecture me over the *coquille St. Jacques* as well?" she snapped.

He stepped back, baffled by her fury. Then he shook his head gently. "I shall talk about the weather and cows, that is all."

"Tomorrow evening," said Helene, making peace.

Bunche walked slowly to the exercise yard and ran his large hands over the chain-link fence. As he looked inside the enclosure, the wind was whipping the tattered volleyball net. He knew now. He knew that the trouble she was in had something to do with Ligur. Ligur. The psychotic who threw quoits to perfection.

Margaret Olsen twirled a black magic marker between her fingers. Down the hall Edward Lupica was waiting for her apology. And she was going to make an apology; the problem was how to phrase it. She realized now that her response had been incorrect. Whether or not he had stolen the pen . . . whether or not . . . there was no excuse to pour coffee on the man. Whether or not he had engaged in a systematic attempt to undermine her position and influence in the agency, there was no excuse to drench him with bad coffee.

She held the magic marker up to the window's light, then let it fall on the fat new file that lay closed on her desk. The file contained data on her new project, her new neighborhood: Washington Heights. It was a good project. It would require months of research, of digging, asking questions and trying to find new questions. Yes, it was a good project. But the Edward Lupica project was more immediate. Project apology.

She took the black magic marker in her hand once again. Her father's penis. Margaret laughed out loud. It was inconceivable. But why had she become hysterical over the loss of a simple writing implement? Why had she gone to the edge over nothing? She recalled with perfect clarity the last session with Stanislas. Buried for so many years, those memories had poured out of her.

What gave Stanislas the power to elicit them? Why did memory break through?

It was, she realized, her usual torment concerning analysis. Ninety-five out of a hundred hours it seemed to be an embarrassing and rather stupid pastime. But once in a great while, it operated with such force of illumination that to abandon it would be absurd.

Margaret lit a cigarette. A written apology to Lupica was certainly possible. But it wouldn't solve a thing. They still had to deal with each other face to face, and a note wouldn't defuse the confrontations. No, she would have to make a classical apology. She would have to appear in his office, present herself to him, and recite a passage.

Suddenly she turned in her chair. For a moment she had the peculiar feeling that Stanislas was in the room, sitting on his chair, ready to give her instructions. No one was there.

Cut this out, Margaret, just cut it out, she cautioned herself. Walk in and apologize. Within the next hour. Before lunch. Just get it done. She had to get it done.

It might be best to be humorous, she thought. But how? By quickly telling him that the reason she got upset about the magic marker was . . . the reason was her father's penis. But he wouldn't think that was funny. He would think she was nuts.

The cigarette was down to the filter. She lit another quickly and listed the various aspects of the apology on an edge of the Washington Heights file: Face to face. Humorous. Brief. She crossed out the list. Opening her purse, she found a comb and combed her hair. It is time, it is time now, she thought.

Margaret stood up, walked to the door, saw that the narrow hallway was empty, and moved slowly toward Edward Lupica.

His chair turned toward the window, Lupica was sitting at his desk, writing. She stood waiting in his doorway. He didn't see or sense her. She knocked twice—small, quiet, undemanding knocks.

Lupica put down his pencil, turned in his chair and saw her. Then he looked fixedly at his pencil.

"May I speak to you for just a minute?"

"Of course," he replied neutrally.

Margaret moved to the edge of his desk, then stepped backward toward the wall to see the whole of his face. She said nothing. Nothing came to her. She thought only that other people's faces were so peculiar. There was his face of which she knew nothing. She would have to speak to it even so, to address it, to please it.

She reached out a hand and touched his desk. Cold. She heard his pencil tapping on the wood. Then he spoke.

"You misjudge me."

She forced herself to look at him once again. The discoloration around his lip seemed inflamed. She had not heard what he said. She had heard some noise.

"You misjudge me," he repeated.

It sounded irrelevant.

"I came to apologize for throwing coffee on you. It was stupid and childish. And I apologize for accusing you of stealing my pen. Stupid and childish. I'm sorry."

Lupica ignored her in turn.

"You seem to think that I've made an effort to destroy your reputation for good work around here. Listen. I'm an ambitious man. Ambitious in the sense of wanting to get ahead, and ambitious in the sense of wanting to make this city viable. But that's not why I criticize your reports. Do you understand? That is *not* the reason. I simply don't agree with your approach. I don't agree with you. And I happen to think my approach is better. Maybe I'm arrogant, but I'm certainly not . . ."

He searched for a word without finding the one he wanted.

"Do you want to close the door?" he finally said.

"No, that won't be necessary. I came to apologize and I've done that."

They stared at each other.

"For God's sake, why do you do these things? Why do you suddenly blow up? What's the matter with you?" His voice was right at the edge of fury.

Margaret felt herself disassembling. She wanted to answer him. What was the way? Her hand trembled on the desk's edge. Finally, she turned up her palms in a gesture of despair.

He moved toward her, about to take her hand. Then he simply dropped the pencil he was holding onto his desk.

"Well. Do me a favor. The next time you decide to water me, please use tea instead of coffee. Tannic acid is medicinal."

They both smiled. Margaret left his office and walked back to her own. Sitting down, she lit a cigarette. The apology had been executed. Now there were other problems. He had made an opening. He was not what he had seemed to be. Again, she had misjudged. He was not what he had seemed to be. She looked down at the file on her desk. This was his work, she now knew. He had gotten her the project she wanted. He was being kind. Or perhaps he was being professional, merely complimenting her, professionally. Yes, the apology was over. But it had bred something else. She was damp with sweat. She was hungry.

Helene Roth watched the afternoon die from the window of her study. She rarely enjoyed this luxury because her hospital work usually kept her occupied until the inmates' dinner hour. The afternoon was dying well, she thought, going bit by bit, with just enough struggle to make it interesting, but no ill-mannered resistance against the inevitable.

In the hour that she had been at home, she had lifted the phone five times, each time determined to call Bunche and cancel the next night's dinner engagement. But each time she had hesitated. And then she gave it up. She would have dinner with the man. She would allow herself a small ration of normalcy. Because certainly she was strong enough to play a little.

When the afternoon was at last gone, she placed a cassette on the machine and sat down, folding her hands in her lap. At the first sound of her own voice, she forgot everything but her patient, her lover, her weapon, her life.

"I spent several hours with Ligur's files. The first question I had to find an answer to was simple: Is there anything in his background that would indicate an ability to expertly execute a drawing such as he made of the green man?

"There was nothing in the files to indicate such a talent. Absolutely nothing.

"The second question: Is there anything in his past, as revealed by the files, that would indicate a knowledge of the green man legend?

"No. There was nothing.

"The third question: Is there anything in his files, any notation by a previous doctor, that would indicate he was obsessed by such an image?

"Again, there was nothing. Nothing in the files.

"Did our sexual involvement produce the drawing? I doubt it. There are limits to the power of fellatio, even when performed by a qualified psychiatrist.

"The indications, though, are clear. Proceed with caution. I am not doing classical analysis with a petit bourgeois neurotic. I am dealing intimately, in every sense of the word, with a killer. A man who is, perhaps, evil, but who has chosen to reveal a minimal portion of himself. And there is nothing I can do, professionally, to elicit more. If what is going on between Ligur and myself is actually a form of love, more will be revealed. More of the green man, more of this reincarnation. More of his beautiful and mystifying drawing. Magical?"

Helene turned off the machine. Darkness now covered the room. Memories of the morning came to her. The quoit landing near her feet. The finely executed arc of Ligur's arm as he threw. The quoit's fall onto the peg. That, too, was normalcy. The normalcy of the elect.

VII

"A lot of people call me Will."

"Why not Billy? Why not William? That's your name."

"I don't know why. My father called me Will. My mother called me Will. So did my friends. On the other hand, my patients call me a great variety of names. One used to call me Dr. Large."

Helene felt comfortable in his car as they drove. She was happy to use the name Will. William brought to mind the mythical brother of a not so mythical patient.

She liked the way he sat at the wheel, back quite straight, hands holding the wheel very lightly. When he turned the car, he seemed to just slide the wheel between his palms, gently. Large men sometimes move like that, she thought. Their size gives them a precarious relation to the world, as though the world were an egg and a slightly bad move might crack it. She grimaced. The last man she had had dinner with was Paul Stanislas, many years ago. Stanislas was intensely fascinated by eggs. But perhaps only as symbols.

"I haven't seen that dress before," Will said suddenly.

"Have you been keeping track of my wardrobe?"

"You are a closely watched woman," he replied, laughing. He was right; she hadn't worn this dress in years. A deep purple in color, it had full, billowing sleeves and a wide cumberbund.

"This is my European dress."

"Ah, that explains all."

"What, in fact, does it explain?"

Will Bunche didn't answer. He was feeling too good for analyt-

121

ical conversations. They drove in silence for about twenty minutes, then the car moved off the highway onto a bumpy truck
road. Suddenly he braked in front of a dimly lit old barn.

"Are you *sure* this is a restaurant?" said Helene.

He laughed and turned off the engine. They climbed out of the
car and walked the few yards from the small gravel parking area
to the barn's door. Helene noticed three other cars parked hap-
hazardly. Bunche opened the door and Helene walked inside. A
simple restaurant with red and white checked tablecloths met
her eyes. The archaic vaulting of the old barn had been left in its
original majestic state. Four horse stalls now served as a bar. A
tall, thin woman led them to a table, handed them menus, and
left.

"Who comes here?" said Helene, entranced.

"The degenerate gentry."

"You're one of them?"

"I'm their very pillar!"

The tall, thin woman came back and asked if they wanted
anything to drink. Bunche ordered a bourbon and water. Helene
declined. She looked down at the menu. *Coquille St. Jacques*,
she remembered. But she wanted calves' brains. It had been such
a long time since the last calf's brain. First snails, then brains.
Yes, that was it. She put down the menu and smiled at Bunche.

"Do you like it?" he said as though the place were his own.

"Very much. Yes, I do. Has it been here a long time?"

"As long as you've been at the hospital," he said, holding the
glass of bourbon between his palms and turning it.

"Does anyone from the hospital eat here?"

"Sometimes."

"Do you come here often?"

He shrugged and sipped his drink. They could hear music
playing in a far-off room. Three other couples were dining. The
woman returned and took their orders. *Coquille St. Jacques* for
Bunche.

"Are you planning to interrogate me now or later?"

"Interrogate you?" he responded. "About what?"

"I don't know. I just had the feeling you were going to."

"If you wish . . ."

"Not really."

He placed his bourbon glass on the table and peered into it.

"Actually, I was intending to," he said without looking up. "But I just couldn't choose between a host of subjects."

"Such as?"

"Oh, the usual things: life, death, eros, destiny, the propagation of cauliflower."

She laughed and took a sip of water. She felt both elated and uncomfortable now. He was looking at her as though he expected something—a confession, a statement, she didn't know what.

"Do you want to hear how I became a psychiatrist?" he said.

The tall, thin woman arrived with food. Helene began to extricate the snails. "Why not?" she said, and put one in her mouth.

Bunche had ordered herring. He broke off and buttered a small piece of bread, cut a piece of the herring in its creamy sauce, then ate bread and herring together.

"I was in Italy during the war. There was a man in my platoon called Horace Sams. Everyone called him Sammy. A very strange man. He rarely spoke to anyone, but he did his job exceptionally well. Of course, his job was to kill Germans. I mean, that was everyone's job—killing Germans—but most of us considered that our real job was to stay alive. Sammy took his job seriously."

Bunche consumed another piece of bread and herring, then continued.

"We had been staying in one of those small mountain villages that seem ready to fall over about any minute. We were ordered to move north again, so we filed out. It was a bit past noon. We were walking on either side of the road, just like you see in the movies. Someone took a shot at us from the village we had just left. No one was hit. We all dived for cover. Except Sammy. He stood there. Another round was fired and kicked up dirt around him. He turned and began walking slowly back toward the village. Right in the middle of the road. He walked about ten yards and was shot through the head. Before he hit the ground he was dead."

"And that was why you became a psychiatrist?"

"Yes."

"I don't, really, understand the connection."

"It came to me that it would be a good thing, before I died, to find out what was in Horace Sams' head."

"Did you?"

"No. Thirty years later I can honestly say that heads have conquered me. I know very little. But then again, my father lived to
be eighty and he never found out what went on in the heads of
his cows."

They finished the herring and snails, and Bunche ordered
another bourbon. The music sounded more loudly now and Helene recognized an Edith Piaf recording. Will Bunche watched
her carefully, ready to spring a question. He wanted to ask if she
had discovered what went on in the head of John Ligur. But he
held himself back. There would be time for that, later. He wondered if she were enjoying herself. He doubted it. He didn't think
Helene Roth enjoyed herself anywhere. She was too engaged.
She thought too much. She was in an antagonistic position vis-à-
vis the world. And since the world was all that there was, enjoy-
ment was virtually impossible.

Helene picked up a knife, moved it an inch from its original
place, and put it down. She did the same thing with a fork. Then
she folded and refolded her napkin. Dinners in restaurants, she
thought, are intelligent, because they have an intelligent sequence. A certain dish follows another and so on until the proper
conclusion: dessert and coffee. There was a precision, a stateli-
ness, a progression. Ah, progression. She fixed on the word. That
was the concept she wanted. Progression from A to Z. Or progression from beginning of treatment to successful conclusion of
treatment. That, above all, was what she missed about psychoanalytic practice. With analytic patients there was at least
the hope of progression. That the progression rarely worked was
no one's concern.

"Do you like Piaf?"

She didn't hear the question, so he repeated it. "Edith Piaf. Do
you like her?"

"Very much. Very much."

"You're smiling. Did I say something funny?"

"No, no. I was remembering something. A colleague in New
York used to say I looked like Piaf."

She moved her knife and fork again. Stanislas had called her
the little sparrow. But soon the little sparrow would send the
sparrow hawk to perdition. At the end of it all the little sparrow
would sing, *"Non, je ne regrette rien."*

The entrées arrived. She looked down at the calves' brains as though she were watching the resurrection of an old friend. Tasting the dish, she found it delicious. Will ordered wine. They ate and drank slowly.

I will not make conversation, he thought, if she doesn't wish it—and she doesn't appear to wish it. So Will Bunche ate silently, giving her quick, small glances which bounced off the walls and the other diners, only to return to her face. She wasn't more than three feet away, and with the slightest effort he could reach across the table and touch her face. That was what he wanted to do—touch her. The *coquille St. Jacques* was as fine as ever, but he consumed it mechanically, without interest. Her face profoundly intrigued him. One moment it was totally in control, the face of a professional woman who had learned to measure and act. And then, for a quick moment, all color would drain and the face seemed to hover above a fearsome abyss. And then the color would return and the face became rapt as she listened to the music.

He refilled her wine glass. She smiled at him.

"Want to taste?" she said, pointing her fork at the brains.

He declined. Edith Piaf stopped singing. They could hear the wind clattering through the old wood of the barn. The couple across the room was laughing loudly. From the kitchen came the ringing of pots and pans. Suddenly Helene became rigid.

"What's wrong?" he said at once.

"Up there, I saw something move up there." She pointed to the dark, vaulted upper reaches of the barn.

"It is the ghost of seductions past," he joked.

Helene let her eyes move, section by section, over the vast dark spaces. She was still nervous.

"Actually, it's probably a fugitive barn swallow," he said. "They never forget that this is really their place."

She returned to the brains. Maybe she had seen something and maybe she hadn't. Perhaps her eyes were only remembering the arc of Ligur's quoit as it came from heaven. Perhaps she was afraid a quoit would land on their table. Or perhaps she believed that if you sat in light, under a dark canopy, something would always emerge from the dark and knock you out, in the light.

Soon the food was finished, the wine was finished, they sat

over coffee and cognac. Helene felt warm, relaxed, tired. Will leaned back in his chair and watched her.

"It was a lovely dinner," she said.

"We can do it as often as you like."

"What do you want of me?"

Her question made him sit forward. "A great deal."

"I'm afraid that can't be arranged."

He didn't answer. He moved the salt and pepper shakers from one side of the table to the other.

"Do you understand?" she said gently.

"I understand very little, in general, and, with respect to you, even less."

"Will, I'm very fond of you. But I told you earlier that—"

"Yes," he interrupted, "you told me about a project. A project? No, it isn't a project."

"I don't care what it's called."

"Could it be called John Ligur?"

He saw her face drain of color. She bent over the table as though she'd been hit in the stomach. He wanted to retract the name, but there it was, spoken. He reached a hand across the table to touch her, to apologize, but she avoided it.

"Listen. Let me pay the bill and we'll get some air."

He waited for a response. There was none. Then her face, ineffably sad, turned up toward him.

"John Ligur is a psychotic. I'm a psychiatrist."

"I know what he is. I know what you are. But that's all I know about both of you."

"And all you will ever know," she hurled at him bitterly.

He shrugged and motioned to the tall, thin woman. She brought the check, and soon Helene and Bunche were walking toward his car. She stumbled once but regained her balance before he could help. "The wine," she said. She began to open the door of the car.

"Wait, please wait," he pleaded quietly.

She turned. He stood very close to her.

"Listen to me. I love you, Helene. Do you understand that? Do you? Is it possible for one psychiatrist to say that to another and not be laughed at? Well, laugh. I have not used that bogus word, that pathetic word, that ludicrous word—I have not used it in polite or written conversation with any human being since I was sixteen."

"I think we should go."

"No, listen. I think I know why it happened, and why I can use the word without embarrassment. Because of you and Ligur. Because of the past. Because, perhaps, I recognize the end of my profession in you. Do you understand that? I became a psychiatrist because I watched a man choose death in Italy, inexplicably. I now love because I see a woman making the same choice in a manner and for a goal that I can't even begin to perceive. It's not possible for me to stand within twenty yards of you without feeling the danger you're in. And, in a sense, the grandeur."

He moved his hand to her face. She was weeping.

"Why? Why are you crying?"

"I don't want to hear what you're saying, Will."

He moved away from her, suddenly furious at his grandiose speech. He could not articulate his position without sounding like an ass. And there was a position. And he had to articulate it. He had to. There were few chances left for him. There were few options. She was the one he wanted.

"Come for a walk with me. Please, come." He turned and began to walk around the far side of the immense barn. A few beams of light filtered through the surrounding evergreens. She followed him tentatively, keeping a distance between them. The wind sounded through the bare-branched trees.

Bunche pointed up at the roof of the barn. "That's where the swallow entered. Probably. If it was a swallow." He leaned against the barn's side, as he had done thousands of times as a child.

It was no use, he realized. The thing couldn't be said. It had to be transmitted, and he was incapable of transmitting it. Maybe he had spent too many years with the crazies. With them, all that was needed was a sudden gesture, or a look, and there would be an understanding. An instant understanding. Or a line, which neither party would cross. Or, some gesture would offer permission to cross. He could take the raving man by the hand and lead him across the line for treatment. Lines. Borders. Zones of at-

traction and repulsion. These were fine. They had allowed him
to survive professionally and remain sane. But this was different.
He did not know how to proceed.

"It's time I took you back," he said.

They drove toward the hospital. Each had come to the same
conclusion: the scene was over; exploration was useless. As they
approached the hospital Helene touched his arm. "I would rather go to my house first. I can make you some coffee. Then we can
pick up my car."

He said nothing and drove to her house. He followed her inside, into the small kitchen, and sat silently at the table as she
prepared coffee.

Helene watched the coffeepot on its flame, her back to Will
Bunche. He sat at the table, still in his overcoat, hands folded in
front of him. He watched her. He observed the slightest movement of her hands. He listened for the first sign of water rising.
This was the house he had watched for so long, hidden in an alcove across the road. Now he was inside, and still he had the
feeling of spying on her. He still felt an outsider, spying.

Helene took off her coat and without looking at him draped it
over a chair. Then she turned back to the coffeepot.

He felt a tremor in one of his legs. What was it? Sexual anticipation? Or the sudden transition from a cold night to a warm
house? He wanted to walk to her and put his hands on her shoulders, then let his hands slide down her back so he could feel,
through her dress, the small of her back and the incline of her
buttocks. It was absurd, he thought, for a man of his age to feel
this way, about any woman.

But he could do nothing about it. There it was. He remained in
his chair. He had never taken eros seriously before in his life. He
had treated sex the way a veterinarian treats hoof-and-mouth
disease. He had progressed as many men progress. A visit to a
prostitute to remove the hated virginity. A few seductions. A
brief period of wild sex with anyone he met who was willing. A
serious courtship, then marriage. In all the years of his marriage
he had never been unfaithful; not because of a belief in fidelity,
but because he simply wasn't interested. His wife would do. In
his daily work he was surrounded by persons whose sexual

drives had led them into states barely human. Were their drives his drives? He hardly thought so.

The coffee was starting to perk. Helene lowered the flame.

Perhaps, he thought, I am recapitulating the last walk of Horace Sams. Perhaps Helene Roth is my death. He sat up straighter. The thought disturbed him. It was stupid. Helene Roth was life for him, another chance, a new way to think, a kind of hope in the daily paralysis. But the thought remained, gnawing. He closed his eyes.

Helene scrutinized the coffeepot. Little brown bubbles were moving up to the glass dome in the lid. Faster and faster came the bubbles. Soon there would be coffee. Three minutes. She walked to the cupboard and brought out two ceramic mugs, placing them on top of the stove.

She adamantly refused to think. He was here and they would make love. Everything happens because of necessity. There are no gratuitous actions. She knew that. She knew that no act takes place by chance, no act is just thrown away. Everything she did had its own necessity. Perhaps a necessity remote and obscure, but all the same, a force like gravity. She wasn't a pill shrink. She knew this.

If I begin to speculate, she thought, I will land on the trash heap. If I begin to speculate on the relationship between Stanislas and Bunche, on the thread between Ligur and Bunche, if I think at all, I will unravel. And then Stanislas will not unravel. Everything will have been in vain.

I am here. He is here. I will serve the coffee.

She picked up the coffeepot with one hand, held the two mugs in the other hand, and walked to the table. She placed a mug in front of Bunche, the other by her hand. She poured coffee.

"What do you take with it?"

"Nothing."

"You always drink coffee black?"

"In certain situations." He took a sip. "You make a very good cup."

"Thank you."

"Do you want to hear about my wife?"

"Not particularly."

"Then I won't tell you."

"Tell me about your dogs. Do you have dogs?"

"The last dog I had died two years ago."

"What was his name?"

"It was a bitch called Willow. Half golden retriever, half God knows what."

"What did she die of?"

"I don't know. One morning we woke up and she was dead."

Helene refilled their cups. They had to converse. They would both keep trying.

"Was she old?"

"Not very."

"Did you call in a vet?"

"She was already dead."

They struggled on. They sipped coffee they had both lost the taste for.

"Perhaps I'll have some sugar," he said.

She got up and brought him a sugar bowl. He lifted half a spoonful of sugar over his cup, hesitated, then poured it in.

"Would you like cream?"

"No. And I really don't want any more coffee."

She nodded, and stood up, and walked into the bedroom. He followed her, leaving his coat in the kitchen.

The new patient in Stanislas's office moved from the chair to the couch. This was his third session. He was in his late forties, short, stocky, and very well dressed. Stanislas had just terminated the professional relationship for the simple reason that the man had lied to him. He was an alcoholic. Stanislas did not treat alcoholics. Treatment was futile. He no longer tried.

The story had finally emerged in the third session. His wife had insisted that he either go to a clinic for alcoholics or see a psychoanalyst. She didn't seem to care which he chose. The man had chosen Stanislas but had not informed him of his condition.

"There is nothing I can do for you until you are dry," said Paul Stanislas.

The man grimaced and moved back to the chair. There was a wicked gash that ran from eye to jaw. When asked about it, the man told five or six stories. He had cut himself with a hand mirror while shaving in a motel. He had been pushed through a glass window. He had been mugged.

The tremendous facility with which alcoholics lied never failed to amaze Stanislas. They lied, he thought, the way saints lived: without thought, without sophistication, without regard for consequences.

The patient fought against termination. He became truculent and then whining. Stanislas was adamant and soft-spoken. Nothing could be done. The patient was wasting money. Dry out. Dry out.

The patient left whistling a tune, shutting the door lightly behind him. Stanislas was alone, and finished for the day. He walked to the sofa where the man had been sitting and touched the fabric. His hand was shaking. Slightly, ever so slightly, but it was shaking. How does one deal with the inexplicable, he thought. How does one probe bizarre actions—car theft, shoplifting, the sudden appearance of objects—when the agent of those actions was himself? He brought his hand down onto the sofa suddenly and savagely. It was the impotence which made him angry. The quaking in his fingers had vanished.

He walked into the bedroom and collected the three hundred dollars he had found in his pocket. Now he would spend it on gifts for Deirdre and Emily.

On the bus going downtown, Stanislas watched an old man in the seat across the aisle. The man had wrapped himself in several worn sweaters and jackets to keep out the cold. A scarf was tied around his neck and another around his waist.

The man wasn't looking at him, but Stanislas felt uncomfortable. His garments are making me uncomfortable, he thought. There are too many of them. The old man should peel the garments off in the bus. I'm allegorizing, he thought. Peel the garments. Peel the cobwebs. Peel the victim. Peel the incidents until the reality emerges.

Stanislas got off the bus six blocks before his destination and walked the rest of the way.

As he entered the department store, his hand automatically went to his pocket. The three hundred was there. He brought his hand out of the pocket, quickly. The paper bills were alien. They

were his but not his. They were, in some dangerous way, coun-
terfeit bills.

He began to walk slowly from aisle to aisle, looking for gifts.
He stopped in front of a tray of woolen mittens. Nice for Deirdre,
he thought. But what was her size? And what color would she
want.

He moved on, passing along the counter slowly, trying to formulate a match—between a gift and Deirdre, between a gift and
Emily. He saw nothing.

Taking the escalator to the second floor, again he moved from
aisle to aisle, looking, trying for a match. Suddenly he stopped.
He had seen a match. A coffee mug. It hung from a hook on the
wall, surrounded by dozens of other mugs. But this one was for
Deirdre. Large and round, it might have been a dwarfed soup tu-
reen. Stanislas picked the mug off its hook and twirled it round
and round in his hand. The color was a dull brick red with little
specks of black. The handle was massive and looked like a plant
sprung up overnight from the red field. Yes, he thought, this is
Deirdre's cup. He could see it in her hand, half filled with coffee,
cigarette smoke curling over the handle.

He put it down on the glass counter and walked off a few feet,
approaching it then from a different direction. In a moment he
felt rather stupid about this, and quickly picking up the mug, he
brought it to the cashier.

It was expensive. The mug cost twenty-five dollars. While the
sales clerk wrote up the order, Stanislas removed the wad of bills
from his pocket. He peeled off the first bill and held it out to the
woman. She reached out her hand and Stanislas pulled the
money back. He felt a vacuum inside himself, as if his will had
been drained. The woman smiled and waited.

"I don't want the mug," he said in a quiet voice. Stanislas
turned on his heel and walked away. The wad of bills was tucked
in his tight fist. Taking the escalator downstairs, he walked out
of the store onto the street. He suddenly realized he was sweating. His forehead was drenched. He looked around and saw a
small coffee and doughnut shop. He walked inside and ordered
black coffee.

He reached for the sugar and then realized he couldn't grasp it
because the wad of bills was still in his fist. This was his own

hand, but it didn't feel like his hand. He pulled his hand down to his lap and tried to open his fist. He felt as though he were performing a surgical operation to open someone's fist. Finally the fingers stretched and the bills dropped into his lap. He picked them up quickly with his other hand and shoved them into his jacket pocket.

He couldn't understand what had happened. Why had he refused to buy the mug after choosing it? Perhaps, he thought, I am falling prey to middle-aged frugality. He finished the coffee and headed uptown. There was still enough time for him to visit his gym and work up a legitimate sweat.

Stanislas belonged to the Fleetwood Club, a small, well-equipped private club that catered to the athletic needs of stockbrokers and surgeons, merchandising executives and actors, politicians and academics. It was open, in fact, to all who had the price.

He opened his locker and removed the wire tray with sneakers and a freshly laundered gym outfit. Five minutes later he started his jog on the circular track that ran around the basketball and squash courts. He decided to do just ten laps, then shoot some baskets, and finish off with a swim.

His usual program called for seven slow laps, then picking up speed on the last three until at the end of the tenth lap he was sprinting. But this night he started to pick up speed at the end of the fourth lap. He felt absolutely no fatigue. Not a single muscle ached in his legs or thighs. He was breathing evenly, just as though he were taking a slow walk around the block. By the sixth lap the temptation to sprint was overwhelming.

He turned on the speed, laughing as he heard his footfalls pound on the wood floor. He realized he was laughing—and he also realized there was a skull in the laughter. It wasn't the joy of speed. It wasn't the pride of accomplishment. It was demonic knowledge. He was laughing, he realized, because he knew there was no barrier he couldn't break.

As he finished the tenth lap he threw out his arms, an Olympic sprinter breaking the tape.

Stanislas didn't walk out for a lap or two, as he usually did to keep his legs from cramping. He merely glided to the basketball court and began to search for a ball. There was one on the far side of the gym. He trotted over, scooped it up with one hand and started to dribble toward the basket.

About twenty feet off he stopped and shot the ball. At the moment of release he realized he'd thrown the ball too high.

It climbed up almost to the circular track, and then slowly, lazily fell toward the floor. Stanislas was transfixed by its trajectory.

The ball went through the basket and made a hissing noise as the net swished.

Stanislas walked toward the ball, which was bouncing slowly to a stop. He put his sneakered foot securely on it, then picked the ball up and twirled it in his hands. It felt like any other ball—round, firm, leathery. But he had never made a shot like that with any other ball. He held it with ten fingertips, each talking.

Slowly he dribbled around the court, bouncing the ball waist high. He felt in absolute control of the sphere. It would do whatever he told it to do. He dribbled to an end line, placed the ball on the very edge of his fingers, turned away from the basket, and brought his arm over on the arc of a hook shot. He released the ball at the top of his stretch.

Again the ball went high, hardly spinning. It drifted up until it was almost obscured by the hazy lights of the gym. Then it came down with increasing velocity. It went right through the basket.

Stanislas started to laugh. He trotted over to the ball and kicked it hard to the far side of the gym.

He had to shower and leave, but he waited. The ball was bouncing crazily. His eyes drank the moment in. The sound of the ball began to reverberate in his ear—like some primeval echoes. He covered them. He looked away. His eyes came back to the ball, as if they were now independent of his will.

"I am watching myself," he whispered, sinking to his knees on the brightly varnished hardwood floor.

A scream gurgled in his chest but did not come out. Instead, it kept him there, kneeling, watching the ball slow its course.

Will Bunche stared at the small, naked body. Helene was lying quietly, one arm spread across the sheet. She appeared neither aroused nor disinterested. Neutral. The room was dark, but slivers of moonlight filtered in through the window and gathered at the foot of the bed.

He reached out a hand and touched the inside of her thigh. As she moved her legs apart, he slipped the hand underneath her. He felt oddly unsure of himself, as though this were his first sexual adventure. He felt that if he made a single wrong move, the spell would be broken forever.

The moment she felt his hand, Helene Roth closed her eyes. Why had he touched her in just that way? That was the way Stanislas always began.

Now he was on his knees, beside her. His hands moved softly up her belly and stomach. When they reached her breasts, he left them there for a long time. He wanted a sign from her, a sign of pleasure, a sign of encouragement, a sign . . . of anything. She remained silent, with closed eyes, breathing evenly. He leaned over and kissed the nipple of one breast.

This is not Ligur with me now, she thought. This is not Ligur.

With a finger he traced a journey along her lips, and then parted her lips and touched her teeth. He stretched out beside her and put his hand back down between her legs. Slowly, she was responding. Slowly. He wanted desperately to kiss her. He wanted to kiss her the way adolescents do, with his whole mouth, as if it meant something. But he couldn't bring himself to attempt it.

Why doesn't she touch me? he wondered. Why not? Then he took her hand and brought it between his legs. Her hand reluctantly folded around his penis. She held it.

He leaned across and kissed her stomach, keeping his lips against the flesh, biting at the loose fold of skin. She smelled good. She tasted good. Then he felt her hand move on him.

I would like to tell her something, he thought, I would like to say something. She was becoming moist, in the way a season changes. She made a sound. A slight sound. But still . . .

It wasn't this way with Stanislas, she thought, and it's not this way with Ligur. This is different. She could feel his stolidity, his carefulness, his tentativeness. She raised herself up and kissed him, on the forehead.

He thought, Nothing is happening. It is sex, nothing else. There is no intimacy. What he was seeking wasn't there.

She brought her hand to his face, wanting to feel what he looked like. She wanted to get a picture of him. He pushed her hand away. He pushed her back down on the bed. He couldn't wait any longer for revelations. He covered Helene. He entered her. He felt the inside of her greet him. Now it was good. He was doing what he wanted to do. He could hardly go deep enough. Deep was intimate. Deep was good. Her body curled under his. His face fell into her hair.

He would ride her over. He would ride Ligur out. He would become forever part of her. He threw his own shudder into Helene. Then, nothing but silence.

She lay on her stomach now, her face on the pillow. His elbow grazed her own. She was happy in the silence. There was nothing to say.

He was very tired. Even so, there was a great deal he wanted to say to her. A hundred sentences swarmed in his mouth. He said nothing. Lying there, he watched the ceiling.

When he had fallen asleep, she moved off the bed. He was breathing evenly, one hand on his chest, the other resting on her pillow. Wrapping a robe around her, she walked quickly out of the room and into her study.

What a long evening it had been. Absurd for her even to try and sort out what had happened, why it had happened, and what damage had been done. Damage. It seemed to her a word that a conspirator would use. She smiled and drew a hand along the row of tape cassettes. She was a conspirator.

Now it was time to work. She selected a tape and put it in the machine, then pressed PLAY. She heard three words spoken by herself and pressed OFF.

No, she thought, this won't do. The past must be reviewed piece by piece, act by act, or she could not control the future. She started the tape again. Helene Roth listened to a whole sentence spoken by Helene Roth and shut the machine off again. She put the cassette back in its niche.

She didn't want to listen. She wanted to be back in bed with that kind, kind man. It was warm there. She went there.

VIII

When Helene replaced the phone, she felt oddly light. It was the first time she had ever called the hospital and said she would not be in. Today she was going to buy a Persian rug. It was that simple. She was feeling very good; she had wanted to buy a good Persian rug for many years, so she would go and buy one.

The simplicity of it amused her. She walked slowly and quietly about the house, relishing her mood. Once, she stopped in front of the tape deck but had no desire to turn it on.

Will Bunche, she knew, had replaced Ligur as the presence in the house. It was astonishing that it had happened so quickly, that one night of lovemaking between old and tired persons could accomplish that. But it was true. The large man was silently in the house, dogging her footsteps, appearing and reappearing. She would turn quickly to look at him—but of course Bunche was not really there now. Tonight he would be.

Usually mornings were the time for coffee and music, but this morning there was no need for any stimulants whatsoever. There was a sense of ease about her, as if the day would consist of petty tasks that could be accomplished.

By ten o'clock she was on the road, beginning the two-hour drive that would take her to the large shopping center in the neighboring suburban county.

Other banal needs surfaced as she drove, in addition to the Persian rug. Light bulbs. Thumb tacks. Tools, such as a rake and a can opener. She noted each one mentally, visualized it, turned it over and over in her head, and then giggled at the absurdity of it.

I am not in love with Will Bunche, she thought, but I am acting like it. I am acting as if I had been presented with a clean, indeed, a whitewashed slate.

It was noon when she pulled the car into the parking lot. She locked the doors and headed for the giant brick department store.

What she saw when she stepped inside dazzled her. Her life for the past few years had been from house to hospital, and she had almost forgotten the wealth of colors and shapes that now displayed themselves in front of her.

Helene walked slowly along the aisle, drinking the sights in, stopping now and then to touch something.

She forgot about the reason for her visit to the store—rug, light bulbs, tools. She just wandered and rode the escalators and watched the people. They were not patients and they were not doctors. They were ciphers.

When she saw a customer engaging a salesperson, she sidled up and tried to listen to the conversation unobtrusively. It fascinated her. Sentences were put together in a coherent manner. What was said was what was meant. Each of the two participants in the conversation tried to understand each other.

Helene Roth realized that she had been so long away from the world of normalcy that it no longer seemed comprehensible. She was moving in a world she had long ago lost contact with.

She stopped at a glass counter, under which were watches.

"Can I help you?"

She looked up. A young man, wearing a suit and tie, was standing behind the counter. He had light brown hair and bluish eyes.

"I'm thinking of a watch," she said, lying, but not wanting to abort the contact.

He opened the case and placed a felt-covered tray of watches on top of the counter.

"Any kind in particular?" he asked.

Her eyes went from the watches on the tray to the face across the counter. Her training made her search the face quickly, and then the body. She was looking for something odd. She was studying the sales clerk diagnostically.

"A thin watch," she said, leading him.

His hands moved over the tray, selected one, and held it up. Helene took it from him.

"Is it a good watch?" she asked.

She wanted him to speak, and to keep on speaking. She wanted to find out once again about neurotic normalcy—where men and women suffer from minor compulsions, or constipation, or insomnia brought on by small disturbances.

"An excellent one," the sales clerk said, "and the price is right."

She wound the watch and held it to her ear. The young man smiled.

Are you the successor to Ligur? She phrased the question silently, and for just a moment could catch the psychotic profile imposed on the clerk.

"How much is it?"

"Seventy-nine ninety-five."

Helene Roth took out her checkbook, wrote a check, and showed her driver's license as identification.

"Would you like it gift-wrapped?"

"Yes."

She watched the young man carefully measure the paper, wrap it, and finish it off with a ribbon.

"Thank you," he said pleasantly, handing the package to her.

"What is your name?" Helene asked.

The young man flushed a bit, then said, "Johnny."

Helene walked out of the store and sat in her car. The package in her hand was perplexing. She didn't want a watch. She didn't need a watch. She had driven two hours for other things.

Perhaps, she thought, it, the package, is my attempt at normalcy—my reindoctrination into normalcy—to Will Bunche and to Johnny the sales clerk.

She placed the package gingerly on top of the dashboard. She was tired. She leaned back in the seat and closed her eyes. There was a feeling in her that something new was appearing, that something different was taking over her life. It was a good feeling. It was a feeling that was, above all, suffused with safety. And quietude—blessed quietude.

* * *

Stanislas stood quietly by the stairs and watched the disembarking passengers. When he spotted Deirdre he walked over quickly, kissed her once on the cheek, and took her arm.

"I want to show you something," he said.

"I hope you'll show me something," she said, laughing. "After all, I don't get on a train to New York on a half hour's notice for nothing."

He steered her to a window of a shop in the station.

"Look."

"I'm looking."

"There. The lighter. Does it look familiar?"

"Vaguely."

Stanislas chuckled and led her away. He had called his wife and asked her to meet him in the city because a few hours after he woke up he felt very healthy. He had realized that all the peculiarities of consciousness and behavior that had been troubling him were spurious. They were just the signs of approaching middle-age angst rather than any kind of dangerous or profound reality.

"I'm glad you came," he said.

She had agreed because she thought something was very wrong. Stanislas hadn't done something this romantic in years.

"You'll never guess where we're going."

She couldn't. He stopped a cab, they climbed in, and Paul gave the driver a downtown address.

Ten minutes later they pulled up in front of a cavernous old bookstore.

"Remember it?" he asked as they stood on the sidewalk.

Of course she remembered it. They used to go there often when they were first married. It was a game they played. Each was allotted a certain amount of money—usually three dollars. Each was required to buy as many used and secondhand books as possible for the three dollars—books that the other person would want. Then they would eat in an inexpensive Italian restaurant and open the gifts.

Her face was impassive. Stanislas waited for her to respond. He needed her to respond, to remember. The last few days had been like a fever, an incomprehensible fever, and now it had abated—and now he wanted to be reassured that there was a place for all of them. In memory if not in fact.

"I remember," she said gently.

They walked inside. He placed three crumpled bills into her palm and vanished behind some stacks.

An hour later they exchanged books in a small restaurant. He was excited, more excited than she had seen him in years. She wanted to participate but felt uncomfortable, as if he was hiding something from her, as if he was going to ask her something.

"What is going on, Paul?"

He sat back, the smile gone, nervous.

"I was going to pieces, Deirdre. I was afraid. I was afraid of something I didn't even know the name of. And no matter how I started to look, no matter how I tried to investigate the fear— there was nothing. Do you understand? All there was—all I could hold were events. I had stolen a car. I had stolen a cigarette lighter. I had procured some money in a way and at a time that couldn't be described. At least the evidence says I did these things. Do you see? How could I deal with something I couldn't remember or place?"

"And now you can deal with it?"

"It's gone, Deirdre. I just woke up and it was gone. So I can start to look at why it was gone. But that would be looking at why it was there. And that's futility. So I accepted the fact that it was a joke. A psychoanalyst moving on in years and getting a bit panicky. So I stopped, and was happy, and wanted to make you happy. And . . . I just began to wonder if what was happening lately was tied in to what was happening between us—the bad things. Am I making sense?"

"Vaguely."

Deirdre felt warm, and hopeful. He was talking the way he used to talk, before he became the analytical machine. Sudden bursts of language—some that made sense and some that didn't, but all of it good to listen to.

"I think I'll have some wine," she said.

They sat in the restaurant for more than two hours talking about nothing—about the neighborhood, about the bookstore, about Emily's latest adventure, about everything and nothing.

"I have to get back," she said finally.

He reached across the table, held her hand for a moment, then released it.

"Thank you for coming in."

He dropped her off at the railroad station in a cab, and pulled away in the same cab. On the ride back to Cold Spring Harbor, Deirdre found nothing clear except the fact that he looked good, that he looked relaxed, that he looked and sounded like the long vanished Paul Stanislas.

Margaret watched the counterman's face. The faces of men are peculiar, she thought. They set so early; moving into a cast they stay there, from birth to death. It was that way with her father. For as long as she could remember, her father's face had always been the same. Set. Formidable. This man serving her coffee had her father's face. It was permanently disgusted. It was always ready to prick balloons.

She looked at the clock on the wall. Ten minutes to kill before Stanislas. The counterman was cleaning a spatula with sweeping strokes, scraping the grease off on the edge of the grill. Stanislas was supposed to scrape off the grimy crusts, those painful, enduring crusts, and let her emerge, someone else.

Five minutes left now. She thought of Lupica. He wasn't what she'd judged him. He was a man who was concerned with her. Hadn't he said she'd misjudged him? Hadn't he asked, with obvious concern, why she behaved so strangely? Suddenly Lupica had become part of her life. In a matter of moments. Without warning, the enemy had turned . . . ally?

The counterman finished cleaning the spatula and hung it up on a hook. Taking a stiff wire brush, he began to clean the grill. The noise sickened her. She paid the check and left.

Stanislas's street was lined with brownstones. In the summer the stoops were full of children. Now they were empty. After walking up and down this street for three years, Margaret knew all the houses with a detailed familiarity. She knew colors of drapes in front windows, which dogs and dog walkers belonged to which houses, which garbage cans were overstuffed and uncovered. And by whom.

She always walked down the street slowly, as though she were going to a tryst. As though she were meeting her lover at the end of the block. Transference notwithstanding.

She walked slowly, close to the curb. She loved him. She loved him beyond transference, beyond good and evil, beyond the horizon of hope. She loved him. That stolid block of a man who sat across from her week after week, trying to put Humpty back together again.

Always, at the end of the block, she stopped and looked over her shoulder. She could not break the habit. In her rural past psychoanalysis was illicit. But perhaps the thing stemmed from something else. Perhaps *she* was illicit?

In the lobby of his building she caught her reflection in a mirror. I am a beautiful woman, she thought, startled. Then she walked into the elevator.

Stanislas wore his usual clothes. His face was set in its usual cast—kindly, concerned, but beneath it all, authoritarian. Margaret chose the chair for this session rather than the sofa. She made her usual search of his face. It was always an exploratory search—for a crack in the therapeutic armor. She never found one. Stanislas, she was aware, knew what she was doing. He allowed himself, inexpressively, to be searched. She admired him for the invariable impassivity of his countenance.

"I apologized to Lupica," she said quietly.

She saw him rapidly engage his memory. He had many patients with many problems. The name registered, and he nodded.

"I apologized to him," she repeated.

"And what did he say?"

"He accepted the apology."

"What else?"

She leaned back and smiled. She would tell this in her own way, her own sequence. It was, after all, her hour.

"Something happened." She waited, a practiced storyteller.

"What happened?"

"The whole thing changed."

"You mean the accusation of theft?"

"No. I mean Lupica and myself."

"Well, from what you told me, any change would be for the better."

"I think I'm going to have an affair with him."

Having said the words quickly, she was astonished to hear them. The thought had not occurred to her before. But she had said it. She leaned back in her chair, almost luxuriously, and said nothing more. Stanislas said nothing.

She took a cigarette from her purse and played with it, peering up slyly at Stanislas to judge his response. Did he think she was going to light it? She wondered if she had made the statement in order to make him jealous.

"Yes. I think Edward Lupica is what I've been waiting for."

"Which is?"

"You know." Her voice was abrupt and savage. She replaced the cigarette in its pack. After all this time she still couldn't talk about a penis entering a vagina. It was too horrible.

"Why do you think it's him?"

"He changed when I apologized. He changed completely. I had misjudged him. Badly. He wanted to know about me. He wanted to know why I thought ill of him."

"Do you still think he stole your pen?"

"I don't know."

"How could you consider someone as a lover who might have stolen your pen?"

Pregnant question, she thought. He was trying to loosen her up again. He was trying to lead her down a certain road. The road would go back to her father. And God knows where else. She stared at him blankly. She would change the subject. He was leaning forward on his desk, one hand supporting his chin. A sudden fury welled up in Margaret. A furious ache to feel, for once, his compassion—not his probing. Where had all the probing got to? Nowhere. She was still the same Margaret, the beautiful Margaret, terrified of the species' most fundamental act. Why hadn't he ever reached across and touched her face? Just once. Just once. Why had he never touched her cheek and told her that . . .

Margaret turned and faced the wall. She removed a cigarette, then replaced it, noticing with little surprise that her hands were trembling. She was cold. Lupica, she realized, was the last hope. It would have to be Lupica. She closed her eyes and saw the discoloration near his lip. Perhaps it was a sign.

"You see," said Stanislas softly, "it's going to take more than will."

What was he telling her? What? He was telling her that Lupica would be the same. That at the critical moment she would feel only horror.

"Well, will is all I have."

"Not true."

"Yes, true. True. True."

"Tell me what you feel about him."

"I don't understand your question."

"Tell me what you feel about him."

"I want him to fuck me," she said. Then her face flushed.

"But why?"

"Because I have to fuck, or I'll die! Or I'll shrivel up and blow away."

"This is the first time you've ever used the word fuck."

"Is that bad?"

"It's just a fact."

"Here's another fact: I don't even know if he wants me. All he said was that I had misjudged him."

"That's all?"

"And he wanted to know why I did the things I did."

"Did you tell him why?"

"I don't *know* why."

Margaret moved around in the chair, crossing and uncrossing her legs.

"You know," she said wearily, "sometimes I think it would be better to go all the way around the bend, to be locked up in an asylum, than to live the way I live. Always hoping, always struggling. Always waiting for the thing that will make everything all right."

"It will arrive."

"So you say."

"If you fight long enough, it will arrive."

"But don't you understand? I'm fighting against myself."

"You are fighting against the past."

"I can't win."

"If I believed that, I wouldn't be sitting here."

But you, she thought, you have a wife and family and you make love and you like your work . . .

"Tell me, as my psychiatric consultant, how shall I proceed with the seduction?"

"I wouldn't be able to help."

"Should I come right out with it?"

She paused. The thought of walking into Lupica's office and inviting him to bed was ludicrous.

"Or should I be subtle?"

Stanislas did not reply. She looked at his impassive face, wondering what seductions he had arranged in his lifetime. She wondered what type of woman he was attracted to. Were there dozens of women in his life? Did he seduce them or did they seduce him?

"Maybe I can entice him with a pen."

The moment the words were out, she realized they were a mistake. Now they were back where they'd started. She tried to recover the detour.

"But this time I'll offer him a multicolor pen."

"What colors do you have in mind?"

She pondered the question. His questions were tricky. Where could this one lead? Should she answer or hedge?

"Purple and blue and blue and purple."

"You mean black and blue, don't you?"

"I mean what I said, purple and blue."

"The color of bruises," he noted.

Margaret did not respond. She waited for the remaining minutes to pass. What if the only way to seduce Lupica, she thought, was over the objections of Stanislas? But he had not suggested that he objected. He had done nothing. Stanislas never did anything.

When the session was over, she lit a cigarette. Then she left the room.

They shuffled into the occupational therapy room. Waiting for them was Elizabeth Diehl, the occupational therapist, and her assistant, Cliff, a tall, brawny man in his late forties who was responsible for the distribution of materials and also functioned as an auxiliary to the attendants.

The room was a very large rectangular space, brightly lit. Along the two long walls were work tables and in front of each work table, a small stool. There was clay on one table, leather on another, basket material on another, and so on. Each patient was meant to report to his current project, but since many couldn't remember what they were working on, Cliff sorted out the confusion.

Elizabeth Diehl had been an occupational therapist for more than two decades. She had spent the last eight years in this hospital. She was a dedicated woman. She believed that the intelligent and aesthetic utilization of hands would ultimately provide balance for brains. Early in her career she had focused on the physically handicapped. But the potential of "the deranged," as she laughingly called them, was more alluring. Psychotics were definitely exciting to work with. Not because of the dangers, but because you never knew what they would do with a piece of clay, or fabric, or wood. You never knew. And they did astonishing things. The annual crafts show at the hospital had been her idea, and the works displayed and sold bore out her confidence.

Elizabeth stood in the center of the room as the patients filed in. She rarely called them patients, preferring to think of them as people. When she addressed a group of inmates, she would start off with "You people should . . ." or "We had some people here the other day . . ." She wore a very long red smock which billowed in waves around her. Four massive pockets were stitched onto the smock and carried pencils, Band-aids, rubber bands, paint brushes.

When the patients were in their proper places and the attendants stationed on each side of the room, Cliff walked to the large metal cabinet near the door. He unlocked it and distributed tools. The sharp instruments, those that could be dangerous, were only given out at the precise time of need, and used only with an attendant present. Then they were removed.

The session commenced. Elizabeth began her rounds, moving from bench to bench, greeting each person, looking over the project, giving suggestions. She was liberal with praise, often holding up a basket or belt and exclaiming loudly over its beauty and worth.

She reached Ligur, who was sitting quietly on his stool, staring at a perplexing pile of leather scraps. This was his new project. To make a belt. To fold the small pieces of leather in a certain way, then to link the pieces together, inch by inch, until a belt's length was achieved. Then it would be finished with a buckle.

Elizabeth was very fond of Ligur. He had never been a problem. Indeed, he had never even spoken in an O.T. session. Yet some of his work was exceptional. For instance, the green beanbag.

She leaned against the work table, facing Ligur. He kept his eyes on the pile of leather scraps.

"Now, watch," she said, picking up a single piece of leather. She folded the leather over, then did the same with another piece. Now she had one in each hand.

"Watch carefully." She joined the two pieces and looked at Ligur for some sign of comprehension. He was staring blankly at her, his right hand making its repetitive motion.

"You're not watching," she gently remonstrated. She unlinked the two pieces. Then she shook her head and reached over to stop his obsessive arm. She linked the pieces together again. She waited. Then she unlinked them and handed them to Ligur.

"Now, you do it."

There was a clattering noise. Elizabeth turned. Someone across the room had dropped a glue pot. Cliff got there swiftly and began to clean up the mess, much to the attendants' amusement.

Elizabeth turned back to Ligur, who held a piece of leather in each hand. "Put one of them down," she suggested.

He complied.

"Now, fold it the way I showed you."

He complied.

"Now, pick up the other one and fold it."

He complied.

"Now, join them."

He joined them.

Elizabeth grinned. She patted Ligur on the shoulder. Instantly, she realized her mistake, for she felt his whole body stiffen at her touch. She moved quickly to the next 'person.'

In front of Ligur was a window. It was a dirty window, and the strong mid-morning sun coming through it blinked and scattered, then reassembled. Ligur dropped the two leather pieces and placed his hands, palms down, on the wooden table. The sun was warm against his face. Sitting erect, his eyes half open, half closed, like a great reptile, he dozed.

"And how is it coming?"

The woman in red clothes was back. There she was, smiling at him.

He said nothing in reply. He picked up two pieces of leather, looped and joined them.

"Excellent, excellent," said the woman in red. Then she left him.

As soon as she had gone, he dropped the leather pieces. The sun was higher in the sky now and shone more intensely through the window. Ligur again dozed. His body fell forward so that the edge of the table supported him.

He awoke and tried to open his eyes. The lids wouldn't move. They would not move at all. Someone was firmly pressing them shut. Ligur brought his feet together under the table. Maybe they were coming for him again. Maybe they were bringing more pain, more torture. But now the fingers on his eyes became gentle. They were stroking his eyelids. Even though his eyes were closed, he began to see.

Immense green hands were directly before his eyes; they had now moved off his eyelids; they were moving back, back, back, until he saw a body standing there just outside the sun-drenched window.

Ligur only waited and watched. The figure was stepping back. It had never spoken. No. But it always told him what to do. Told him with a gesture, a movement of the head, a step of the feet.

Ligur saw him moving, heard him moving. It was like a locomotive pulling a train, and Ligur loved trains, had always loved trains. It moved slowly, and the sound of it was steady and made beautiful things happen in his ears. The green man moved his legs; he moved his arms; he moved his head, like the longest and most beautiful train in the world.

Ligur suddenly knew why he had come now. Of course. To save him from the torturers. He had not revealed the secret, and they had burned him and tried to break him. So now God was here to reward the saint. And to protect him.

The green man stopped moving. Ligur looked at his chest, because he couldn't bear the splendor of his face. That he could not stand. The green man held out a hand. Ligur saw that his last finger, the little finger, was not green. It was a vile pink. And it throbbed. It throbbed.

Then he vanished. Ligur opened his eyes and saw the green stain on the window. He could see the green stain on all the leather pieces, and on the table, and on the floor, and there was a green stain on all the people in the room.

He picked up a piece of leather. He let it fall. He picked up another piece, and let that fall. He pushed all the leather pieces together in a pile. There were beads of sweat on his forehead. They formed, vanished, formed again.

Elizabeth Diehl was standing in front of a large piece of clay. Holding a small knife in her hand, she was talking to the sculptor about symmetry. She rarely made aesthetic judgments about work done here—that wasn't her job—but in this case the patient had made one side of the face so grotesque that she had to intervene.

"It would look much better this way." She began to reshape one side of the face, using her hands and the knife. She worked slowly. From time to time she stopped and looked at the patient to see if he was following.

Finally she was finished. Stepping back, she looked hard at the head. It was good now, a well-done portrait in clay. But who did it resemble? Perhaps it was a relative. Or a figment of the patient's imagination.

"Keep up the good work," she said.

Elizabeth Diehl turned and walked into Ligur.

"What are you doing here?" she said as though he were a lost dog.

Ligur made no reply. He reached out with a hand, swiftly, quietly, and took the knife away from her. She never knew what was happening until she saw the knife in his hand.

"Give it back!" she shouted, and grabbed his wrist. She felt the power of his hand, his grasp. She couldn't pull the knife away, could never do that. She dropped his wrist and screamed.

Instantly, Ligur turned toward the center of the room. The attendants saw the knife. Everyone saw the knife. There was an absolute silence in the room.

Ligur walked back to his work table. The attendants began to usher the other patients quickly out of the O.T. room. Some of the patients giggled at Ligur. One raised his hand in a salute.

Soon Ligur was left in the room with the knife. Surrounding him, but keeping their distance, were Elizabeth Diehl, Cliff, and one attendant.

"Be careful, be careful," the attendant said to the others. The meaning of his cautious tone was clear: Ligur is a killer; Ligur would use that knife.

Staring at Ligur, Elizabeth tried to understand how this could have happened. The patient was sedated. The patient was medicated. He was given therapeutic drugs. How then . . . ? Why? Why did he take the knife?

"Wait it out. Wait it out," the attendant said.

Ligur stood with his back against the table. Looking at the three people in the room, he didn't know them.

"Give it back, John," said the attendant, shortening the distance between himself and Ligur with a small, shuffling movement. Ligur watched his feet.

"Isn't there someone we can call?" Elizabeth whispered to Cliff. Cliff shook his head. He was watching the attendant carefully for a cue.

Ligur turned and placed his right hand on the work table, palm down. His left hand held the knife now, the blade turned away from the onlookers.

"That's right, John. Relax. Put it away. Just follow me out of the room."

Ligur did not move. The attendant took another step toward him, motioning to Elizabeth to stay clear. Suddenly, Ligur raised the knife high above his head. His face was blank, unmovable. Then he exhaled so forcefully it might have been a scream, and he brought the knife down with a rush. The knife broke the flesh of his little finger, cut through the center of the bone, and nailed the finger to the table.

The room circled around Elizabeth. She grabbed hold of Cliff's shoulder for balance. They all watched the blood drenching the work table. On Ligur's forehead, the beads of sweat had evaporated.

* * *

"You didn't know I was a regular Daniel Boone," he said, pulling away some twigs and pointing to a yellow stain on the frozen slush.

Helene was cold but exhilarated. A muffler was wrapped around her head, partially obscuring her face. They had spent the morning hiking on a nameless mountain. Now she looked at the stain on the ground.

"What is it?"

"Deer markings," he said, squatting on the ground. She was always astonished by the grace with which this large man moved. One moment he was standing and the next moment he was squatting. The motion was fluid, as if done with no effort, as if his body changed gears without thought.

"Doe or buck?" she asked him with a grin.

"Buck. Does are too intelligent to mark."

They had walked a long way in silence. From time to time he had touched her arm as if to say she was doing fine, she was holding her own. But that was all, and Helene had been grateful for the sense of separateness.

"Can we see them?" she wondered now.

"Hunting season isn't far off and the bucks are getting wary. If we stayed here a few hours, we would see them. Do you want to?"

She stamped her feet on the ground and smiled. No, she thought, that would be a bit much. She shook her head and stamped her feet again to show that she was too cold.

They began to walk back toward the car, Helene walking slightly behind him, moving in Bunch's footsteps when they ran into thickets and brambles. She was surprised by the terrain, that it still existed in such a primeval state in an area that was now almost suburban. They stopped for a moment to breathe. The view was magnificent: a panoply of densely wooded forests broken by low hills of pasture land, with here and there a farmhouse, a barn, a cluster of old outbuildings.

Will Bunche reached down and picked up a twig, then broke it in half. It made a noise like a shot.

"Do you like that sound?" he asked her.

"It sounds," she replied, "like a twig breaking."

Bunche laughed. "I wasn't asking a philosophical question."

"What kind of question were you asking?"

"You know, sometimes you are strangely combative."

"So I've been told, yes," she admitted.

Bunche quickly stepped beside her. He took off his glove and ran his hand along her cheek. He couldn't remember ever being so happy. He couldn't remember looking forward so much to each step, each word, each touch. He wanted to hold her—right there—on the mountain. But he put his hand back in the glove. They walked on.

Reaching the car, she said, "Let me make you a cup of coffee." Half an hour later, flushed, they walked into her kitchen, tingling in the sudden warmth. As she began to prepare the coffee, she felt him walk behind her, then felt his hands go under her sweater, around to the front of her, cupping her breasts. She closed her eyes. She was safe. She was warm. She thought that there was no way this man could want her, or touch her, or take her, that would be bad, ugly, demeaning.

She felt his mouth on her neck and turned to dig herself into his chest. He smelled of the mountain, not of the hospital. He smelled of something in the past which she could not recall.

The coffee was perking behind them. They didn't move. They didn't speak. What, after all, could they say? Nothing. They had salvaged bits of love and bits of lust from the wreckages of both their lives. They were hesitant to speak of it. Yet the desire to name it was strong.

"There are many other places. I can take you to all of them," he suddenly said, disentangling himself and pouring two cups of coffee.

She sat down, and he put a cup of coffee in front of her and sat down across the table.

"What kind of places?"

"A mountain. A brook. A forest."

"The next thing you're going to tell me is that you have access to a green glade."

"A green glade," he repeated, savoring the sound on his tongue, imagining the look of it.

"Can't you produce a green glade?"

"I think," he said in slow, serious tones, "that for you, I can."

She was made uncomfortable by his statement and sipped her

coffee in silence. Bunche stared past her, at the far wall. He didn't want to push her. He made conversation to suit her mood. If she wanted silence, he was silent. If she wanted banter, he bantered. That's the way it had to be. She had told him nothing about her life. Nothing. He didn't even know where she was born. She had told him nothing and he wanted to know everything. He wanted minutiae. What she had eaten at twelve. What books she had read. What music she had heard. He wanted to know all about her mother and father, about . . .

"What are you thinking?" she said.

"How reluctant you are."

She looked at him with a cold glint in her eyes, momentary. He never saw it. "I'm doing what I can do."

He nodded, sipped his coffee. They watched each other by looking past each other.

"Sometimes," he said, "I forget that we're both psychiatrists."

A phone was ringing. Helene went into the small, adjoining room to answer it. Bunche filled his cup again and sat down. It seemed to him that she was talking forever. He watched the circles his coffee cup made on the plastic tablecloth.

When she came back into the kitchen, she sat down. Wrapping her hand around the coffee cup, she stared at Bunche with wide-open eyes. She loosened her grasp on the cup, then closed her hand tightly again. Finally she took her eyes from his face and stared down at the hot black coffee.

Something was wrong, he knew. Bunche moved his chair back, as if preparing to rise. Her hand on the coffee cup had started to tremble. She was watching it as something not a part of her. Bunche reached forward and wrapped his hand around hers on the cup.

Savagely, she pulled away. She resumed her uncomprehending stare at him.

"A patient of mine tried to mutilate himself. His name is John Ligur."

She spoke the words carefully and slowly, as if addressing someone who had just learned the language.

A spasm of stomach cramps made her lean over suddenly, wrapping her arms around herself. Bunche rose from his chair and kneeled beside her.

"Get away from me," she hissed.

Then she was off the chair, still doubled over. The coffee cup was flung against the far wall. It fell, splintering.

"Get away from me, get away from me," she repeated in a whisper.

Bunche sat down at the table again. He would wait.

Helene stood up and brought her hands to her hair, smoothing it. He watched the performance of her reconstruction. Slowly, silently, she put in the steel wires. She took deep breaths until the cramps were gone. Now her face was set in its mold. Pale, yes—but set.

"It is not the way for one doctor to behave in front of another," she said grimly.

"No," he said, "not even if they are lovers."

"Not even if they *were* lovers," said Helene.

Helene retrieved the shattered coffee cup, gathering the splinters carefully. Then she got another cup, half filled it with coffee, and sat down across the table from Bunche. She smiled at him, gently, kindly, as if forgiving him for an indiscretion.

"I know about Ligur," he said evenly.

"What do you know about Ligur?" She was smiling.

"I know what you feel for him."

She reached across the table and placed a hand on his for just a moment.

"You know nothing about Ligur. You know nothing about Ligur and you know nothing about me."

"Do you want me to come back later?" he asked.

She reached out and touched his hand again. Then she began to speak, in a low voice, as though tremendous effort were required to enunciate. She tried to cast out the sadness in her voice, but it kept returning.

"I think, Will Bunche, that you are one of the finest men I have ever met. I am glad we made love. I am glad we had dinner in a barn. I am glad we walked up and down a mountain together."

As she abruptly stopped speaking, he saw her trying to replace the steel wires.

"I want you to go away," Helene Roth said.

"Can I come back?"

"I think . . . you see . . ." She was using her hands now, spreading her fingers and staring at them. "He tried to mutilate himself."

"What do you want me to do?" His face suggested that he would do anything.

"I want you to go away."

He couldn't understand what she was saying. He wanted to touch her. He would make everything all right.

She slammed the coffee cup down on the table. "I am sorry this began and now I am ending it. Do you understand? I am ending it because I must. I must."

"No. I don't understand."

"Your understanding is not necessary."

Will Bunche rose from the table, put on his jacket, and walked to the door. "Are you saying that you don't wish to continue?" His back was to her; he was facing the door.

"Precisely."

It sounded like a cat spitting. He turned and saw her, and wanted to hold her. She was so small, and weak, he wanted to pick her up and carry her into the bedroom.

"Precisely," she said again.

"Precisely," he whispered.

He was out of the house. He was in his car, starting it. Helene was standing just outside the door, arms folded across her chest. What a picture, he thought. And would it ever leave him? The woman psychiatrist chattering with cold. The other psychiatrist sitting in a car, idling the engine, just like a sixteen-year-old schoolboy saying good night to his date.

What was it she had said? "Your understanding is not necessary." He turned the radio on, then off. She was there, standing there. He pulled out of the driveway and began to drive toward the hospital. Then he made a sudden U-turn. He would first go home and see his wife.

As he had driven off, Helene had gone inside and closed the door. She felt it was necessary not to think. She would clean up the house and then go to see Ligur. In the kitchen she sponged the table, emptied the coffeepot and washed it thoroughly, inside and outside, then washed the coffee cups and stacked them in the rubber tray. She straightened the chairs around the table.

Standing in the center of the kitchen, she thought, I do not know
what I am wearing. She looked down at her arms, at her legs and
feet. The nurse had said only that Ligur had tried to mutilate
himself. He was in the F ward, the physical ailment ward,
among pneumonia patients, cancer victims, kidney disorders,
gonorrhea, and mutilations.

Slowly she clothed herself in the psychiatric guise. It steadied
her. After all, she had seen mutilations before. They were like
the common cold in an institution. She looked in a mirror and
felt, for an instant, complete revulsion for herself. She had felt
that once before—after she understood the motives of Paul Stanislas.

She drove at a leisurely speed toward the hospital. She started
the windshield wipers although the day was clear and sunny.
Counting the number of seconds it took for the wipers to make a
complete sweep, she then calculated half sweeps and quarter
sweeps. She looked at the speedometer and noted twenty miles
per hour. She turned the wipers off, then on again, then off, then
on at a faster speed. She calculated the high speed sweep. Then
she pulled the car off the road. She saw the word 'mutilation'
written across the windshield, and on her hands.

English was not her first language. Although she had learned it
thoroughly, the language did not impress her. She felt that it was
often vague and had lost most of its resemblance to life. But
there were some words which retained an absolute fidelity to
the act, she thought. Mutilate was one of them. There was no
confusion about the word. It wasn't used in place of another. It
wasn't used allegorically, the way, say, "betrayal" often was.
Mutilate was mutilate. Someone did it to someone. Flesh and
bone were severed. There was pain. There was . . .

Helene drove back onto the road and continued at fifty miles
per hour.

The F ward jutted out from the main complex of buildings. It
was one of the few edifices with two legal entrances. It had its
own parking lot, a small square of gravel surrounded by stunted
pines and junipers. Helene parked close to an entrance and hurried inside. A nurse behind a small desk greeted her by name.

"I'm looking for one of my patients, John Ligur."

"Second door on your right," said the nurse.

The ward had sixteen rooms, eight on each side. There was nothing to distinguish it from an ordinary hospital except for the fact that all the doors to all the rooms had been removed. Helene stood at the entrance to his room. Wrapped in a white smock, Ligur was lying on the bed, on his back. A folded screen stood off to one side.

Because the ward was so silent, Helene wondered if there were patients in other rooms and what might be wrong with them. She wondered where the nurses were, the quiet bustle, the sounds of people being ministered to.

Taking one step into the room, she could see that his eyes were open. She walked to the bed and wrapped her hands around the steel bar at its foot. Cold, ice cold. Ligur did not move. Behind the bed was a small window, high up on the wall.

"What did you do to yourself?" she whispered. She walked around the side of the bed. His open eyes made no sign of recognition. She touched his forehead lightly with the palm of her hand, as though wiping away a stain.

He was awake. Wide awake. And calm, so very calm. She touched the sleeves of the white smock which clothed him.

"I never deserted you," she said, "never!"

But she was thinking of mutilation, of what he had done to his body. She put a hand on his knee, under the smock.

"You and I are together," she whispered.

She moved her hand up his thigh, past his thigh. She felt the bulk of his testicles and penis and withdrew her hand. He was not mutilated that way. Not. An immense flood of well-being invaded her. Then, for the first time, she saw the bandaged finger. She stared down at the thing wrapped in gauze which dangled from his hand over the bed's edge. She reached out, tentatively.

"Are you Dr. Roth?"

Helene turned quickly. A large woman in a red smock was standing in the doorway. Helene backed away from the bed as if trapped. The response was automatic; she was thinking of nothing.

Elizabeth Diehl took a step into the room. "Are you Dr. Roth?" she repeated.

Helene nodded and moved farther away from Ligur. The woman now seemed familiar to her.

"I'm John's occupational therapist."

Helene nodded again. What did this woman want? She didn't know, but she wanted her out of the room.

"He simply took the knife away from me. I was doing something with it for another patient, and then suddenly he was there, and he took the knife."

"Did he say anything?"

"Nothing. Nothing at all. He just took the knife away. And then he did it. He just did it."

Elizabeth Diehl walked farther into the room and circled the bed.

"Why would he do it? Why?" She turned to Helene for an answer.

"John Ligur is violent," Helene said finally.

"But the drugs are supposed to prevent that."

"Sometimes they work quite well."

Elizabeth Diehl turned back to Ligur and watched his face.

"Is he awake? Is he in pain?"

She waited, watching. When it was obvious that no answer was forthcoming, that she would discover nothing, that she could not manage to understand the persons who made baskets with her help, then she turned and left the room.

Helene watched her go and listened to her shoes clattering on the ward's silent floor. She returned to Ligur's bed.

"Can you hear me?"

The wide-open eyes did not blink, did not move. They remained fixed on the ceiling.

Very quickly she leaned over and kissed him on the neck. Then she stepped back.

"We are in this together. You and I. I shall not be unworthy of you again."

She left the room with a great surge of tranquillity. Ligur was alive. Ligur was well. She had erred, but she had recovered. Their connection was intact.

"He seems fine," said the nurse as Helene walked past the front desk.

"Yes, fine," Helene Roth agreed. The air was cold and clear. She felt remarkably strong. She felt adult.

Margaret stared at the words on the pad. She had written them herself, but she hadn't realized what she was writing. Above the words were a doodle, a cross, and a slash mark. Now she read the words aloud.

"It is the blight man was born for—it is Margaret you mourn for."

A line from a poem by Gerard Manley Hopkins. She hadn't thought of the poem for years. Her father used to recite it to her when she misbehaved. What were the opening lines? The ones she had written down were the last. She remembered that the first line started with her name, Margaret, and then something about distress.

"Margaret, are you weeping . . ." No, that wasn't it. "Margaret, are you grieving . . ." Grieving, yes. But nothing else would come to her. She crumpled the note paper and threw it into the wastepaper basket.

She and Edward Lupica had passed in the hallway twice that day. Each time she had thought of opening a conversation, of beginning the seduction. But nothing happened. They passed, and nodded, and once he smiled. A grim smile.

Margaret walked to the window and looked out. It was growing dark. Soon Lupica would leave, and she would leave. And the whole project would have to be put forward another day . . . then another day . . . and another . . .

She had sensed, as they passed each other, that he knew what was going on. That he realized there was a change in the connection between them. She could feel that.

She ran her hand along the window ledge and looked at her fingers. Clean. The whole office was spotlessly clean. She sat down at her desk and listed possible opening gambits.

"I want to talk to you about something."

"I understand your criticisms now."

"I would like to see you for a few minutes outside the office."

She tore up the page. It would have to begin outside the office. That was true. Suddenly it came to her. The plan came like a blueprint. No one cared if she left early; she usually did leave early. Putting on her coat, she switched off the light, walked out of her office and down the hallway. She took the elevator down, left the building, crossed the street, and stationed herself in an alcove of another building from which she could see her fellow workers exit.

She would wait there for Lupica. She would confront him on the street, as if by accident.

Walking through the revolving doors, groups of people came out of the building and separated. A girl paused, looked up at the sky, made some decision, and walked uptown quickly. A man stumbled as he reached the sidewalk, grinned, and stiffly resumed his journey. One woman rolled up a newspaper, then threw it into the gutter, staring after it as though contemplating the ultimate significance of her act.

She did not see Lupica emerge. Pulling up the collar of her coat, she wondered if he was working late, or if he had already left and hidden himself in the crowd. She shifted her weight from one foot to the other. She decided not to light a cigarette.

A huge, old limousine pulled up in front of the building. The driver stepped out, opened the rear door, and a man in a wheelchair wheeled himself out of the building and up to the car. The driver helped him climb inside.

Wearing a small, crushed gray hat, Lupica came out. He looks like a newspaper reporter, she thought. He paused and stared across the street. Margaret knew he wasn't looking at her. He stood there, his shoulders hunched more than usual, his gaze definitely furtive. She moved back into the shadow of the doorway.

Finally, he began to walk. Margaret gave him a block's lead and then followed. He was walking too fast for her. She was almost trotting. Four blocks farther she caught him, at a light. For a moment she stood beside him, uncertain of what to say.

"Hello," she said, slightly breathless.

He turned his head and looked at her uncomprehendingly. Then he smiled. "Which way are you going?" he said.

The light turned green. She said nothing. He didn't press for an answer. They walked together, at a much slower pace. He stepped to the outside.

They passed a bar and he said, "Would you like a drink?"

It was a working-class bar, with a hot table in front. There were no booths and the room was thick with the smell of smoke and damp clothing. They moved toward the rear, to the end of the bar. There was a single stool unoccupied and he motioned her to sit down. Lupica stood beside her. On her other side a short, thick-set man sat with his elbows on the bar, his head cradled in his hands. It was quite hot. She opened her coat. Down at the front of the bar, the television was tuned to the news.

Lupica ordered a beer, and Margaret, a Bloody Mary. She watched the bartender proceed. She found it fascinating. He opened a small can of tomato juice, poured it into a glass, threw in sauce, pepper, salt, a slice of lemon. Placing a shot glass on the bar, he poured vodka into it, then emptied the shot glass into the brew and splashed more vodka from the bottle.

She waited until Lupica tasted his beer, then sipped her drink.

"Where are you from?" asked Lupica.

"Maryland."

He nodded as if she had told him something impressive and revealing. She noticed that he was keeping his eyes averted, staring first into his beer, then at the television, then at some imperfection on his coat.

Now is the time, she thought. Proceed to converse.

"I want to thank you for giving me that new project. It's something I wanted."

He nodded assent. She spun her Bloody Mary on the bar. That was the wrong way to begin, she thought. The wrong way. She had to take it away from cities and planning.

"Do you like Hopkins?" she said.

"Who?"

"Never mind. It doesn't matter."

The drowsy man on her other side was leaning against her. She moved just slightly into Lupica. We're touching, she thought.

"Do you want another drink?" said Lupica.

She indicated her half full glass. He wants to know what he's doing here, she thought. He wants to know what's happening. And what would Stanislas think if he knew? Knew they were here, in a bar, making preliminary noises. What would he think?

She turned to say something. He turned to say something. They were looking straight on at each other. In the dimness of the bar his face seemed twisted, nearly evil. The discoloration above his lip looked fluorescent. She turned away. He was talking now, but she didn't hear him.

She looked down at his shoes. Her eyes traveled up his leg. Why didn't she just say why she was here? What she wanted. Now he was talking about the city. The city he loved. He was planning, he would make the pieces fall into place, he was aiming for balance . . . She pulled her eyes away from his leg.

"Balance," he said again. "I guess that's my favorite word."

She laughed.

"Does it strike you as funny?"

She laughed again. It was too funny.

"That's why we have the problem in the office," he said. "You refuse to deal with balance."

Now she was laughing uproariously into her drink, pushing against Lupica and the man on her other side. He was talking about balance. She was in this lousy bar to balance her life.

"Look," he said, "I have to go."

So he had to go. Why doesn't he go?

Lupica ordered another beer. The change made a clatter on the bar and she wanted to reach out and quiet the coins.

I can say it, she thought. I can. I'm going to say it. Before he takes another sip of beer I will have said it. I can, she thought. I can. No, no! I can't do it!

Lupica drank his beer in silence. When he finished he touched her hand, lightly. Then he was gone. She saw the two quarters he had left on the bar as a tip. The beer bottle still had beer in it. So did his glass. A man sat down on the empty stool. She lit a cigarette. The stench in the bar grew thicker.

Helene Roth sat quietly in her study, a shawl wrapped around her shoulders. Darkness filled the night and the room; there was no moon. From time to time something stirred just outside the house, made a noise, rustled branches. It is an animal, she thought. An owl, or a dog.

When the phone rang she let it ring. It stopped after nine. She knew it was Bunche. He would call again, she knew, again and again. It would be a long time before he accepted her decision. But accept it he must.

She held out a hand in the darkness. Just a blur. The fingers indistinguishable. It looked rather like a mitten. She remembered her hand's slow crawl up Ligur's thigh . . . the relief.

When the phone rang again, "No use, no use," she whispered to it.

Outside the house there was a sound like small feet scurring. Perhaps one animal chasing another. Perhaps a kill. An owl swooping onto a field mouse. Perhaps a feral cat seeking a mate.

As the phone stopped ringing, she closed her eyes. Envisioning Bunche, she saw him dial, calmly, confidently, sure that she would eventually answer. "No use, no use," she whispered.

Without knowing why or how, she knew she was the genuine cause of the event. *She* caused that uplifted knife, the glint of the sun across the blade, the plunge of steel into his finger. She was now the cause of all Ligur's fortune, good and bad. And he was the cause of her triumphs and failures.

She stood abruptly and walked to the phonograph. Choosing a record, she put it on the turntable. The music of an obscure eighteenth century composer, Galuppi, played on the harpsichord by Fernando Valenti, sounded in the darkened room.

She had played the harpsichord as a child. Poorly, but passionately. The instrument provoked her intellectually. She loved music with a sensual joy. But the harpsichord was different. The sound of it made her edgy, almost irritable. There was nothing quite like it. It took her ears apart. It lodged in her spine. It battered the central nervous system.

As Galuppi filled the air, she wrapped her shawl more tightly around her shoulders. As though from a vast distance she heard the telephone ring, then stop, then start again. In a while the record ended. Although it occurred to her to play the other side, she did not move. She was constructing a catechism.

Question: Why did I sleep with Will Bunche?

Answer: Because I was weak. Because I did not have absolute faith.

Question: Why didn't I have absolute faith in the power of Ligur, and his vision?

Answer: Because I am still a scientist. A psychoanalyst. A psychiatrist. Because I'm unable to deal with the unknown.

Question: Do I still want to destroy Paul Stanislas?

Answer: More than ever.

Question: Why do I want to destroy Stanislas?

Answer: Because he destroyed me.

Question: What is to become of me?

Question: What is to become of Ligur?

Question: What is to become . . .

She had run out of answers, then out of questions. The telephone began to ring again. She put the record back in its cover. Then she approached the shelf where the tape cassettes were filed, selected one, and put it in the machine. By the time her own words sounded, she had resumed her seat and wrapped the shawl tightly around her shoulders.

"A most astonishing dream. I was traveling somewhere in Europe. It was winter. Houses and streets and even the people were covered with snow. It was night, and I was traveling alone. I walked into an inn and asked for a room for the night. The innkeeper looked familiar, but I couldn't place him. He gave me the key to room 41. The number appeared in large print on the key holder. The key itself was large. As I walk up the stairs, the key gets larger and larger. Until I can hardly hold it. A man appears at the top of the staircase. He speaks German and is dressed in evening clothes. He helps me to my room.

"When we are inside, without a word spoken, we undress. We lie down on the bed. The sheets are bright yellow. I say that I have never seen such bright yellow sheets. He replies that his feet are yellow. I stare at his feet. They are yellow. They are the color of the sheets. He turns the light out.

"We begin to make love. We make love all night long. When morning comes I am exhausted. The man is standing across the room, holding a bathrobe over his whole body. I say good morning. He drops the bathrobe.

"He is not the man I slept with. He is a gigantic green man. He is bestial. He seems to grow, to inflate, to fill and control the whole room. I scream. Then I wake.

"The figure in this dream is the same figure that Ligur drew. I dreamed his vision, or his knowledge, or his madness, or his dream."

Helene walked swiftly to the machine and turned it off. The telephone was ringing. She peered out of the window into the pitch-black night. The sounds had ceased. Perhaps, she thought, the kill was made, the predator is satisfied.

She resumed her catechism.

Question: Do I still love Stanislas?

Answer: I have no answer.

Question: Do I love Ligur?

Answer: I have no answer.

Question: What is the relation between mutilation and love?

She had no answer.

For the first time the ringing phone intruded on her. She wanted to rip the wires from the walls. Placing her hand on the cold receiver, she waited for it to stop.

IX

The young man was wearing a dark blue Navy watch cap, pulled low over his eyes. He hadn't removed it when he entered Paul Stanislas's office, and he didn't remove it or lift it from his eyes when he sat down on the couch. He started to speak quickly, punctuating his words with frowns and occasional grins.

"They fired me. Good. I'm an actor, not a fuckin' file clerk. I had finished what I was supposed to do and I was sitting, minding my own business, reading a book. You want to know what book I was reading?"

He didn't wait for an answer: "I was reading *Mein Kampf.*"

He laughed out loud and pulled off his wool cap with a flourish, flinging it upward into the air.

"Don't you know a lie when you hear one? I wasn't reading that book. I wasn't reading anything. I was staring at my shoes. This lady comes over with another batch of files. I tell her to go fuck herself. They call the temporary agency, and boom, here I am again. What a shame. I was doing so well. So well. So well. Did you know I could sing?"

Stanislas made no reply. He was waiting for the jag to subside. The young man was now off the couch and on the chair, throwing his hat up and trying to catch it on the tip of his shoe. His dress was shabby, except for his shoes, which were spit shined into a high gloss.

"Of course. I can sing and dance and . . . and file. I am one good file clerk when the situation demands it. But they were fucking over me. Do you understand?"

171

On and on he rambled. His sentences began slowly, picked up speed and volume and ended in a crescendo. Stanislas wasn't listening to what he was saying. He listened to the movement of the words. It seemed familiar. The young man was speaking in some sort of meter. Shakespearean? He wondered. Or the meter of classical Greek poetry? He didn't know.

The sentences became weaker and weaker. He seemed to be devouring himself verbally. Finally he stopped talking.

He reached down, picked the hat off the tip of his shoe, shined his shoes with it, then pulled it back over his eyes.

"So there it is," he said.

For the first time in the session the young man couldn't look at Stanislas. His eyes were cast to the floor.

"So there it is," he mumbled again, as though a great fatigue had settled on him.

Then he perked up and held out his hands.

"I also have good hands. Very good hands. Like an all-pro quarterback. Like Vladimir Horowitz."

And then he was silent. After a while he put his hands in his lap and leaned back in the chair. He closed his eyes.

Stanislas was staring at the picture on his desk. He moved it to the left. He knew that nothing productive could be done in this session. His only job was to get the man level. He had been way up, and now he was way down. He just had to be leveled out and sent onto the street.

A point had once been made to him—very clearly. The great majority of patients are not helped by psychoanalysis because the basic ingredient is never present during the session. That basic ingredient is simply that peculiar calmness needed to enter into the transference, and thereby enter into the process.

As he looked at the young man, he realized more than ever the truth of that statement. There had been another point: that a doctor cannot perform serviceable root canal work unless the patient is anaesthetized. Psychoanalysis has not been able to develop an anaesthesia that would put the patient into the correct mood of sedation. Alert, but quiet. In touch with the past. In touch with the fingertips and the head. Close to the passions. Close to the horrors of every childhood. Close to incest. Close to patricide. Close to feces and death. But calm.

His mind shuffled through the past, seeking the source of those comments. It registered, the file card was obtained—Helene Roth.

Drip, drip, drip, Stanislas thought, she is seeping through—water through the hand. A steady sequence; not the manufactured meter of the young man's speech.

"How is your career progressing?" Stanislas asked.

"Better than yours," the young man retorted.

Stanislas smiled. That was fine. Then the young man offered up a brief, carefully reasoned analysis of why he hated psychoanalysis. And then the hour was over—he left.

The last appointment for the day had canceled earlier. Stanislas left his office and walked through the rest of the apartment, checking to see if there were any household chores to be done. A cleaning lady came once a week, but he had his clothes to look after, and a food supply.

Briefly, he thought of going to the gym. I'm too tired, he concluded. The bed looked inviting. Each morning he made the bed so that it looked inviting. The blanket was stretched taut. The pillows were fluffed. The sheet was folded over the top of the blanket.

He lay down fully clothed, keeping his feet over the edge of the bed. A small lamp near the clock was the only illumination in the room. He wondered how Emily and Deirdre were progressing in the ordeal of dinner. He grinned as he pictured mother and daughter silently battling over lamb chops or stew or spaghetti. My function in the family, he thought, is to act as a dinner-hour mediator.

Stanislas closed his eyes and slept. He dreamed that he was alone in the North. In a country of perpetual ice. He was dressed in animal skins and lived in an igloo. Outside, the wind howled. Inside, quarters were so cramped he was forced to remain hunched over. It was dark inside the igloo and not that much warmer than outside. He was rubbing oil on his hands and feet, the fat from an unknown animal. He spent hour after hour rubbing himself with the oil. Then he rubbed his harpoon, a short, stubby branch attached to a bronzed blade. He rubbed the shaft carefully, until he could see each definition in the grain of the wood. Then he carefully oiled the blade until it shone.

The wind stopped and all was absolutely still. He knew it was time to go outside. He began to take off all his clothes. When he was entirely naked, he rubbed his body with oil. He rubbed oil all over himself: eyes, genitals, ears, navel, everywhere. The more he applied the more it began to stink, to take on the most putrid odor.

He picked up his harpoon and crawled toward the opening of the igloo. His feet, which were oiled, kept sliding on the ice. Finally he emerged and stood up. It was surprisingly warm. He stood in front of the igloo and turned suddenly when he heard a wall crashing. The igloo was melting. He felt terrible fear. He plunged his harpoon into the melting house. It vanished. It became part of the ice.

He began to walk, then to trot, holding the weapon lightly in his hand. A green spout was visible, pushing up through the ice. He plucked it, chewed it, and found it delicious. The taste was like licorice. He found another and consumed it. And then another and yet another.

Throwing the harpoon away, he began to amble, stark naked, along the ice, plucking the sprouts and eating them.

Then he came upon one that was bigger than the rest and a dull yellow rather than green. He reached down and pulled the sprout. It did not move. He grabbed hold of it with both hands. Slowly, it began to yield. His face was drenched in sweat. Every muscle in his body ached. He pulled and tugged and finally the sprout came up, and as it emerged the ice around him splintered with a roar.

Before him was a massive white geyser. Ice and water and cold and wind filled the air. Then the white geyser dissolved and he was staring at a giant green figure—part man, part nothing, part anything.

Stanislas awoke with a scream on his lips. He sat up straight on the bed and didn't know where he was. His clothes were drenched with sweat. He might have had a high fever, he thought. He looked dumbly around the room, his eyes lighting on the clock. Six-thirty P.M. He had slept for more than an hour. He threw his legs over the side of the bed and tried to blink away the drowsiness.

Stanislas remembered only bits and pieces of his dream: ice, a harpoon, the color green. He stood up and looked around. It was no use, he had to go back to bed. Sitting down on the bed once more, he took off his shoes. He stretched out and sank into a deep sleep.

When he awoke, it was ten minutes after nine. He sat up, fully awake now. He didn't remember dreaming anything. He had an erection. He undressed and showered. Outside it was raining; Stanislas could hear the slow drizzle against the glass.

He walked into the kitchen and made himself a cup of coffee. Then he took the coffee into the living room and put a record on the phonograph. He listened for a moment. It wasn't what he wanted to hear. He exchanged it for another. Again it was the wrong music. He changed records. Then he thought the needle was too worn. He turned off the phonograph. Rummaging through a cupboard, he found a new needle. He replaced the old one and turned the phonograph on. Better, he thought, and sipped the coffee.

He looked around the room and realized that he didn't like the drapes. Wondering whether there were other drapes available, he walked into a large closet and pulled out boxes. There were no drapes. He tried another closet. Nothing. The drapes would have to stay. Too bad, he thought, sitting down. The music began to irritate him. He got up and shut off the phonograph.

It continued to rain. Stanislas walked to the window and stared at the river. He was too far away to see the drops pelting the water but could envision the little splashes and the staccato sounds they made. That was the sound he wanted to hear. He turned and studied his record collection. It was large and diverse, but there was nothing in it to approximate the river sounds.

He walked into the kitchen and threw the remaining coffee into the sink. He began to rinse the cup. The handle snapped off suddenly.

It lay in his hand. He stared at the two pieces of the cup.

He couldn't understand how it had happened. How could he have broken the cup when he wasn't even aware of applying any pressure? Where did the strength come from? Or had he lost contact with his strength?

A chill enveloped him. It was not over, he realized. It had only just begun. The well-being he had felt when he called Deirdre had been a lie. Someone or something had misled him. He was being played with. He was entering into delusion after delusion.

The pieces of the cup seemed to grow in his hand.

Is this the sign that I am going to break? I want to, he thought savagely. I want these stupid mysteries to end. I want control—some kind of control—even death or psychosis or senility. Anything that can be named. Anything but this slow horror of the will seeping away. Anything but this paroxysm of dream and motiveless action.

A sudden memory intruded: the basketball going high, high, high into the air and then descending unconsciously through the net, as if he had not thrown it.

Stanislas placed a finger on either side of his mouth and pressed. No, he had not lost contact with the reality of his body. There was pressure. He felt his fingers. He pressed harder. He felt the gradations of strength.

Aspects of the dream resurfaced—the green sprouts coming through the ice, the taste of licorice.

He opened the cupboard. There were several cups of the same kind. That made him feel good. He threw the broken cup into the garbage bag, then returned to the living room and sat down. He wasn't tired yet, but hardly energetic, either. He felt very calm. He thought of nothing. He just sat there.

Margaret lay, naked, on the bed in her room. She lay on top of the quilt. The apartment was always too hot in fall and winter. As the heat was sent up through a central system, there was no way to control it.

It was ten o'clock at night. The bedroom was flooded with oblique light from the kitchen which adjoined it. Margaret could hear the rain outside beating against the windows. She was evaluating the Lupica episode, trying to understand just what had happened. Deciding that this evaluation warranted a cigarette, she lit one and made a slash mark on the inside of the match cover. Her fourteenth cigarette of the day. A bit much, she thought.

She turned the radio on to a country music station. Her Maryland childhood persisted in this way. She liked country music. Or, rather, she liked the lyrics of country songs. Often absurd, often embarrassing, even so, they dealt with the things she dealt with: impotence, jobs, love, death. And in country music everything turned out badly. Yes, badly—that was the crux.

She stared down at her body. As a child she had often had the feeling that her body was not born with her at birth, that at a certain time (she knew not when) it was given to her. And that was why it was so beautiful.

A man was singing a song about a girl who drowned in a river. She turned up the volume to learn the girl's name, and the river's name, and the train of events that led to the tragedy. Yes, she loved country music. And she loved the city. She was proud of the paradox.

She looked at the clock and saw 10:15. What did Stanislas do in the evening? What did Lupica do? She could imagine both of them pacing. Were they thinking of her as she thought of them?

Maybe she should take a walk to the river, the East River. Maybe she should amuse herself by going to the little park by the river and making believe she was a poor little country girl about to leap. It was a safe park; the entrance was at the end of a street littered with doormen. She touched her thigh, then her knee. But I am not a poor little country girl, she thought. Not at all.

She got up and dressed, slowly and calmly. It was a short walk, so she wouldn't need a raincoat, just her long winter coat, modeled, perhaps, on some nineteenth-century dragoon. It made her appear even taller than she was, and thinner.

She reached to the top of the closet and pulled down a water-repellent fisherman's hat that her father had given her when she left for New York years ago. He had made a joke about the hat and the city, but she couldn't remember it. She hardly ever wore the hat.

Margaret looked at herself in the mirror. All of a sudden she grinned. She felt so good! She didn't know why. Loose, easy, strong. And here she was going to throw herself in the river. She grinned at herself. Her image grinned back. She stuck out her tongue. She made face after face, and the mirror was faithful.

Margaret slowly walked toward the park. It was warm for the season and a steady drizzle beat on her hat. She turned down Fifty-first. There were the doormen, waiting under awnings or just to the side of entrances. Margaret liked to watch doormen. She couldn't quite understand what they were doing. Some looked permanently energetic. Others drearily lounged, only to be energized when a taxi pulled up or a package arrived.

At the end of Fifty-first was the park. One entered by a stone staircase, very steep, that led to a long ramp at the bottom. Once on the ramp the East River became dramatically visible. Now one had two choices: to walk straight ahead, cross over the highway, then climb down another flight of stairs to the walkway right along the river; or one could take a flight of stairs which led to the little park on the near side of the highway. Margaret would descend to the park. But first she stood quietly watching the river. The current was rapidly swirling. So this was the place for the jump. The thought was oddly amusing. If things ever got so bad that suicide was the right move, the one place she would certainly not fling herself was in that river. Never mind what the country song said. Not that river.

The park was almost empty. Two dog walkers were making their rounds. There were scattered groves of trees, a large, unused stone building, and a very ornate massive water fountain which, to Margaret's knowledge, had never worked. A few stone benches completed the park's landscape.

The park lamps had long ago fallen into disrepair, but illumination was plentiful from lamps on the highway. Margaret walked along, smiling at the dampness. She could see and hear the cars on the highway. A sudden flash of headlights, then nothing, then another set of headlights, and another. It seemed to her a form of entertainment. And she loved the sound of the highway on a rainy night. A sizzle as the tires slapped the wet road, then a low, hollow sound, then the sound of sheer speed. Lights and sound and speed, observed from a pastoral enclave. She loved the city not for its monolithic cement, but because the city provided such unlikely amusement.

Behind her were massive apartment buildings, covered with ivy, thrusting out a bizarre pattern of trees and shrubs from terraces. Looking uptown, she saw that rain had coated the bridge.

The steel looked flimsy. A car on the highway hit a puddle, sending a torrent of water into the park. It came over in a sheet and drenched her. Margaret laughed aloud and retreated to the center of the park.

She looked around. The dog walkers had vanished. No one at all was in the park. She turned to the river and saw that no one was walking on the walkway. There was only the river, the cars, herself. She held out a hand; the rain was steady and light.

She walked over to the water fountain, noting the basin stuffed with dead leaves and twigs. Cupping her hands against the rain, she lit a cigarette and looked downtown. The old wharf was still there, jutting out about twenty feet into the water. It was accessible from a footpath across the water, and Margaret had walked there many times. It was an old-fashioned four-poster wharf, with a sea gull perched on each post. The water was clearly visible through the cracks in the wood. She supposed the wharf to be nineteenth century. She could stand on the highway, take one step onto wood, and drop one hundred years. Of course, the wharf smelled. It smelled of decaying wood, of gulls, of seaweed, and that pungent scent of port cities. Sweet, perhaps. Sour, certainly. Like a dead fish drenched in Chanel.

Margaret thought it would be nice to stand on the wharf in the rain. Nice but dangerous. She was having a good enough time here in the park, smoking, listening to cars, keeping her back straight.

A cold wind came up suddenly and almost tore her hat off. She whirled around, away from the river. When the wind subsided, she turned back to the river. She searched her pockets for gloves, without success. With gloves she could have cleaned the basin of leaves and twigs. She loved the basin, a beautiful bronze bowl that offered up one's distorted image.

Another sheet of water came up off the highway. Margaret caught only the end of it, the rest plummeting beyond her. She dropped her wet cigarette to the ground. There was a sound behind her. She started to turn but found herself in absolute darkness. There was no light at all. She smelled wet wool. She took a step forward. Something stopped her. She was being held. There were arms. It had to be arms. She stood still.

Now she understood. Someone was behind her. That someone

had thrown her long coat over her head. He had his arms wrapped around her. She was a wrapped bundle.

She felt no fear. It was as if she had entered a foreign, not dreadful, country. It was necessary merely to understand the terrain. These arms wrapped loosely around her—if she didn't move she could only sense them. Perhaps this was a joke? Is it someone she knows? One of the doormen of East Fifty-first?

The arms quickly tightened. She was immobilized. She could feel muscle and sinew through her coat. Now fear seized her. Paralyzing fear that drained her limbs, her mind. She was incapable of thought. The arms tightened again and crushed her breasts. She could hardly breathe. The darkness darkened.

Then she realized that it was happening. Happening to her. Fear turned to panic. She struggled against the arms, making little animal sounds in the confines of her coat. The arms were impervious.

Panting for breath, she stopped the struggle and felt perspiration drip down her back and legs. She smelled something funny, and then knew it was herself. The pressure of arms lessened. One arm was removed. Where was it? Where had it gone?

The arm moved underneath her dress and tore off the panties that covered her flesh. Feeling fingers on her buttocks, hungrily grasping, she closed her eyes in the darkness. The fingers moved between her legs, slid up and down her thighs, reached under and up over her belly. She felt that an animal was crawling on her flesh. It was unbearable. She began to sob. Her knees refused to support her. The animal went on crawling.

I am going to die, she thought. She was being auctioned off. The fingers were weighing her. The fingers were the buyer. She was the meat. The fingers were inspecting the meat. Soon she would be slaughtered. Good. That was what she wanted. To be out of it. To be in the clear light of death so she could breathe and not be afraid. The fingers were going to pay for her by the pound. They were rubbing against her clitoris. She felt revulsion and some pain. She felt obscene. She thought she would die in the next moment. Yes, she thought, let me die! The animal was rubbing her slowly, very slowly, to get her ready. To prepare her for death.

Where is the rain? Where is the highway? Where is Margaret?

For an instant, a finger penetrated her. She straightened her back and tried to scream. Then she was being dragged. She could feel her feet slide along the concrete. Now they were on softer ground and she was on her back. The coat over her face was wet and a chill ran through her body. From the waist down she was bare of clothing.

She tried to pull the coat from her face to see what was happening, to see her fate. A blow landed on the side of her head, making her dizzy. She felt a hand slip under her buttocks and raise her slightly off the ground.

There was something between her legs. Large and stiff, it slapped alongside her thighs. It started to move into her. She tried to bring her legs together. Another blow landed, stunning her through the coat on her face. She felt no pain, but tasted blood.

Now it was inside her. In pain and fury she tried to scream. She tried to turn, to escape. There was no scream, there was no escape. The horror was crawling through her. It wanted more and more of her. It wanted to bury her there in the rain.

On the other side of my coat is his face, she thought. His face. The horror has a face. The pain was scalding. Scalding. Wet leaves were clinging to her buttocks. Pain. Horror. Pain. And then the body on top of her shuddered—and the agony slid out.

The weight rose from her. She lay there under her coat. She heard noises. Then she heard a laugh. A deep, long laugh. The laugh of a happy person. A laugh of joy. And then there was nothing. Silence.

I have dreamed this, she thought. I have dreamed everything. She pulled the coat from her face. She was weak, and could not sit up. Her body ached in all its parts. But she knew it was only a dream. Then she looked down at herself and pulled the coat back over her face in horror.

What shall I do? she thought. She lifted the coat and looked out at the river. It was still there. The highway was still there. She turned to look at the fountain with the bronze basin. The rain was still falling. And over there near the fountain was something familiar. After a while she realized it was her rain hat.

Slowly she stood up. Her underclothes were strewn about and torn. She left them where they lay. Buttoning her coat, she walked to the rain hat, picked it up, and put it on her head.

Each step hurt her. Home seemed miles away. I have been for a walk in the park, she whispered. She stared up at the steep flight of stone steps. She would have to climb them.

Will Bunche sat parked in his car on the strip of highway across from Helene Roth's house. It was the usual morning hour. Two bluejays were performing their aerial tricks over the house, flying in circular paths, coming very close to each other at the apogee of each path, then picking up speed as they spiraled downward for another run.

He waited there until he saw light and movement in the house. Then he left the car, crossed the road, and knocked on her door. No one answered. He rang the doorbell.

Helene opened the door. There was no surprise on her face when she saw him; neither was there the slightest greeting. She was dressed in a severe brown suit. He had never before realized how small she was, how fine her features were, how beautifully arranged, the entire woman.

She moved her eyes from his face to his jacket. Behind him, over him, he could hear the raucous calls of the jays.

"I thought it had been settled," she said slowly and carefully.

"What had been settled?"

"You and I."

"Death is the only settlement."

She looked up at him quickly, with just a trace of a smile. He wanted to kiss the smile.

"Are you telling me," he continued, "that you can also make such settlements?"

"I presume you have come for a cup of coffee."

"Oh, yes," he said formally, "I have come for a cup, one cup, of coffee."

She stepped aside and he walked past her into the house. He sat down in the familiar kitchen chair. She poured him a cup of coffee and sat down across the table.

"How is Ligur?" he asked.

"He seems to be fine."

"It was not as bad as you thought then."

"There was blood. And pain. And terror. That is enough badness."

He took a sip of coffee. "I have never had the impression that you shrink from violence."

"Our time together was short. Therefore your impressions of me may lack accuracy."

"May I speculate that this withdrawal is temporary?"

"What withdrawal are you speaking of, Will?"

She had pronounced his name as though she had known it for decades, and as though his name itself were a crime.

"Your withdrawal from me."

"That is not temporary."

"Therefore you would rather I did not arrive in the morning for coffee?"

"Coffee is intimacy. And we won't be that way anymore."

"What way will we be?"

"I don't know. I really don't know."

"What you want is a professional relationship." He laughed out loud, sardonically. He turned to face the window. The sight of her now was painful. He would not continue this absurd conversation. He loved the woman who sat across the table from him. He wanted to talk to her about circling bluejays. Or French food. Anything but the current topic.

"I have hurt you, and I am sorry."

He looked quickly at her face and then away from it. She didn't know how much she had hurt. She didn't know.

I am going to pull myself together, he thought, and say a few things to her. He heard the jays again, more raucous now. The only songbirds that were truly beasts. They ate anything: grain, young birds, young mammals, eggs. In their evolutionary wisdom they had given up migration. Season after season they stayed put. They were dazzling—the blue and the white, the fierce eyes staring with full comprehension . . . She was staring at him now. She, too, was fierce and beautiful.

"I accept your judgment," he said finally. "I accept your judgment on me."

"Thank you," she replied simply.

"But may I speak for a moment?"

She nodded, then went to the stove, brought the coffeepot to the table, and filled his cup.

Will Bunche began a sentence, then broke off swiftly. He felt as if he were about to make a formal statement of enduring importance. He felt as if he were addressing her at a significant function, and she was listening carefully. The function, he knew, was his own dismemberment. But the goal was to save her. Nothing must happen to Helene Roth. That was the creed. He knew he must do everything possible to ensure her survival. Nothing else mattered. He would age and wither and be blown away like his father. But she must be saved. For someone else, if not for him. Someone else. He remembered her body under his hands. How many hours ago? He remembered the way . . .

"Are you going to lecture me?"

It brought him back. "Yes. I want to give you my views on the psychiatric balance."

"By all means. Give me your views."

Bunche lifted his cup, noticed the circle it had made in the saucer, and placed the cup back in the circle.

"I divide psychiatrists into four categories. The first consists of those who want to heal. Quite simply, they want to heal. They want to make sick people well. They want to alleviate suffering. They want to heal. Let's call them the Christian residue of the psychiatric community."

"And I am not among them," she noted.

"No, you are not."

"What's your second category?"

"Those who are curious, like myself. Men and women who became psychiatrists because they wanted to solve certain mysteries. Because they wanted answers."

"I'm not among them, either," she said, almost triumphantly.

"No, you are not. But I am."

"I congratulate you." She could not mask the contempt.

"Then there is the third category. It consists of those who seek power. Power is there, vast power. Money and prestige, and the ability to prescribe drugs and institutions, to change a man's life

in an instant, to kill, to save, to commit, to confuse. Power.
There's power in all of it."

"And that is my category, Dr. Bunche?"

"No. That is not your category, Dr. Roth."

"Who, then, am I?"

He reached across the table and encircled her wrist with one of
his long, large hands. She let herself be held for a moment, then
pulled away. She continued to look at him.

"There is a fourth category. Those who go over."

"Over where?"

"To those on the other side. This fourth category is strange.
Few belong to it. Very few. They have found something in the
madness of their patients. They have found *something they desire.* And as time passes they lose the sense of distinction; soon
it is madness, alone, which pulls them. So they go over. Some go
mad. Some merely change the way they look at their patients.
They continue to appear as practitioners, but in reality, they are
listening and watching and trying to absorb the madness and put
it in more palatable forms."

Helene stood up and began to sponge the table. He watched
her steadily.

"So you think I have gone over," she said mildly.

"I know it."

"Tell me what happens to those in your fourth category. What
happens to those who go over?"

"They die."

"We all die."

"They die in a certain way."

"And what is that way, Dr. Bunche?"

He held up his palms in a a gesture of unknowing. He wanted
her to sit down again, across from him.

"Are you sure I have gone over?"

"Quite sure."

"What are my symptoms?"

"Your withdrawal from me. From the real. From love."

She piled the coffee cups in the sink, then wiped her hands on
a dish towel. She was staring out the window. He could hear the
jays again. She turned to him.

"I thank you for your analysis, and for your professional opinions. Time will tell whether or not you are right."

He was beside her in a second, his hands on her shoulders, his thumbs along her collarbones.

"Helene, it's a false god." His voice was thick, and unsteady. "It's a false god like the rest. There is no beauty, no power, nothing sacred in madness. It is just another form. That's all. That's all."

He let his hands fall away. A smile was frozen on her face. She was still dismissing him.

He stepped back. "I will not come here again, unless you wish it. Unless you ask me to."

He left the house and crossed the highway and got into his car. His hands shook too violently to start the engine. He sat and waited. The bluejays were no longer cavorting. He saw only one, resting on a telephone wire, its eyes moving over the landscape.

Finally he was able to start the engine, and he drove to the hospital, parking in his usual space. It was too early to go to his office. It was too early to be there at all. A maintenance worker was emptying trash from wire baskets into large plastic bags. They greeted each other. Bunche walked along the path that paralleled one of the hospital wings. The maniacs are inside and I am outside, he thought. The maniacs are inside and Helene Roth is still outside.

He stopped walking and listened. A little song was coming from one section of the building. Perhaps it came from the women's wing. Perhaps one of his patients was singing. Perhaps she was the lady who defecated on the floor, then scattered hair ribbons on her feces. Perhaps it was the woman who spoke in sentences of four words, not one of which was a verb. Perhaps the little song was being sung by old Mary, who had been at the hospital half a century, who mutilated herself, year after year, until now every part of her had something missing.

Perhaps it was the young girl who had murdered her three children. She hung them with dish towels in a closet and said nothing to her husband when he came home. So he opened the closet to get his bedroom slippers and found the children.

Well, once in a while they said something that knocked your

eyes out with revelation of truth. But that was all. That was the end of it. They weren't any better on the other side. They were decidedly worse.

He turned and started to walk back to the entrance. Helene Roth's car was coming through the gate. He watched her drive slowly into her spot. She got out of her car and walked toward the entrance. Seeing him, she stopped. They were fifty yards apart. They gazed across the fifty yards. Then she walked inside.

She is going to see Ligur, he thought. She is going to continue her dialogue with the other side. For only a moment, he wanted, desperately, to fall to his knees and pray for her.

Emily was sitting on the floor of her room. In front of her were a large pad and several crayons. She had been drawing a horse. He was very attractive, but something was wrong with his head. She knew that something was wrong. She picked up the pad and held it at arm's length. The head was too small, she decided. Taking up a purple crayon, she drew another head over the small one. That was better. Now, however, the horse had a small head and a big head. She giggled. It was a two-headed horse.

She spread out all the crayons. The orange one had a nice point. She colored the horse orange.

Her father could ride horses if he wanted to. She knew that. He could get on the biggest horse in the stable, gallop down to a fence, and jump over the fence. Emily knew that her father could be the greatest horseman in the world, if he wanted to, if he wasn't so busy.

Now an orange-bodied, black-headed horse filled the page. There had to be some grass. Emily took a green crayon and made slash marks at the bottom of the picture. And there had to be a sun. She made a bright purple sun in the upper right-hand corner.

Emily wasn't finished yet. She looked on the floor for a crayon, the right crayon. There was a brown one, but it was stubby and overused. There was a red one. And a thick yellow crayon that came from another set. She took the red crayon and drew her father sitting on the horse. It was hard to get both his legs around the horse. But she managed finally, and gave him a yellow feather in a yellow hat on his head. Then she pushed the pad away. She was tired of drawing. She wanted to read.

Emily's books were scattered about the room. Her father gave her books about horses, and . . . and there was the *Mother Goose* book. She pulled it out of a pile. He had given her this one and it was her favorite. It was large and square and the pictures were big. Sometimes her father read the rhymes out loud to her and they both laughed. Emily wanted to know all the rhymes in the book. She opened to the middle.

> Curly locks, Curly locks,
>   Wilt thou be mine?
> Thou shalt not wash dishes
>   Nor yet feed the swine,
> But sit on a cushion
>   And sew a fine seam,
> And feed upon strawberries,
>   Sugar and cream.

She read it aloud, once, twice, three times. Each time she read it at a faster pace, until, by the third time, she was going so fast she stumbled over the words.

Emily lay on her back and put the book over her nose. She loved strawberries and cream. Sometimes she and her mother would pour heavy sweet cream over big red berries bought from a truck farmer.

She sat up suddenly, perplexed. Her mother had never made her feed the swine. But that was probably because there were no swine around. Swine were pigs. That she knew.

Emily put down the book and returned to her drawing pad. In a corner of the horse picture she drew five pigs. When she was finished, she realized that their snouts were too long. They looked almost like wolves. So she made their bodies longer.

She turned over on her stomach and took up the book.

> Dance to your daddy,
>   My little babby,
> Dance to your daddy, my little lamb;

You shall have a fishy
In a little dishy,
You shall have a fishy when the boat comes in.

It was hard to recite. It didn't go smoothly. She tried again, more slowly, in a sing-song fashion like they did in school.

No, she didn't like that one. Not at all. And she didn't even like the picture with it. She flipped the page and sat up. This was her favorite page. Truly her favorite. In the picture was a beautiful coat, and a beautiful little girl was crying because there was a hole in the coat.

I'll tell my own daddy, when he comes home
What little good work my mammy has done;
She has earned a penny and spent a groat,
And burnt a hole in the child's new coat.

That was her absolute favorite, and when she came to the last phrase, she sat up regally and proclaimed to the wall: "And burnt a hole in the child's new coat."

Then she hopped up and left her room and walked down the hall. The door to her parents' room was half open, as it always was. Her mother was out of the house. There was no one in the house but Emily.

She pushed open the door and walked inside. Standing on the carpet, she folded her arms. It was always cold in this room. The bed was so large, so much bigger than hers. She walked over to it and touched the bedspread. Then she sat down on the bed, rocking softly, bouncing on the springs. Her mother slept here, on the right, she knew. And her father slept on the left.

If her mother were to catch her in here, she would get yelled at. Her mother didn't like her in this room. But her mother wasn't home, was she. Emily walked over to the large chest of drawers and opened the top drawer. It was filled with papers and envelopes and old wallets and checkbooks. She found a batch of photographs in the back of the drawer, held together by a rubber band stiff with age. Emily looked through the pictures one at a time. There was one of her mother and father, holding hands on the beach. There was one of her father, smiling, holding a base-

ball bat just as if he was going to hit a ball. She liked that one.
There were pictures of other people she didn't know. When she
tried to replace the rubber band, it snapped. Emily felt afraid. But
she shoved the photographs back where she had found them and
thrust the rubber band into her pocket.

The next drawer was full of her mother's underclothes. Emily
picked up a camisole and held it over her head. She could see
right through it. She flung it high into the air and it floated lazily
back to the carpet. Digging through the drawer, she found another. She tossed it and it drifted across the room and landed on the
bed. Emily leapt after it onto the bed and grappled with it,
bouncing up and down on the bed springs. Suddenly, she became
still and sad. She had heard this noise before, and she didn't like
this noise.

Quickly, she gathered up the lingerie and thrust it all back
into the drawer, making no effort to leave things as she had
found them. Then she walked through a door into her parents'
bathroom.

The bathroom was filled with implements of wonder to Emily. Thick towels, sponges, bottles, and sprays. Sweet-smelling
soaps, and lotions and creams. She picked up everything and everything dazzled her.

On the sink was a pair of scissors, long and slender, with an ornate handle. Emily used both hands to open and close the scissors. They made a beautiful sound—snip, snip, snip.

Near the shower a huge yellow towel hung from a towel rack.
Bright blue flowers nestled in the yellow background, and bright
blue fringes edged it.

Emily snipped off the fringes. She looked around. There was
plenty to snip. She could go back to her mother's camisoles. She
snipped more towel. No, it was better to stop. Her mother would
be home soon. She put the scissors, the beautiful scissors, back.
Stopping to bounce just twice on the bed, she left her parents'
bedroom.

In her own room, she picked up the horse drawing. She didn't
like the color of the horse. She didn't like the way her father
looked on the horse. She didn't like the swine's snouts.

The pad went spinning across the room.

Emily took up the *Mother Goose* book and put it on her lap. Slowly, she turned the pages. There. That was a good one.

> Baby and I
> Were baked in a pie,
> The gravy was wonderful hot.
> We had nothing to pay
> To the baker that day
> And so we crept out of the pot.

Margaret sat up in bed. She was in her apartment, but she didn't remember returning there. The sun was streaming in through the window. She had her coat and dress on. The bedspread was crumpled and strewn with bits of leaves and twigs and dirt.

She remembered. Her legs sought the floor and she stood. Dizziness and nausea, nausea and dizziness. She reached down and held on to the bed to steady herself. A circle of sunlight fell round her legs. They were black with dirt.

Her thighs and back ached. There was an awful tightness in her neck and shoulders. It felt as though the slightest movement would split a vital bone.

She had to take her clothes off. She had to get rid of everything that smelled of the park. When the clothes lay in a heap on the floor, Margaret moved unsteadily away from the bed and into a pool of warm sunlight. Her body seemed disgusting to her. She felt like an old old woman. Tears poured from her eyes. She didn't know why she was crying now. She wanted to sit down on the floor in the sun. Ten feet away, the rain hat was perched on a chair. Beyond the chair was the bathroom, and a shower.

Slowly, she began the walk. A step at a time. I am very old, she thought, very old. Reaching the shower, she turned on the water and listened to it drum on the tiles.

The water eased her pain. As she stepped out of the shower, her back brushed against the shower curtain and she started to tremble, as if something was about to wrap around her again.

I must not think, not touch, not explore, she thought. I must deal with mundane things. The news. That would be right. She would turn on the radio and listen to the news. Margaret walked naked out of the bathroom and turned on the radio. They were talking about the Middle East. That was good. She listened. She stood still and listened. It has to be a little louder, she thought. She turned up the volume. Then she brushed off the bedspread, depositing the debris in a paper bag in the kitchen. Now the commentator was talking about unemployment. Statistics. She tried to memorize the statistics—fourteen point seven. Eight point three. "Anacin stops the pain three times faster," said the man on the radio.

She had to fold those clothes on the floor. Picking up the coat, she brushed it off, then carried it to the closet at arm's length. She folded her dress. I won't look for my panties, she thought, because they're gone. Gone. Rip. She heard the rip again. She turned up the radio. Discussion of weather, report on the rain last night. Her eyes closed. She saw a sheet of water come spiraling up from the highway. She turned down the radio and walked to her bed. She lay down.

Decide what must be done, Margaret, decide. The first thing was to contact the agency. It was not possible to go to work, not right now. Next, call Stanislas. She had to see him. Why? She just had to.

But these acts were difficult to execute. The phone by her bed seemed miles away. Sunlight now hurt her eyes. She knew it was possible to close the blinds. It was possible.

The sounds from the radio came to her as a hopeless jumble. Perhaps, she thought, I have lost the gift of language. Perhaps English is no longer my native tongue.

She began to move toward the phone, crawling across the bed as if it were a bramble patch. Each time part of her touched the bedspread, she felt pain. It wasn't the pain of an open wound; it was the pain of anticipation: what awful thing was about to happen?

Finally she placed a call to the office. She spoke quietly and without agitation. "I will not be in today." It was as simple as that. The person on the other end of the wire noted the statement, the name of its author, then hung up.

She dialed Stanislas. A tape recording asked her to briefly state her message. She said, "I would like to see you this afternoon."

For three hours she lay on her back on the bed. From time to time she raised a knee to her chest, then lowered it, as though testing the mechanical function of her parts. She tried to keep her eyes focused on the point where wall and ceiling joined. She tried to envision buildings she had seen, courtyards she had photographed, squares she had been enamored of during the past few years. If she lost the focus for an instant, memory of pain assaulted her, memory of penetration, a scalding sense of shame and futility and dirt.

The phone rang. Stanislas was returning her call. He did, in fact, have a cancellation. An hour was available at four. Could she be there? Yes, she could. There were no questions. An extra session always implied a crisis.

Her moods and responses began to change rapidly. One moment the light would blind her; the next she opened her eyes wide to absorb the sun. One moment she would be absolutely calm; the next, her leg muscles went into spasm. Sometimes the words coming from the radio were crystal clear and of great import; sometimes they lost all meaning.

She realized, after three hours, that she had to get up from the bed. Finally she made it, and stumbled into the kitchen. Now she had to find something to occupy herself. She took a grapefruit from the refrigerator and sat down at the table. Starting to peel it, she found the skin was difficult to separate. But she kept at it, pulling off piece after piece. When the task was completed, she gathered all the skin into a heap. Then she began to section the fruit. Then that was done.

I was raped, she thought. That is all that happened. I was raped just like other women are raped. She moved the pieces of grapefruit skin into a circle. She gathered them together again. Lifting up a grapefruit section, she bit into it. Sour, very sour. Margaret got up and walked to the refrigerator, opened the door, and looked for something else to do. No more grapefruits. She picked up a sponge and began to sponge the refrigerator. Front, top, left side and right side.

I was raped, she repeated to herself, and that is all that happened to me. But Margaret did not believe that. She believed that something else had happened.

The refrigerator was bright and clean now, the sunlight sparkling on its surface. And what will I do tomorrow? she thought. And what will I do the next day, now that I have been raped? She could find no answer. Could she stay in the apartment forever?

It is time to look in the mirror, she realized. It is time to do that. With slow, deliberate steps she walked to the mirror in the bedroom. She stood in front of the glass. What she saw was good. Hideous bruises on her hips and breasts. It looked like she had been marked with blue and black crayons, and here and there, with a sickening orange one.

These marks made her feel better, much better. They upheld the theory that she had only been raped. She turned and looked over her shoulder and saw the bruises along her back and buttocks. Then she faced the mirror again and moved close to it. Her upper lip was swollen.

She stood with her legs together, afraid to allow any space between her thighs. She trembled. What if he, the rapist, were at this moment studying his own bruises? What if he should come again? What if he lives down the block? Or around the corner? What if he wasn't yet through with her?

Margaret retreated from the mirror and turned off the radio. Until three-thirty in the afternoon she sat quite still on the edge of her bed. Then she dressed, left the apartment, and took a cab up to Stanislas.

She had arrived early and she waited, standing in the anteroom. Ordinarily she used the time to search for opening lines, gambits, ways to intrigue or irritate or provoke him. But now she searched for nothing.

Stanislas was sitting behind the desk as he always sat. She walked in calmly, sat down on the chair rather than the sofa, and smiled at him.

"How are you doing?" he said.

It was an intelligent question, she thought. It was the proper question.

"Quite well," she replied.

He cocked his head to one side in a gesture that said she could hardly be doing well and needing an emergency appointment at the same time.

For a moment she savored the mystery, enjoyed her refusal to commence. Then delay became impossible.

"I was raped." She looked at him, still smiling.

"I don't understand you."

She had expected some confusion at the start.

"I was raped."

Stanislas seemed to sigh, then leaned forward in his chair.

"Allegorically? Or in fact?"

"I was *raped!*" she screamed, and stood up, pulling up her dress to show him the bruise that snaked down one leg. Then, feeling ashamed, she sat down again.

"When did it happen?" His question was short and terse.

"Last night."

"Where?"

"In the park near the river."

"Did you report it to the police?"

"No."

"Why not?"

"I don't know. What's the difference?"

"What sort of man was he?"

"I don't know. He threw my coat over my head."

His interrogation was controlling her hysteria. He knew she would rather sit on his knee and be comforted. But now she was starting to relax.

"Do you often go to that park at night?"

"Not often. Sometimes."

"Did he say anything?"

"No."

"Did you go to work this morning?"

"No."

"Why not?"

"Why should I?"

"Will you go to work tomorrow?"

"I don't know."

Margaret wanted to tell him about the rape. She wanted to delineate the agony. But she just sat there answering questions. Then she stopped answering. Finally, she said, "Do you know what happened to me?"

Stanislas pursued his method.

"What did you do this morning?"

"I lay in bed."

"That's all?"

"That's all."

"How did you get here?"

"By cab."

"Why a cab?"

"I didn't want to walk."

"Do you feel dizzy?"

Margaret laughed. He was being evasive, she thought. He was being childish. He didn't want to talk about the issue.

"I felt very old," she said.

"Why old?"

"I don't know. But I felt very old. And sometimes the light hurt my eyes. Don't you want to know what happened to me?"

"I do know. You were raped."

"No. That is not really what happened to me."

"What then?"

"It's difficult to say."

"If you can feel it, you can say it."

"It's not difficult for you to say because you're not afraid."

"I'm afraid of many things."

"No, you're not afraid like I'm afraid. You're not caught like I'm caught."

"What was done to you?"

She let her eyes circle the room, searching for a single word.

"I was made futile. Yes, that's it. That's what was done to me. My own coat was thrown over my head and then someone took my body away from me."

"Try to be clearer."

"No, I don't have to be clearer. That's clear enough. It's not clear to you because you don't understand."

"I understand."

"Someone did to me what I couldn't tolerate. Someone isolated what was intolerable. And did it."

"The man probably never saw you before."

"Yes. I know that. But that makes it worse. Don't you see? There are millions of women in this city, and he chose me."

"Rape is a common occurrence."

"No. I was picked out."

Stanislas sat back and pondered the incipient paranoia of his patient.

Margaret looked down at her shoes. "He did not only rape me," she said almost inaudibly.

"What did he do?"

"It was more than . . ."

"What else did he do?"

"He touched me with his hand."

Now her eyes were closed. The memory was clear. A hand, like an animal, moving over her body.

"He touched me with his hand," she repeated.

"Your lip is swollen."

"I tried to fight through the coat."

"Why did you go to the park last night?"

"I couldn't sleep."

"Why to the park in the rain? It was raining."

"The park is beautiful in the rain. The bridge is beautiful. The highway is beautiful. The river is beautiful. So I went. I was listening to the radio. There was a country music song about a girl who killed herself by jumping in a river. So I went to a river."

"To kill yourself?"

"No. To mimic."

"It might be a good idea to call the police."

"No."

"Why not?"

"You already asked me that."

"Why don't you want to? It's the usual procedure."

"If I can't tell you what happened, I couldn't tell them."

"But you have told me what happened. You were raped."

"I couldn't scream. I couldn't say a word. The coat was in my face. My face. His hand moved over me and I couldn't say a word. He tore my clothes off and I couldn't say anything. I began to smell. It was all over my body. And then he threw me on the ground and I couldn't scream, and the coat was in my mouth. And then he . . . he . . . there was nothing I could do. And then he was gone. I was lying in the rain and the dirt and the leaves. They stuck to me. Leaves were on my bed this morning. I

could scream now. To let you know what happened. So you
don't forget."

"Why do you think I would forget?"

"What do you care? I'm a patient."

"Yes, you are my patient."

"You're trying to help me, isn't that the case? If you're trying
to help people, you can't share their pain."

"Are you in pain?"

"Yes! I'm in pain."

"Where?"

"Here," she said, pointing to her stomach, where the disgust
had knotted.

Then she shook her head slowly from side to side. "No, not
here—here." Her hands were between her legs.

"It will pass."

"Do I have your sacred promise?" she said bitterly.

He picked up a pencil and tapped the eraser end on his desk.
He welcomed her sarcasm. Years of experience had taught him
that sarcasm was a civilized response. People who are about to
kill themselves, or people who are about to step over the line,
never use sarcasm. Sarcasm belongs to the tired, the disabled,
the despairing, but these, of course, are still sane.

She was a strong woman, he realized. She had a resiliency
which always brought her back. An essential wisdom that surfaced, when things were bad, in sarcasm or wit.

"I think you should go home, go to sleep, go to work in the
morning, and be back for your regular session."

"I had other plans," she returned.

"What plans?"

"I plan to write a country song. It's about forcible entry. I
think I'll call it 'Red River Valley.'"

Stanislas laughed, loudly. He dropped his pencil on the desk.
He leaned forward, watching Margaret. The mask of fear was
back on her face and she was fighting for control. He laughed
again, until she began to smile.

Margaret then stood up, staring past him to the window. She
straightened her shoulders and then shrugged, as if to say all
would be well. She left.

It was already dark on the street. Margaret began to walk. Her usual apprehension of other people was gone. The worst had been done to her, the very worst. After eight blocks she realized she was hungry. She'd had nothing all day but a section of grapefruit.

She remembered a restaurant a few blocks south. Mama's. The place served good chopped sirloin platters, and, she recalled, good tomatoes.

Mama's was open. Small tables were covered with red checkered tablecloths and each had a fake kerosine lamp. She sat down at a table nearest the bar. A waiter approached, smiled a bit grimly, and put a menu on the table. She read it quickly as a formality and ordered the sirloin steak and a Bloody Mary.

When the drink came she sipped it, grimaced, and smiled. She lit a cigarette and sat there, in the near darkness, sipping the drink and smoking, the pain receding from her stomach and her crotch and her head.

Fifteen minutes passed with no sign of the chopped sirloin steak. Margaret ordered another drink. This one wasn't as good. The bartender had weakened the sauce.

Finally the food came. Margaret picked up her fork and made an incision. They had done it the right way—inside rare and outside charcoaled black. She threw a bit of salt on the meat and the sliced tomatoes. Now she tasted the meat. Perfect. She looked down at the perfect meal. A small rivulet of blood flowed from the center of the meat. "Red River Valley," she thought. What a nice thing it had been to make Stanislas laugh. He laughed so rarely. She cut another piece of meat and raised it to her mouth.

The fork stayed there, just outside her mouth. Then she lowered it back to the plate. She shifted in her chair. She picked up her napkin, folded it, then opened it and replaced it on her lap. She watched her waiter reading a newspaper at an empty table.

Stanislas's laugh. Margaret had heard it before. She knew she had heard it before. Her neck tightened abruptly.

She had heard that laugh last night, when she lay on the wet ground in the park.

Margaret fell over the table as though struck by cramps. There had to be some mistake. A laugh is nothing, a movement of the mouth and an extension of the vocal cords. Nothing.

The meat on her plate kept giving up its blood. Now there was a large red circle of it.

Stanislas had raped her. Stanislas had raped her. Stanislas had thrown the coat over her head. His hand had gone between her legs. Stanislas had thrown her down. It was Stanislas who had raped her.

She rose to her feet and looked around. The waiter approached. Margaret waved him away. There had to be a phone here. Somewhere. Yes, over near the bar. She walked to the pay phone. But who could she call? What could she say?

She returned to her table and sat down. She had made a mistake. The laugh was a coincidence. It was a sign of her unbalanced state. A bizarre response to the transference. It was a mistake, a lunacy, a little residue of her past.

Margaret tried to finish the meat but could eat no more. The waiter brought the check and she paid it. I'm scared to walk out on the street, she thought, and stayed in her seat. Not possible. Could not have been Stanislas. She would have known. Known the moment he touched her.

She signaled the waiter and ordered another Bloody Mary. When it came she stirred it in an agitated way, clockwise then counterclockwise.

No. It was his laugh. Certainly his laugh. He was the man who had laughed in the park. Stanislas. She fumbled for two dollar bills and left them by her drink. Then she was out on the street.

Stanislas loved her. Stanislas hated her. Stanislas! Stanislas raped her! She put her fingers into her mouth and pressed up against a window. She looked and saw nothing. The glass was cold on her cheek.

She had to go home. Which way was home? She turned from the window. It was that way. She walked, moving between people, taking chances with cars, ignoring red lights. Home was closer all the time. Stanislas raped her. He gave her that pain. But she loved Stanislas. How could his body cause her pain? She stopped and closed her eyes, remembering. She opened her eyes and walked home.

Margaret sat by the telephone. If she dialed his number, what was there to say? She thought this over for several hours.

The director lounged easily in his chair which sat along the paneled wall of the conference room. His eye met that of each physician who entered, to show that he appreciated the man's presence.

Helene was already seated in a straight-backed chair toward the rear of the room. It was to be a full-blown conference. Rarely called by the director, these were thereby infused with enough importance to warrant the attendance of virtually the entire professional staff.

She knew them all. They knew her. They had compared dossiers on patients, mapped out strategies, debated dosages, traded labels of madness.

Will Bunche was seated toward the front of the room. She could see his profile clearly, and the professional face he always wore at such gatherings.

The director was chatting with someone now, making small talk. He glanced down at the watch which sheathed his bony wrist. A man Helene had never seen before entered the room and walked quickly to the front. The director greeted him and shook his hand. He carried an old-fashioned leather briefcase with straps and eyed the assembled doctors nervously. Someone rose to help him off with his coat.

The director raised a hand for silence.

"I would like to thank all of you for coming here, for taking time out of a busy schedule. Hopefully, this meeting will be brief." He looked around, as if there might be some dissent. "Charles Moreno is here, and he will do most of the talking. As you know, Mr. Moreno is associate warden at the Attica State Prison."

The director sat down. There was no further introduction. Moreno rose and moved to the place his predecessor had been standing. He was short and thick set, with a bushy head of gray and white hair. He wore a conservative brown suit and a brown tie.

"I appreciate very much the time you are giving me, very much. We have a problem up at Attica—"

There was a muffled guffaw from the center of the room. The director looked around suspiciously.

Moreno, his face impassive, continued. "One of the problems we have up at Attica is the fact that inmates consider a tour in your hospital a form of rest and recreation. Currently, as you know, the length of the observation period for an inmate sent here is approximately four weeks. That space of time is long and attractive enough for inmates to feign psychosis."

He paused and looked around. The director was solemnly nodding his head. Helene stared at the paneled wall. The grain ran vertically and there were a few dark knots in the wood. She wondered if they were real or false.

"Your hospital is one of three which accepts Attica inmates for observation. But since yours is obviously the best, and by far the most progressive, I've come here to ask you a question. Is it possible to cut the observation time? Your director told me he wouldn't make a decision without the advice of the professional staff."

The director rose and let his eyes move over the assembled physicians, anxiously soliciting comments.

One of the newer staff members stood up, pushing back his seat with a loud scrape. "I don't see how you can cut the time required. In fact, time is the most essential element in an observation."

"I thought tests are the most essential element," said Moreno.

"No, time," corrected the other. "Because it's possible to feign psychosis very well for a short period, but much harder over a space of time. Ultimately, it becomes too uncomfortable. So he gives it up. Time is all."

The director was nodding his head in agreement. There were murmurs throughout the room as colleagues talked it over.

Helene was staring at the young psychiatrist who had just spoken. She wondered which of Bunche's categories he inhabited. Someone else made a suggestion concerning the psychiatric staff at the prison itself, which was minimal and not highly qualified. Helene leaned back in her chair. It was too warm in the room and she felt sweat on her back. Nothing, she knew, would be said here that might interest her. The common path of pursuit was overgrown.

Now, one after another, doctors rose to speak. Conversation grew spirited. A few challenged the entire Attica administration, and a few took themselves to task for lack of diagnostic tools.

Bunche had said nothing. He sat playing with his tie, flipping it up toward his chin and letting it fall.

They are babbling, she thought. They are talking about the control of madmen rather than the utilization of madmen, or the . . . She caught Bunche's eye for a moment. He had looked at her and then looked quickly away. Was he seeking proof that she had gone over? Should she feign interest in these proceedings? It didn't matter. She was in her land and they were in their land.

Moreno was talking again, outlining steps the Attica administration was taking to cut the incidence of feigned psychosis. His report elicited more comments from the doctors and soon the room was buzzing.

She wanted them all to be quiet again. She wanted them to look at the grain in the wood, the sutures in their past. A tremendous wave of contempt rolled through her, contempt for all of them. Here they were, sitting and talking, while their superiors were sequestered away, lulled into tranquillity by a handful of pills. These men were masters of chemical metabolism and cretins of the heart. She nearly giggled. The heart? Was she going to drag that into it? The heart. And the will.

It's too warm in here, she thought, too warm. She imagined the face of Moreno changing before their eyes into a massive green face, with foliage for hair. And what would the director say to that?

"Dr. Roth, would you like to make any comments? Surely you have had firsthand knowledge of these problems."

The director's smile was urging her to speak. She saw Bunche suddenly lean forward and run a hand through his hair.

"Dr. Roth," explained the director to Moreno, "is one of the few here with extensive psychoanalytic training and practice."

He leaned heavily on the word 'psychoanalytic.' Do they want me to stand up? she wondered. Moreno was staring at her. Do they want me to exhibit my Freudian past? To tie a ribbon around someone's penis?

She stayed seated. "Two thoughts come to mind. The first is simply that if a person can feign psychosis flawlessly, there is a very good chance that he is psychotic."

There was a pause.

"And the second?" urged the director.

"The second is that if a person feigns a psychotic act that is dangerous to himself, he is psychotic. The diagnosis will be different. He won't be the type of psychotic that he feigned, but another kind."

"You mean apples and oranges?" queried Moreno.

"I mean grapes and yams," she replied, and the room rocked with laughter.

She didn't want this laughter. She didn't want them to laugh *with* her. It was a bogus camaraderie. Bunche was not laughing.

The director moved on, briefly questioning those who had not thus far contributed. Then, suddenly, the conference was over. Moreno put on his coat, shook hands vigorously with the director, and was ushered out. No one waited for a formal dismissal. They casually hurried to their cars.

Helene looked up and saw that Bunche was still in his seat. He stared straight ahead. The empty chairs between them were scattered in all positions, some facing each other, or the wall, or jammed under the table. Was he going to say something? She didn't want him to say anything. But he sat there.

Finally, looking away from her, he said, "Are you sure you mean grapes and yams?"

"I've never liked the phrase 'apples and oranges' used to signify differences."

"And why not?"

Now he had turned to face her. His eyes were blank, academic.

"I don't know," she replied.

"But you think grapes and yams does the trick?"

The trick. The trick. Something was wrong here. She stood up and looked at the door. It was open.

"We are having a professional conversation, Dr. Roth, that is all."

"That is no longer possible."

"And why not?"

"Because, as you observed, I am in the fourth category."

"Ah, yes, the fourth category."

He pointed to a manila envelope lying on the floor against the leg of a chair. He retrieved it. Now they were only five feet apart. He held up the envelope.

"You see how sloppy those in the other three categories can be. They leave their papers all over."

"I can be sloppy, too."

"Can Ligur be sloppy?" he wondered.

She left the room and walked down the hall. When she heard him calling her name, she stopped.

"I apologize for that question," he said. "It was not professional."

She turned and smiled at him, professionally. He waved goodbye with the manila envelope and, professionally, smiled.

Helene vanished down the hallway. Bunche walked to the window and watched her cross the yard. She walked stiffly. She looked only at what was in front of her.

He sat down in a chair. Bunche was exhausted. During the conference he had been acutely conscious of her presence. When she had spoken, he felt a great ache. Grapes and yams. Grapes and yams. He hadn't seen a bunch of grapes since the summer and he hadn't seen a yam in years.

He tried to remember what had been said during the past hour, by Moreno, by all of them. He remembered nothing. Not a word. I am getting old, he thought. The great ache had exhausted him. He leaned back and closed his eyes. Helene.

Margaret sat in the smoking car of the 6:38 A.M. train to Cold Spring Harbor. The usual commuter flow, of course, is from Long Island to New York, so the entire eight-car train was sparsely populated.

The smoking car was new, but its windows were already filthy. As the train emerged from the tunnel in Queens, the sun was just rising on the horizon, and she saw the filth with great clarity. She had passed the night second by second, minute by minute, and hour by torturous hour. She had substituted analysis for fear. She had thought it out. First, there was the possibility that she had imagined the man she wanted to be raped by to have raped her. In that case the laugh, the identifying laugh, was an illusion, a hallucination, and there was no connection between her analyst's laugh and her rapist's laugh. Lying in bed, she moved from point to point, from possibility to possibility, with no interference but the very slow passage of time.

When she eventually reached the conclusion that Stanislas had raped her, that the laugh, no hallucination, was as indelible as a thumb print, she was faced with the monumental question, Why had Stanislas raped her? She was his for the asking. And how had he been able to face her later, with such calm, even if he knew she couldn't identify him? For a few moments she considered an alternate scenario. Stanislas had raped her as a therapeutic act. It was a seductive thesis but hardly convincing. How could rape be therapeutic? Could terror do anything but destroy? Did violence speak of anything but doom?

Night became morning and Margaret was alone with the fact that Stanislas had raped her. She had to share that fact with someone. She had to share it with his wife. Only his wife.

Therefore she was on the 6:38 to Cold Spring Harbor with Stanislas's address printed in pencil on a piece of paper crumpled into the pocket of her long dragoon's coat. She had, at first, considered calling. But the notion of imparting this information to his wife on the telephone made her uncomfortable. She had to go there, and present herself, and tell the story.

The train made a stop. Margaret looked out at the commuters on the other side of the tracks, waiting for trains bound for New York. They huddled in small groups about twenty yards apart, where they knew each car would stop.

At the next station a conductor took her ticket and told her that Cold Spring Harbor was next.

The train stopped again. Hurriedly, almost in a panic, she searched for her luggage. In a moment she realized there was no luggage. She had brought nothing.

It was an old wooden landing, cluttered with commuters. A small ticket office was boarded up, unused. She got in a cab that had just delivered a commuter and thrust her crumpled piece of paper in front of the driver.

The ride was short. The cab pulled up a long driveway, and she paid the fare and got out. She looked at the house. This was the house where Stanislas lived. She hadn't expected this kind of house. No, not at all.

Perhaps, she thought, no one is home. Perhaps his wife will shut the door in my face. Perhaps, perhaps . . . Twenty feet separated her from the doorbell. She shoved her hands into her pockets and walked to the door. She pressed the bell.

In less than a minute, the door opened a few inches. The chain was still attached inside.

"Mrs. Stanislas?" said Margaret.

"Yes."

"I'm Margaret Olsen. I came out here on the train from the city this morning. I want to speak to you about your husband."

Deirdre looked closely at the tall woman at her door. As an analyst's wife she had occasionally been accosted by patients in one way or another. She knew that the only intelligent response was to avoid contact at all costs. No conversation, no meeting, nothing.

"Are you a patient of my husband's?" she asked gently.

Margaret knew instantly which way they were going. She stepped back, searching for the right words. It was cold on the steps and somehow her feet had gotten wet. They throbbed with cold and dampness.

Oh, God, it's bad enough, Deirdre thought, surviving as Paul's wife—now I have to pick up his professional pieces.

"Are you a patient of my husband's?" she repeated, this time with no gentleness, but an edge of animosity.

"It is not what you think it is," said Margaret suddenly, and trying to smile.

Deirdre gave her a cold stare and released the chain on the door. It swung open. Margaret walked inside and followed Deirdre to the kitchen. Deirdre made a gesture that told her to sit down, and she did, grateful for the warmth of the house.

"I didn't know that trains run out here so early," Deirdre said, pouring coffee into a cup and bringing it to her.

Margaret said nothing. She drank the coffee slowly and searched her purse for a cigarette. On the table were two books of matches and an overflowing ashtray.

Deirdre leaned against the sink and smoked, watching the young woman trying to compose herself.

This can't be the woman he loves, Margaret thought. This can't be her. Not this pale, drawn, chain-smoking wreck in an old housecoat. Margaret didn't want to look at her. Maybe she ought to get up, excuse herself, and go right back to the train station.

"I'm sorry, I didn't get your name," said Deirdre.

"Margaret. Margaret Olsen," she said, still looking away from the other woman. "I've been a patient of your husband's for three years, or a little more."

Finally Margaret turned in her chair and faced Deirdre. She looked directly at her analyst's wife.

"Your husband did something . . . I think I have made a mistake."

Deirdre laughed and refilled the younger woman's cup.

"Well, if you've made a mistake, let me share it."

Margaret opened her coat and let it slide off her shoulders. Then she pushed a shoe from one foot with the other. She said nothing.

Deirdre was uncomfortable in the silence. "Do you live in the city?" she said.

"I live there and work there."

Margaret could not put the two of them together. She couldn't see them sharing a bed.

"Why have you come here?" Her voice was demanding.

"I want to tell you something about your husband."

Deirdre laughed. "I doubt that you can tell me anything I don't know."

"Paul Stanislas raped me."

There was nothing dramatic in her tone. Deirdre stared at Margaret. She tried to read her face. Were the words literal, a statement describing an actual event, or were they meant to signify something else? She sat down across the table from Margaret and lit another cigarette.

"You mean, of course, that after three years of analysis nothing good has happened to you. You mean that the process was, how shall I say, a bust."

"I mean Paul Stanislas raped me."

"Paul Stanislas raped you," Deirdre repeated, mimicking Margaret's inflection. Oh, God, she thought, mornings are bad enough and now I have crazies coming right to the door, crazies taking trains at dawn.

"Well, in that case you ought to call the police."

"I am not interested in talking to the police. I am interested in talking to you."

"Okay. Talk to me."

"Your husband raped me. I was alone in a park. He threw my coat over my head and raped me."

"You saw him?"

"Not really."

Deirdre laughed. "You mean you didn't see him?"

"I never saw his face."

"But it was Paul Stanislas?"

"It was."

"And how do you know that?"

"I heard the rapist laugh. And the next day I heard your husband laugh."

"You can't be serious."

"I am serious."

"A laugh? Tell me, was it a trilling laugh, or a guffaw? Or was it one of those deep-throated erotic laughs? You mean to say that you came out here to tell me that my husband raped you—a patient of his—and you recognized him by his laugh? What an astonishing story."

"I understand that you wish to protect your husband."

"Me? Protect Paul Stanislas? Listen to me. I'm married to him, but I don't protect him. In fact, I'm sure my view of him is far less complimentary than yours. But a rapist—no. Definitely not."

"I don't know why I came here. I really don't. All I wanted to do was tell someone, tell you—his wife."

Deirdre sat back and stared at Margaret.

"Well, you've told me, haven't you. Now you want me to believe it. And even if I believed it—which I don't—how would that help you? What would you want me to do?"

"I don't know."

"When did this . . . this thing happen?"

"Two nights ago."

"And you've seen Paul since then?"

"The following afternoon. When I heard his laugh."

"When you heard his laugh."

"It was not pretty."

"I'm aware that rape isn't pretty."

"I have not slept in two days. I cannot put this thing together. I can't understand it."

Deirdre stood up and walked to the window. She turned, sighed, and shrugged her shoulders.

"You come here with the most flimsy evidence. And you want my support?"

"No, not your support."

"What then? Sympathy? All right. You have that. All victims of rape have my sympathy."

"I don't want sympathy either."

Margaret was standing now, putting on her coat, slipping her foot into the shoe she had removed.

"Listen to me," Deirdre said wearily, "let me tell you something about marriage. I'm tired of being married to Paul Stanislas. Very tired. There is nothing he can do anymore that will excite me or interest me. But that is what happens to marriages. Isn't it? You're thrown into a cage with a man. Year in and year out. And finally, in spite of yourself, you know that man. You know him very well. And when you know someone, you find out . . . you find out what some very smart people have been saying for thousands of years: we are all ugly. Stanislas is ugly. I am ugly. Even you are ugly. But Stanislas did not rape you."

Margaret smiled at her. "Perhaps you are right."

"Where are you going now?"

"Back to New York."

"The train doesn't leave for another hour."

"I'll wait at the station."

Deirdre grabbed a coat from a closet, threw it around her, and picked up the car keys from a shelf over the sink. She opened the kitchen door and they walked to the car.

"Are you like all the other patients?" Deirdre asked, backing the car down the driveway and onto the road.

"Yes, like all of them. I love Paul Stanislas."

"And who does Paul Stanislas love?"

"Why you, of course."

Deirdre's hands tightened on the wheel. She had a child on the seat beside her. A child more naive than Emily, and ultimately, more dangerous.

"Do you really believe that?"

Margaret made no answer. She was in a haze. The lack of sleep was crawling through her, fastening on her shoulders, pushing her head down.

The car pulled up to the railroad station and Deirdre turned off the engine.

"We can wait here until the train comes," she said. "At least it's warm."

Margaret nodded and sank deeper into the front seat. She didn't want to think about Stanislas, or his wife, or rape. She wanted warmth and quiet.

"What will you do now?"

"Do?" she murmured.

"Yes. What will you do?"

"I don't know."

For an instant, Deirdre wanted to reach over and brush away the curl that had fallen over Margaret's eye. Instead she lit a cigarette and stared at the ramshackle station. How many hundreds of times during the last few years had she picked up Stanislas at this station? How many times had she driven him to it? How many thousands of times had she been here in this car with a coat thrown over her housedress?

She turned and wedged herself against the door for a clear, unimpeded look at her visitor. Margaret was almost asleep, her coat pulled around her face. Was she crazy? Had she really been raped? Why would she accuse Paul?

But, thought Deirdre, this woman has integrity. Yes, that was the word—integrity. And it oozed from her. If she hadn't been raped, then she had suffered something equally horrible. And she had suffered recently. The message was on her face.

Margaret straightened her back. Her eyes opened. For a moment she didn't know where she was. She tried to rub the exhaustion from her eyes.

"Is the train coming?" she wondered.

Deirdre nodded and pointed to the clock on the dashboard. "Fifteen more minutes."

Feeling a sudden and immense tenderness for her, Margaret reached over and covered Deirdre's hand with her own. Deirdre pulled away quickly. They sat in silence, watching the few commuters who had missed the earlier trains gather near the tracks, watching the dry leaves dance over the frozen ground.

"I could not live out here," said Margaret.

"Why not?"

"Look there."

Deirdre followed the direction of her hand. A single leaf was moving along the station landing.

"It would be too sad. Just too sad," said Margaret.

"The city is sadder."

"The city is life and death."

From the distance, like a sound from the past, a whistle blew. A low and long sound. Margaret shivered.

"In a minute or so," said Deirdre.

"I should not have come out here."

"No. You shouldn't have."

"Are you angry with me?"

"I don't know what to say. How to respond."

The whistle sounded once again, louder, entering the car, drowning them.

"Why did you put your hand on mine?" said Deirdre.

"I don't know."

"You must know."

"But I don't."

"Did you think we have a kind of suffering in common?"

"I don't know why."

"Do you think I have been raped by Stanislas? You mustn't think that. I'm his wife."

Suddenly, from the east, a massive steel locomotive came into view.

"Pull up the button. Then you can open the door."

Margaret stepped out of the car and stood by it until the train stopped. Then she thrust her head inside.

"He raped me. I swear it. You must know I wasn't lying."

Deirdre watched her turn and run to the train, climb the steps, and vanish inside. In three minutes the train pulled slowly out of the station. She started the car and drove into town. All the stores were now open. She sat parked in front of the candy store and smoked a cigarette. Margaret Olsen seemed to her profoundly connected to truth.

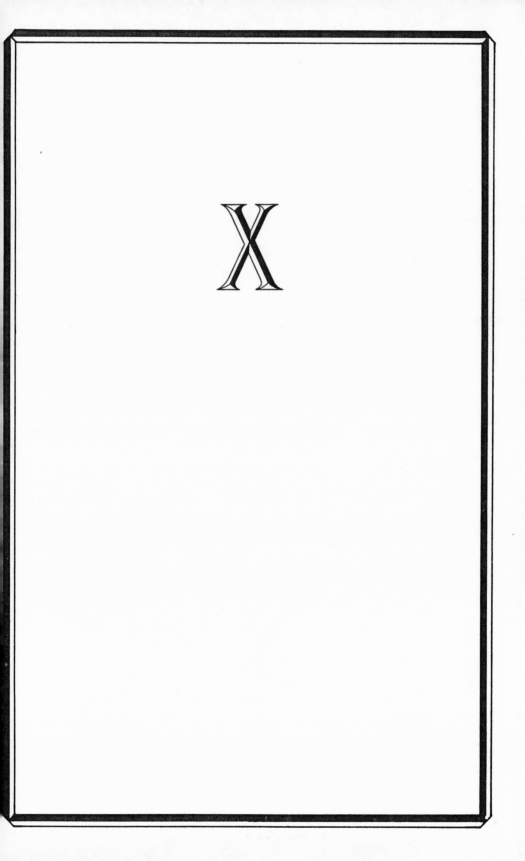

X

Stanislas was standing at the edge of the club pool. It was a luxury for him to have the afternoon off, a great luxury. He looked around. The pool was empty, as was the surrounding area. He stared down into the greenish water. Small ripples crested, then rose again. He was standing quite close to the edge. If he should move forward an inch, his toes would hang over the side.

I am beginning to live with fear, he thought, but that fear is like a wisp of smoke; grab at it and it flees, ignore it and one chokes.

From somewhere else in the club came a heavy clanging noise, as though one of the members had dropped a weight to the floor. Then silence again. The walls and windows were thick enough to shut out all the noise from the street.

He wished Emily was with him. They could swim together.

Stanislas wore an old-fashioned bathing suit that hung loosely around his thighs. It was time for him to set his goal, and he did so: ten laps.

He crouched, then flung himself at the water in a racing dive. The moment he hit, his arms began the crawl. When he reached the far side, he submerged and kicked off from the base of the pool. So it went for ten laps. Finishing the last, he submerged again and stayed under until he felt his chest constrict. Then he propelled himself to the surface, grasped the edge of the pool, and rolled onto the dry tiles.

He waited until he caught his breath, then collected the

sneakers which he had carefully placed against the wall. He laced them on and walked to the exercise room, still dripping.

Stanislas confronted the punching bag on its swivel. Slowly he began to make the bag dance, hitting it twice with each hand, bringing his fist across the body and then in the opposite direction. Left hand—back and forth. Right hand—back and forth. The bag was starting to hum.

Stanislas hit faster and faster, until he missed once and the rhythm was broken. The bag rocked crazily on its swivel. He steadied it and began to hit again.

Sweat was breaking through the thin film of water that still covered his body. Stanislas began to pick up each leg with each blow, to increase the thrust of his hands. Low and steady came the sounds of his punches—drum rolls, heartbeats, boots.

He wanted to close his eyes. He would do it when the rhythm was truly established. That was the goal: to close his eyes and let his hands proceed. But not yet, not yet. His hands moved faster, his legs strained to keep up with the speed. And then he shut his eyes. He kept them shut, without altering in space or time a single movement of his body.

He heard only the collisions of fist and leather. This was the way he had orchestrated his life, intellectually. A steady, progressive, climbing beat—from stupidity to knowledge, from barbarism to sophistication, from impotence to love. That was the way he had planned it; the only way it made sense.

Then his fist misjudged the distance and the beat was broken forever. The bag careened wildly on its swivel. Stanislas opened his eyes, stepped back, and watched it. He was breathing heavily and the sweat poured from his shoulders.

The leather bag slowed down, then stopped moving. The grains in the leather were visible. Stanislas stepped forward and put his hands along the seams. It was like holding a face that had suffered greatly. Like consoling a face that was beaten.

"Unlust," he whispered to himself, and then grinned. It was Freud's word for pain, used in his discussions of masochism.

As he held the leather face, he remembered, dimly, a book he had once wanted to write concerning the physical body. It had to do with a synthesis between Freud and the rhythmic utilization of the body. It had to do with the reasons that athletes suffer less from mental disorders than the rest of the population. It had to do with the athlete's ability to place the body into a certain beat, to run a certain distance, to take the body out of its usual time and send it into that other time. He let the leather bag fall back.

No, he remembered, it had been more. He had, at that time, thought it theoretically possible to diagnose a severe neurosis or psychosis, treat it psychoanalytically, and at the same time provide the patient with a physical goal. No, he recalled, it was something else. It was more. Much more.

There were mats along the wall and wooden rungs fastened to the wall for sit-ups. Stanislas lay down, thrust his feet under the rungs, clasped his hands behind his head, and brought his chest up to his knees. He did twenty-five, the last ten laboriously.

He stood up and jogged in place, shaking his hands loosely by his sides. Perhaps, he thought, his long dead theory was the reason why he had never gained any professional friendships, in spite of being a good classical analyst.

From the exercise room he went to the sauna. There were two factions in the club—those who liked the steam room and those who liked the sauna. Stanislas was with the latter. The sauna always sapped him of the will to exercise and gave him a feeling of almost joyous fatigue.

After the sauna he showered and returned to his locker to dress. He sat on the bench and stared at all the clothes he would have to put on. He felt very good. He could hear a man whistling in the next aisle. The tune was familiar, but he couldn't name it.

Stanislas got into his trousers. Then he leaned over and reached for a shoe.

On the inside of his arm, running along the bicep muscle, was a wicked bruise. Stanislas stared, then ran his finger around the perimeter of the bruise.

It couldn't have occurred while he was swimming, it wasn't that fresh. It was beginning to yellow around the edges. He looked at his left arm. There was a similar bruise just below the bicep.

Stanislas held both arms out in front of him. It astonished him that he had bruised himself so severely, and yet he didn't have any idea as to their source. The bruises were situated as though he had wrapped his arms around something heavy and tried to move it. Or as if he had attempted to wrestle a large German shepherd to the ground.

He touched the bruise on his right arm with his left hand. Just a slight bit of pain. He reversed the procedure. Again, nothing much. It could be a rash, he thought. No. They were bruises.

Suddenly his mood changed. The lighter, the car, the money, and now the bruises. A progression had emerged. First an insignificant object, then a moving vehicle, then a psychoanalytically pregnant symbol—and now this.

He kicked the half-retrieved shoe, sending it spiraling under the bench. Then he was bewildered by his act. He picked up the shoe, finished dressing, and returned to his office.

Sitting down behind his desk, he stared at the empty couch. In twenty-five minutes someone would be lying on it. He could not remember who was due, so he looked at the calendar for a name. Leaning back in the chair, he recalled the important elements of the last session and planned an approach for this one.

He realized that his left hand was inside his jacket and fingering the bruise through his shirt. He pulled his hand away quickly and sat forward in his chair.

> No pain, no palm;
> No thorn, no throne;
> No gall, no glory.

He recited the phrases out loud to the empty couch, not remembering where he had heard them or who had spoken them. He started another line. "No bruise, no . . ."

But he couldn't manage it. He tapped a pencil on the desk. No bruise, no butter. No bruise, no battle. No bruise, no brightness. None of them were any good. They didn't match the tone of the other lines. No bruise, no bronze.

He stood up. The impotence infuriated him. The pencil broke in his fingers. No bruise, no brine.

Perhaps he needed to see the bruises again. Perhaps their color, their shape, would give him a clue. Carefully he took off his jacket and hung it on the back of the chair. Then he rolled up his shirtsleeves and stared.

It was no use. He picked up a pencil and tried to break that one, also. He was too weak. A wave of tenderness infused him, and he realized he was being compassionate toward himself.

Helene Roth closed the ward doors behind her and began the long walk down the hall which led to the exit. It was midday and the hospital was reaching a peak of activity. White coated doctors and nurses moved with precision, holding dull gray envelopes or clipboards fastened with bright brass hardware.

There were other nonuniformed persons about, those shadowy officials who presided over the transfer of inmates from prison to hospital and back again. And there were those who represented the state's interest, making sure the insane were kept in and the sane kept out.

At midday the hospital's ambience altered. One seemed to be in a thriving business firm where deals were being consummated, where items of value were being planned, produced, and marketed. At midday, everyone was caught up in the activity. Even the psychotics reacted, reaching for their pills with dispatch, obeying orders, correcting their postures.

Helene was wearing low-heeled shoes and enjoyed the clickety-clack of her feet as she walked. She passed the receptionist's desk and started to open the glass door to the parking lot.

"Dr. Roth."

It was her name so she turned, wearing her professional smile, the one that is passed down from generation to generation of healers. The smile that will assure everyone that all is well, that comfort is manifestly desired, that the doctor was engaged in saving a limb or a life. Helene, like others, no longer thought about this smile. It was there; it happened automatically.

Standing twenty feet away from her was a woman. A woman younger than herself, dressed simply, in very good taste.

"Dr. Helene Roth?"

Helene cut the distance in half, folded her arms, and kept the same smile on her face.

"Yes, I am Dr. Roth."

The woman sat down on the visitors' sofa and fumbled for a cigarette. Then she fumbled with the match. Helene noticed that her purse was of the softest kid leather and fastened with a large gold clasp.

"May I speak with you for a moment?" asked the woman.

Helene moved closer, inclined her head solicitously and increased the intensity of her psychiatric smile. This might be a relative of a patient, she thought, or an agency official.

"You knew my husband. Paul Stanislas."

Helene stood there with her smile frozen.

"I'm his wife. Deirdre." Deirdre was staring at Helene. She looked exactly as Deirdre had known she would look: small, dark, competent. And, above all, wise. Deirdre always knew Paul had lied about the affair. It had not happened in order to further his career, as he had stated. But, until now, she hadn't known its reason. Now she knew. Wisdom. Paul had wanted Helene Roth's wisdom. Wisdom was what he had always desired. Not medical wisdom. The wisdom which, in the old days, had been a religious province.

For a moment she felt tender toward Paul, and felt pride in his pathetic quest.

"What can I do for you?" said Helene. Her mouth moved stiffly.

"My husband is in trouble."

"Everybody's husband is in trouble."

The phones behind the reception desk were now jangling. People hurried past the two women, pulling other people behind them, pulling packages.

"Can we go somewhere else?" wondered Deirdre.

"I am no longer in private practice," Helene said in a low voice. "Here is where I work."

"I need your help."

"I am no longer in private practice," she repeated.

Deirdre picked up her purse from the sofa and put it on her lap. It was a gesture which indicated that now there was an empty space on the sofa. The other woman could sit down. It was an invitation. Helene Roth thrust her hands into the pockets of her long white coat.

"Please," said Deirdre.

Helene sat down, her eyes focused on the large glass window.

"I've driven a long way and I'm very tired. But, you see, I didn't know where else to turn."

"Please be specific."

Deirdre caught just the slightest hint that English was not her original tongue. This woman came from a different time and a different place. It was the merest inflection.

"A woman patient accused my husband of rape."

"Is that what you have driven all this way to tell me?"

"My husband stole a car and didn't know he stole it."

"As you must know, men have peculiar relationships with motor vehicles."

"He finds things in his pockets, things he can't account for."

"Such as?"

"Money. Cigarette lighters."

"What are you trying to tell me?"

"I think Paul is going crazy."

Helene stared at her. "Crazy?"

Deirdre started to speak again but her voice caught. She had lost control in front of Helene Roth and would have to regain it. She played with her cigarette, moving the ashes around in the ashtray. She waited until she was sure she could speak.

"He is doing these things, but there is nothing, absolutely nothing in his manner to let you know. He's the same as he has always been. Exactly the same."

"Then let him seek competent help."

Deirdre came close to panic. There was something wrong with this woman. She wasn't understanding the problem.

"I don't think you understand me," said Deirdre.

"I heard what you said."

"Something awful is happening to Paul."

"So you have said."

"I need your help."

"Why mine?"

"Because I assume that you once loved him."

Helene turned her head and looked at the wife of Paul Stanislas. She took in every feature, every flaw of the woman's face.

"What was that you said?"

"I assume," Deirdre repeated slowly, "that you once loved him."

"I did."

"Then you must help him."

"Why must I?"

"Because you are probably the only person he will listen to."

"There is nothing I can do for your husband."

"All I want you to do is drive down with me. Just look at him. Talk to him. Maybe I'm wrong. Maybe everything's fine."

·"No."

"It will take only a few hours. Listen, I know there is some bitterness in these things, but—"

"What things?"

"Old love stories." Deirdre almost put her hand on Helene's, but remembering Margaret's gesture in the car, she stopped.

Helene engaged her psychiatric smile. "No."

"I have a daughter," said Deirdre, as though she hadn't heard the refusal, as though Helene might want to see Emily, too.

"How nice for you."

"Her name is Emily. She's exactly what you'd assume the child of an analyst would be. Smart. Very smart."

There was a noise behind the reception desk. Deirdre looked up to see a man being dragged, held under each arm by an attendant. She turned to Helene to shut out her horror.

"We can be there and back in a few hours."

"No."

"You're dealing with someone's life now!"

"Aren't we always?"

"Why won't you go with me? Why?"

"I prefer not to go."

"I won't beg you," said Deirdre, nearly in tears.

"But you are begging me."

Deirdre suddenly stood up. It had been a fool's errand. This small, competent, wise woman would do nothing for Paul.

"Do you love your husband?" said Helene.

Deirdre sat down again, feeling tired and weak.

"I don't know."

"Are you uncomfortable in this hospital?"

"Very."

"Well, you should be," Helene said gently. "This place is filled with psychotics. With a great many dangerous people. And this is where I live and work. I don't understand that other world. I don't want anything to do with it."

"Why did you ask if I loved Paul?"

"Just curious."

"If you won't see him, then tell me what to do."

"Seek competent help."

"What else? What can I do?"

"Speak to him. Tell him the things he has done. Point out the contradictions in his life."

"I don't know what you mean."

"Contradictions. He appears to be one thing, he acts otherwise. He acts in contradiction."

Deirdre, exhausted and confused, leaned back on the sofa and closed her eyes. The woman would not help. Something was wrong. She hadn't yet made the correct approach, said the proper word. What was it? She heard Helene Roth talking:

"You thought we shared something, didn't you? You thought we had been broken on the same wheel. Alas, they were different wheels. Only the turner was the same."

Deirdre opened her eyes to see Helene Roth standing, ready to leave.

Deirdre leaned forward. "Please," was all she could say.

"Point out the contradictions," Helene replied.

Deirdre left through the glass door. Helene watched her with no expression, watched her walk all the way to her car.

When Deirdre got into her car, she closed her eyes again. It was a long drive home. The trip was a wasted trip. Why had she come? To play the good wife, the loyal, concerned wife? She opened her eyes and looked in the mirror. No, it wasn't that. That long trip was all to see Helene Roth. To stare at her. To hear her talk.

She opened the glove compartment and pulled out maps, little flashlights, at least a dozen books of matches. She shoved it all back without looking at a map.

Is he really going mad? she wondered. Is he really doing things he's not aware of doing? Was that Margaret Olsen really telling the truth?

She would have to start the car and start driving. Sooner or later she would have to do that.

Helene Roth didn't like her, she thought. Or she did not like Helene Roth. More than Paul stood between them. Deirdre rolled down the window and the cold air swirled in at her.

I've made an ass of myself, she thought. I've acted in a manner designed to bring Helene Roth back to Paul. But for what? To help him? Or to throw a lie in his face?

She laughed, recalling her mention of Emily. The grieving wife asks help for her poor daughter. Deirdre flushed. She lit a cigarette. Cars were moving in and out of the parking area.

Perhaps, she speculated, it was the scene itself I wanted. The moment when they both stood in front of Paul's door, rang the bell . . . when he looked up and saw Helene Roth and his wife before him on a mission of mercy . . .

Or did she drive up to ask the woman one question: Who is Stanislas?

She started the engine and peered down at the heat gauge. It would take some minutes to warm up properly. Of course, she could leave it running and go back inside and find Helene Roth and start all over again. But she couldn't think of an opening line. She rolled up the window and inched the car out of the hospital grounds.

Helene Roth, after watching her visitor leave, had sat down on the sofa and folded her hands on her lap. For five minutes or so she didn't move. The hospital sounds came to her only dimly, like background music in a movie. Eventually she rose and walked outside. Instead of walking to her car she drifted along one side of the building. The air was cold, but she felt no chill.

Bits of paper blew across the ground, and a crushed paper cup was visible in one of the bushes. She thought of picking it up and depositing it in the nearest trash basket. But she backed off the path until her arm touched the building's wall. She turned quickly and stared up at the structure. She felt safe there, in the cold shadow of the wall.

And then it came. It came from her belly and moved up through her chest and neck and into her face. Her whole body was quivering. It was victory.

It was victory. It was triumph. It was beyond her dreams. There was no cold air. There was only this warm infusion of joy. She began to laugh, and then to cry, and then her laugh broke through the tears. She turned to the wall and pressed her face against it.

Stanislas was on the point of the spear. She had envisioned something, and proceeded to try it, and it had worked. Each aspect, each component, had beautifully worked. This was no longer a deserted woman's rage. It was no longer a romantic lark. It was no longer an affair with a madman. It was reality. She had broken into reality, with Stanislas on the point of the spear.

I must stop laughing, she thought. I must stop crying. I must . . . Suddenly she whirled around like a dancer, moved quickly to the crushed paper cup, plucked it from the bushes, and threw it high into the air.

Deirdre was keeping the car in the right-hand lane, going slowly. The more she drove the more furious she became—at everything. At the way she had spoken to Helene Roth, at Paul, at the car, at the road she was on. She lit a cigarette and threw the match out the half-inch open window. The wind blew the match back onto her lap. It left a dark smudge on her dress.

The car behind her honked because she was driving so slowly. She rapidly accelerated, then slowed down, accelerated and slowed down again. The car behind her shifted lanes.

She couldn't afford to connect with the world like this. When she got back to Cold Spring Harbor, she would say nothing. There was nothing to say. If, in fact, her husband was doing what the circumstantial evidence pointed to, one could only watch and wait.

She tossed the cigarette out the window and watched the flying orange sparks in the mirror.

Helene Roth heard a sound that came from above her. She stepped back a few feet from the wall and looked up. Through the grill she could make out a face, the face of a patient she had never seen before. The man was grimacing at her with his tongue hanging out, and his hands crawled over the inside of the grating. Helene smiled at him and then walked off.

She felt strong. She felt ecstatic. Her feet were crunching away a year, and then another year, and then another. She could see Paul Stanislas as he had been then, strong and intelligent and loving. She laughed out loud and stamped her foot down the way a flamenco dancer stamps the floor. She crushed out the year; she crushed his face and his betrayal.

Helene reached the end of the building. She cornered it and continued walking down the path. She was starting to feel the cold now and clasped her arms and laughed. Good, she thought, let the cold come. Let everything come. Nothing mattered, not anymore. She had performed an elaborate circumcision. Helene paused, astonished at the word—circumcision. But the task had been a cosmic circumcision of Paul Stanislas. An awesome operation, performed from a distance through an intermediary, and performed with the smallest hope of success. But it had succeeded.

She thought, I should drink a bottle of champagne. I should put on a beautiful dress and toast Ligur. Toast both of us.

The wind blew some leaves around her feet. She kneeled down and picked up a few and crumbled them in her hands. Paul's wife had asked for help. There was no help now for Stanislas. He was sleeping in the bed he had made. But what a subtle, deadly bed it was, with all the silk one could possibly desire and all the snakes one could tolerate.

She looked up at the entire side of the building, seeing the brick, the stone, the windows, the gratings, the shape and coherence of the whole. Helene Roth knew what she had done. There was a heart in that building, and in all buildings like it. This heart was not like other hearts. It did not concern itself with the pumping of blood or the construction of romantic fallacies.

It was a heart that expanded in human ignorance—the biology and mechanics that no one knew, the theories that never did match the reality, the therapies that consoled their creators. She had grasped this heart of madness and flung it to the world, in the person of a man called Stanislas.

Helene wondered when the euphoria would cease. She was al-

most delirious now with triumph. I must slow down, she
thought, I must gather my wits.

She came around to the front of the building again and could
see her car and started to walk toward it. Mid-stride she turned
and walked into the building, then to the rest room reserved for
the women staff. She threw cold water on her face. The triumph
was not dissipated.

Deirdre sat in the car and sipped coffee. The car was parked in
one of the small gas stations which lined the highway. The
coffee came from a machine and she thought it vile. But she
sipped and smoked and watched the cars whiz by.

Helene Roth was forcing herself back into Deirdre's head. She
knew the *why* of the affair—Paul's quest for wisdom—but she
couldn't understand just precisely how it had happened. She
could not, for instance, imagine that woman in bed with Paul.
But they had been there. They had made love. Perhaps they had
even loved each other.

Was the wisdom transferred in bed? Deirdre laughed out loud
and tossed the coffee cup out the window. It landed on a little
plot of grass with a trash basket sitting in the middle. She realized she could have put it there. Too late now.

How was the wisdom transferred?

There had been no transfer, of course. And that was why he
had terminated the affair. Deirdre thought back. She tried to remember why she had terminated affairs. It was usually a matter
of disgust. But Paul was too fastidious to feel disgust. He wouldn't
have one day looked at Helene, afterward, and felt disgust.

Paul making love to Helene Roth. Paul raping the Olsen girl.
What insurmountable absurdities!

Helene was standing in the hall, watching the midday thrust
slowly wear itself down. Doctors passed and greeted her warmly.
She nodded and returned the greetings. She had never before felt
so entirely at ease in the hospital, and at the same time, she had
never before felt so acutely the difference between herself and
the others.

The difference was now extreme. She existed in a different realm. A psychiatrist passed without noticing her. She greeted him loudly. The man turned, looked at Helene in astonishment, said hello with enthusiasm, and continued on his way.

The flush of victory was beginning to subside. Helene contemplated the ancient custom of casting a memorial coin in triumph. That would be appropriate, she thought, a single gold coin to commemorate the triumph. But who would be on the front of the coin and who would be on the back? Whose face would be hammered into gold?

"Good afternoon, Dr. Roth."

Helene turned and saw Will Bunche. He was walking quickly but steadily past her. She held out a hand, as if to stop him. He did stop, perplexed. He was trying to keep his professional demeanor intact. She pulled her hand down; it was a mistake. She had somehow wanted him to share her joy. That was not possible.

"Can I help you?" he asked.

"Not at all. Good afternoon, Dr. Bunche."

He looked at her, then walked on.

I cannot share this with anyone, she thought, but the man who is being destroyed or the man who is destroying him. And neither one is conversant with the truth. Which means I'm alone with the truth, the mystery, and this joy. But the joy was receding for not being shared.

"How have you been?"

Margaret stared at her analyst. The question seemed bizarre. It had no bearing on anything. The man who had raped her was asking with obvious but controlled concern about her condition.

"Much better."

"Did you report to the police?"

"No police."

"In other words, you have survived."

"I have survived."

"And you will survive other things as well."

"I suppose I will."

She watched him carefully. She watched the way he phrased

the questions, the way he sat, the way he moved, the way his face was set.

"Have you been to that park again?"

"No."

"Will you go again?"

"Someday."

He is either a consummate actor, she thought, or a madman. Those were the only two options. She wondered what he would say about her trip to Cold Spring Harbor, if she told him.

"And now you're back at work?"

"Yes, of course. I have to pay for these sessions."

She knew that she ought to stand up and accuse him. That was the thing to do. But it couldn't be done. She laughed inwardly at the thought of accusing her analyst of rape during an analytical session. Would it go down as resistance? But she had to do something. This nonsense couldn't continue. There he was, with his infernal questions, sitting behind his desk. Her rapist. Look for a sign, she told herself, look for a sign in his face or his hands, and keep looking until you find it.

"Tell me," she said, "what kind of people are rapists?"

"What kind do you think they are?"

"I think they're indistinguishable."

"Indistinguishable?"

"From anyone else. They look like you and me."

"What makes you think that?"

"I just feel it."

"And the man who raped you?"

"Perhaps he looked like Lupica. Perhaps he looked like you."

She watched his face even more closely now, leaning forward as if to stare at the carpet but really focusing on his mouth. There was no telltale twitch, not the slightest indication of distress.

"Why do men rape? Why don't they pay for it?"

"For the same reason men kill."

"Why do men kill?"

Stanislas turned up the palms of his hands. The gesture was his only answer.

Margaret closed her eyes. The session was going nowhere. She had meant the confrontation to take place. That she had decided. Now she could see the pair in the park. The woman in the long coat. Stanislas creeping up on her, throwing the coat over her head. The set of his face was the same as it was in this room. No lust, no violence appeared on his face. The lust and violence showed in the hand that ripped her panties. She saw him do it again, felt his hand.

"Why are your eyes closed?"

"I'm looking at something."

"What are you looking at?"

"Something you wouldn't like."

"What?"

"Your penis," she cried out savagely.

Stanislas, waiting, said nothing.

"I'm sorry," she said softly.

"About what?"

"About what I said."

"There's nothing to be sorry about in what you said. How do you mean, you were looking at it?"

He was back to his questions again, back to his incessant fixing of motive. He was trying to force her into it once more. This time she would break out.

"I was envisioning a line of penises, and they were all labeled," she said caustically.

He ignored this. "Your hand is shaking."

Margaret looked down at her right hand. He was right. It was trembling in her lap.

"Does it bother you if it trembles?" she asked.

Stanislas said nothing. She could tell he was anticipating an outburst from her. Well, there would be no outburst. She formulated the statement: I know who raped me. It was right on the edge of her lips. It was hanging there. She only had to let it fall. Why couldn't she do that?

No, she thought, watching him watch her. No, Stanislas is not an actor. He's a madman. I'm being treated by a madman. It was funny. Margaret nearly laughed.

"Were you ever prevented from saying something that you had to say?" she asked.

"Are you being prevented?"

"Yes. I can't say it."

"Are you sure?"

"I can't say it."

"Can you talk around it, or—"

"You don't understand."

"Can you draw it?"

"It deals with you."

"Then why can't you say it?"

He's mad, she thought, truly and irrevocably mad. Now he is asking to be named, to be identified. But he knew she wasn't capable of it.

Suddenly she wondered if she had been the first. There could have been others. He could have raped all his patients, year after year. And then what? After rape—what?

"Have you been seeing that man in your office?"

"You mean Edward Lupica?"

"Have you seen him?"

"No."

Did he know what she was thinking? Was he afraid? Was he trying to change her tack? No, that couldn't be. For even if he knew her thoughts, he wouldn't mind. He was mad. Dr. Stanislas was mad.

"I had a strange dream," she lied.

"Tell me."

"I was lying on the ground. It was springtime," she improvised. "I was wearing a strange dress I had never worn before. And suddenly, as I lay there, I saw a fire on the ground. The fire was creeping along the ground and approaching my strange dress. The dress caught fire and I felt a lot of pain and woke up."

"Why was the dress strange?"

"I don't know."

"The color?"

"I don't remember the color."

"And you'd never worn it before?"

"Never."

Margaret was proud of her skill at lying.

"Where did all this take place?"

"I don't know."

"You said you were lying on the ground. Was it in the city or the country?"

"The country. Definitely the country. I remember seeing trees in the distance."

"Was it familiar?"

"No."

"Are you sure? There was nothing recognizable? Was it the park where you were raped?"

"No."

"Where you grew up?"

"No."

She was enjoying the lie, playing it for all it was worth. What did it matter? The man was mad. He had raped her. He had violated her. He had lain on top of her. He had forced her legs apart. He had . . .

"Tell me about the fire you saw."

"It was like . . ."

"Like what?"

"Like a fuse."

"And you saw it coming?"

"Yes."

"But you didn't try to run."

"I just lay there."

"Why didn't you run?"

"I don't know."

"When you woke up, were you in a sweat?"

"I don't remember."

"When did you have the dream?"

"Last night."

There was silence then. He was gnawing on the dream, she knew, as he gnawed on all her dreams. But this one was all a lie.

There was little distance between them, but she felt no sense of intimacy. She had loved him. He had raped her. Why didn't she feel that she knew him?

Margaret leaned back and recalled his wife, chain-smoking in a housecoat in the kitchen. She could see them now, together, caught in their net.

She thought, I hate him. I hate him. I hate the madman who is trying to interpret my bogus dream. I hate the way he sits there and plucks pencils from the desk. I hate his arrogance. I hate his goals. I hate him.

"Tell me more about the dress."

"Now I remember. It was a dress made of beads. Orange beads and green beads. Beads of precious stone and beads of coal. And through it my nipples were visible. Yes, I remember that."

"What joined the beads?"

"Semen. Semen joined the beads."

He gave her a blank look. She returned it.

"Semen?"

"Yes, yes, yes!" she shouted. She was standing. His face suddenly frightened her. He would come for her again. He would hurt her. She fled stumbling against furniture and doors.

Helene Roth closed the door softly behind her. Ligur was already seated on the examining table. She leaned against the door and smiled at him. He was looking elsewhere. She thought, How can I tell him we have conquered? He doesn't care. He doesn't know what I'm doing. He doesn't think the way I think.

The ecstasy had gone. In its place was a constant buzz of joy which seemed to seep through each part of her. She walked over to Ligur and touched him briefly on the arm.

Each time the distance diminished between herself and Ligur, Paul Stanislas was closer to his deserved fate. She touched Ligur again, hurrying the fate along.

Now he looked at her with those strange, wholly frank eyes. Never inquisitive, never threatening, eyes as clear as the sky itself on the clearest June day. Eyes that hid nothing because they revealed nothing.

She had a strong desire to sing to him, to sing a kind of lullaby, or a marching song. If only she could do something to communicate her joy. She stifled the desire. What was joy to John Ligur? He was far beyond that.

She could see his legs beginning to move as they dangled over the edge of the table. In a slow rhythm, first one foot moving up, then the other. It was the slow stroke of a train cylinder.

She held out her hand, placing it almost in front of his eyes. He stared at it for a moment, then pushed it back a little with his own hand, then pulled it forward to his face again. Then he began to explore her hand with his fingers. She shivered under his touch. He turned her palm over and looked at it.

She held out her other hand. He stared at both of them.

For an instant she felt he was looking upon her hands as an offering. That was as it should be. Things and limbs should be offered to John Ligur. Now she understood how people used to worship Dionysus, how they would offer themselves, laughing. Yes, Dionysus was the laughing god, and Ligur was . . .

What was he? She brought her hands to her sides. What was he? A god. He was the god of the head, made flesh. He was the god of the night sent full-blown and psychotic into the golden day.

She felt good standing next to him. There was nothing else in the world she desired. Only this god.

"Yellow."

She heard the name of a color. The sound had come from Ligur in his colorless, godly voice.

"Yellow," Ligur said again.

"What do you want?" said Helene.

"Green," he said.

She was moving her hands in confusion.

"Black," said Ligur.

Yellow. Green. Black. What was he talking about? She wanted to know. She was paying homage to the god and had to know his every cryptic utterance.

"William," he said.

She thrust her hand into her pockets, searching for the photograph. Finding it, she put it in front of his eyes. He stared at the figure for minutes. He stared at it, then all at once looked at her. She felt herself shriveling. He lay down on the examining table.

Helene Roth undressed the young god, who moved not a muscle as each garment dropped off. She stepped back to look. He lay like a corpse on the table. She moved close to him.

She wondered at the absolute quietude of his body, the absolute serenity of every muscle. The comprehensive pattern of his veins made her weak. How was she to absorb his body, as she had already absorbed and used his power?

Her lips sought his naked stomach. She pressed down with them and felt his stomach muscles against her teeth. Then she backed off until she felt the wall behind her. It was better to look at him now, not to touch him. It was better to watch the body, the breath.

If only she could draw him. If only she could capture just what
he was, even though she hardly knew what he was. But even if
she could put him on drawing paper, well, so what? Bunche and
the others would never understand. They would simply say
she'd 'gone over.' But it was not to madness that she had
traversed. It was to a realm that only madness could enter. Psychosis was merely the veil. Draw it away and see John Ligur. No,
she hadn't gone over to the psychotics; she had harnessed herself
to one of them—to a god.

Then she thought, I am thinking like a child, like a very young
girl. But is that bad? Is it bad, finally, to worship? He had destroyed her scientific beliefs.

"So," she could hear Bunche say in his infinite sobriety,
"write a book." She laughed. Yes, a book was being written.
Written with the bones of Paul Stanislas. Yes, it was a lovely
book, a very, very old-fashioned book that said violence must
visit those who profane love. Tears suddenly came to her eyes.
For Paul had profaned, and broken her, and changed her, and
forced her to come to this place.

She moved back to Ligur's side. She took his genitals in her
hands. Ligur was still, always still. She stared down at his flesh
and knew she was holding Paul Stanislas's life and death in her
hands.

She wondered if she loved Ligur now. Did she love the man
who lay there? Or did she only love what was in her hands, that
strange bundle, that message sender?

As she leaned over and kissed his flesh, she felt with nearly
painful intensity the raw sense of worship. It wasn't the way she
used to worship Stanislas, that peculiar worship belonging to
love which annihilates intelligence. This was the ancient worship of a god. It was the worship of the god who brings corn to
starving people, of the fisher-king who brings fertility back to
the parched land, of the god who searched for and found the
grail.

I want that strength, she thought. I want that gift. I want
that . . . Her mouth slid over his erection. Now she was
suffused with her god, suffused with his power. She could do
what she wanted.

She grabbed his thighs and her nails dug deeply. He lay still.

Very still. Helene drew him into her. There was not enough.
There could never be enough. She left his body tense. Once more
she sucked on him. And then he cried out—but without a sound.
It was the seed of the god.

Stepping away from him, she was confused. The walls were
moving toward the center of the room. He was quite still. She
flung herself over him. Even so he did not move. She cradled his
head in her hands and kissed his eyes. He kept them open.

They remained like that for some minutes.

Finally Helene began to smoothe her hair, button her long
white coat. She helped Ligur to dress. When she opened the door,
doctor and patient walked down the hall toward the central
ward. An attendant met them and Ligur was transferred. He
shuffled off, the attendant walking two steps behind, watching.

Helene followed but stopped at the ward's entrance. Other inmates were wandering about. Ligur had put himself into a corner
and was making his obsessive hand motion.

One inmate was staring fixedly at her. Helene smiled. He took
a tentative step toward her, then changed his mind and made a
grotesque hop to the side. He waited a moment, then hopped
again. He hopped back and forth, looking at her, until his drug
took effect. Then he slowed down and looked at the floor.

Observing Ligur, Helene folded her arms. It is possible, she
thought, to watch him now for hours, to spin out a web of explanation. But what was there that could be explicated? She could
only participate. She watched his arm move with continuous
precision from point to point.

Leaving the god at last, she made her way to the coffee room.
No one else was there. She sat down at a table and circled the
cup with her hands. The coffee was bitter but hot. She realized
that her own past had been obliterated at the moment she
learned what was happening to Stanislas. She was no longer Helene Roth, psychiatrist. Not anymore. She was still a practitioner, but of what skill? What art?

A tall man in white coat entered the room. Helene stared at
him openly. It was some time before she realized he was a colleague. He poured a cup of coffee, sat down, and proceeded to
read a dossier.

She watched him carefully. He was thinking as he was reading. She could sense the relentless activity of his brain. This process was one they had all engaged in. A new inmate had arrived. His doctor obtains the dossier. He reads the record. Interviews are arranged. Medication would be prescribed. Most important of all, the diagnosis must be confirmed. Is the young man really a paranoid schizophrenic? Yes. No. Maybe.

She wondered if she had done all that for all these years. It seemed unbelievable. But she had, indeed. She had done it all.

Because she was staring at him so intently, her colleague looked up suddenly.

"I enjoyed your comments at that meeting," he said.

It took her a while to remember the meeting with the director and a man from Attica. She couldn't recall what she had said.

He tapped the dossier. "Some new luminary."

"Yes," she said, having to say something, "they keep coming."

She suddenly recalled the name of this doctor—Dwyer.

"Luminary. I like that word. Luminary," Dwyer chuckled.

What a strange world I used to inhabit, she thought, staring at him again. Then she wrenched away her eyes and looked down at the bitter coffee in her cup.

She was thinking, It is a quiet, lovely freedom I have now. The situation is clear. I have Ligur in silence. Stanislas is dying in silence. The doctors and their dossiers, the nurses and their pills in white paper cups. The days of light and the nights of darkness.

When she looked up, Dr. Dwyer was gone.

XI

There's too much heat in this house, thought Stanislas as he swung his legs over the side of the bed. The clock read two A.M. Deirdre was asleep, her body making the small, sharp movements that had always distinguished her sleep pattern. An occasional stifled moan would coincide with a brief jerk of her arm.

Stanislas left the bedroom, walked down the hall, and passed Emily's room. She, too, was fast asleep. The room was a shambles—small mountains of toys and books, clothes with sleeves turned inside out, and colored crayons strewn across the floor. Emily slept peacefully amid the chaos.

He went down to the kitchen and placed a glass under the faucet. Then he turned on the water and let it run. When he thought it cold enough he turned off the faucet, took the glass of water to the table, sat down, and drank it. Even the kitchen was too hot. The night light outside at the kitchen door threw a beam into the window and then down onto the floor. Stanislas slid a foot into the light, then pulled it back. He repeated this, faster and faster. Tired of the game, he finished the water and opened the kitchen door. A gush of cold air sailed into him. It was welcome after the heat of the house. Half an obscured moon was visible, and he stepped outside, closing the door, and stood staring up at the silvery presence. Soon he became aware that the gravel was digging into his bare feet.

Where were the sounds of tree limbs swaying, the crackling of branches? Where was the noise of the night? He heard nothing. He took a fistful of gravel and threw it as far as he could. At last he heard something. He took up another fistful, this time toss-

ing it directly above his head. Some of the stones bounced off
him as they came down, others missed him. Randomness. He
had dealt with that concept in his youth and despised it. While
other young men were contemplating suicide over love, or despair, or ennui, or whatever, only randomness had attracted him.
It attracted him to such an extent that eventually he decided to
destroy himself over it. If everything was truly random, there
was an absolute imperative to proceed with randomness. He
would go into a library and move quickly through the shelves,
making random selections from random categories. Then he
would read the books randomly and return them randomly. The
engagement with randomness had lasted perhaps a month.

He threw another fistful of gravel into the air. This time virtually the entire rain of pebbles fell on him. Stanislas laughed. And
then he began to feel cold. It was astonishing, he thought, how
adolescent fantasies returned. Here he was, nearly forty, flinging
pebbles up to the sky to capture their random patterns. A gust of
wind tore into his neck. Now he wanted some warmth. He
walked back into the house and up the stairs. As he climbed, he
realized that he wanted Deirdre. She was still sleeping. He sat
down on the bed and slipped a hand down the front of her nightgown. He watched her face.

The movement of her chest against his hand was not random.
Not random, the slow, steady beat of a living heart. He touched
her nipple. The heartbeat slowed, then quickened. Her eyes
opened. They stared at each other. Then he leaned forward and
kissed her forehead.

He felt confused. He wanted to make love to her but lacked all
passion.

"What do you want?" she whispered, her voice deep with
sleep.

"I don't know."

"But you always know what you want, Paul."

He moved his hand down onto her stomach. "I woke you. I'm
sorry."

She closed her eyes. He began to massage her softly, kneading
her flesh with his hands. She moaned a little. He reached her
neck and dug the stiffness out of its sinews with his fingers.

"What do you want?" she asked again.

Suddenly he pulled his hands away and thrust his face onto her stomach. Her arm circled his head, mother and child.

"But you've never wanted this," said Deirdre, cradling him with both arms.

He disengaged himself quickly. He no longer wanted her. He walked to the other side of the bed.

"I have to sleep," he said. "I'm tired."

Once again he crawled beneath the sheets, making sure no part of his body touched hers.

It would be nice, he thought, if one could mimic the rhythm of another heart. If one could lie in bed next to someone else and control the heartbeat so that the two beats were synchronized. And if one could induce sleep in the other . . . He felt himself becoming drowsy and turned to face Deirdre. Her shape began to blur, to grow soft and colorless . . .

Something was hurting him. Something was causing him pain. It was a sound. The sound of his name. Someone was calling his name.

He looked around and saw the bed. Deirdre was sitting up, calling his name. Where was he? He looked around again. It was his room. He was standing in the center of his room. Deirdre was abruptly next to him.

"Are you okay?" she said.

Stanislas said nothing. Something was in his hands. The pillow. He dropped it.

"You're sweating," said Deirdre.

Stanislas pushed her hand away.

"What happened?" he said at last.

"You were screaming. I heard you screaming and woke up. You were standing right here."

The sweat dropped from him in large drops. His shorts were transparent with dampness. He felt as if he had just performed an incredible feat of physical endurance.

He walked over to the bed and lay down. Deirdre sat just beside him. Although his body was exhausted, his head felt light and strong and as though it were dancing on top of his shoulders.

"A dream?" she said.

He didn't answer but looked at the questioner. Eventually he knew who she was. Deirdre, his wife.

Suddenly he was very cold and pulled up the covers.

"Yes, a dream," he said.

He remembered it now. A woman was walking with her back to him. He knew who she was, but he couldn't pronounce her name. The woman vanished and another woman took her place. Deirdre. Then Deirdre vanished and there was no one. He was on a flat, grassless plain with smooth pebbles all over. The pebbles were rust colored.

Hands began to pop out of the ground. A hand pushed through the pebbles, extended its fingers, flexed them, then vanished. Another hand, then another hand. He was able to identify each hand. One was Deirdre's. Then the other woman's hand. Then Deirdre's. And so on.

He began to try and grab each hand as it came up, before it vanished again in the ground. He grabbed and missed. Then he grabbed and caught, but the fingers slipped through his own. The hands appeared faster and faster, and he tried his best to catch each one.

Finally he caught a hand, firmly. He held on. He began to pull the hand out of the rust-colored pebbles. It became easier to pull, but was changing within his grasp. It was getting larger, and more powerful, and more masculine.

Then it became green. He was pulling a massive green hand from the ground. He tried to release it, but the hand was cemented to his own.

He recalled the dream with utter clarity.

"Did you see me leave the bed?" he asked Deirdre.

"No. When I woke you were there, in the center of the room with your pillow. Screaming."

She had lit a cigarette and was sitting hunched over on the bed.

"What time is it?"

"About three-thirty."

The green hand had just appeared again. It was somewhere in his brain. He was awake, but the hand appeared anyway. The sweat began to pour from him once more.

"What's wrong, Paul? What's the matter?"

Stanislas shook his head. He was not able to speak. The hand vanished. He turned and lay his face on the sheet.

"Can I get you something?"

"Some water."

She brought him a glass of water from the bathroom. He tried to sit up, but could not do so. He was much too weak. She helped him, holding the glass and supporting him with one arm.

"What's wrong?"

"A bad dream. Just a bad dream."

He sipped the water, which tasted foul and metallic. The notion of rust came to him, and then the rust-colored pebbles and then the massive green hand moving out of the ground. His own hand flew up in a gesture of self-protection, and the glass was knocked from Deirdre's grasp. She stood up quickly, holding her hands at her sides. She had no idea what to do.

"Leave me alone for a while."

She nodded and left the room. He could hear her steps down the hall stop short of the staircase.

I'll be all right in a moment, he thought. I'll be all right if I can just relax. He started to breathe deeply, forcing the air into his lungs and then exhaling through his mouth. He arched his back off the bed with each inhalation and then fell back down as he exhaled.

It was passing. He could actually feel the sweat dry up on his skin. It was passing. He sat up. Deirdre was standing in the doorway.

"It's okay," he said with a wan smile.

Tentatively, she entered the room and stood at the foot of the bed.

"Don't you know," he said, "that analysts eventually develop sleeping problems?"

She tried to laugh. He patted the bed and she sat down, looking carefully at her husband's ashen face. She thought, Perhaps this is the face that girl was talking about . . . and perhaps this is the man she was talking about.

"Keep the covers on," she cautioned.

He nodded and let her pull the covers up to his neck.

The ward was silent and dark. A few slivers of moonlight worked their way through the meshed windows, and a strong bulb near the exit penetrated several feet into the ward. The shift between midnight Saturday and eight A.M. Sunday was always understaffed. Sunday was visitors' day. Sunday was the day for church. And Saturday night was the focus of exhaustion in a long week, for staff and inmates alike.

So this particular eight-hour shift was a shift of great gentleness. The inmates, many of whom rarely slept, slept during this shift. Petty animosities between attendants dissolved. Those on duty felt a sense of solidarity with their fellows, and visits—to chat, to play cards—were common.

John Ligur, however, was not asleep. The little finger into which he had plunged the knife was throbbing. The wound had already healed, the bandages were off, but the finger throbbed. The pain didn't bother him. He was listening to the throbs, trying to ascertain a meaning from them.

Tears rolled down his face. He dipped the bad finger in the wetness. He was crying because he felt very weak. The drugs had made him weak. And if he remained weak, the task could not be accomplished. He put his wounded finger in his mouth and ground his teeth into the flesh until he tasted his own bone.

He felt something. It was pain. It did not reach his entire body. He ground his teeth again on the finger, and this time the feeling began to reach out, to thrust toward his toes and toward the muscles of his back. Pain suffused his body.

The Lord of heaven and earth, the Lord of little children and dying animals had spoken to him. The Lord had given him three words: *black, green, yellow*. The Lord had commanded him to speak them to the woman. She had not answered. The Lord of Light had given him three words. But she had not answered.

So John Ligur knew. He knew that before the sun was once again furious in the sky, before the day had warmth and dazzling color, she would come for him. She had been unveiled. She was their leader. She had forced them to hurt his body, to cause him the agony of confession.

He spat out blood. Then he removed his pajama bottoms. He placed his bleeding finger crosswise over his penis and felt the blood dripping on it.

His ears were beginning to hear things. There was a light tapping. There was a muffled cry. There was the movement of a bed on the floor.

Now he stood up. His eyes were beginning to see in the darkness. He could make out the whole ward. Silently, he moved to the very center and then stood there. Inmates slept on either side of him. He breathed in deeply.

There was a sound from the ceiling. He looked up. A round disk appeared to him. It was black. Then it was yellow. Then it was green. The disc was turning slowly. He stared into the disc and could see himself. There he was. He was beautiful. "That is me, that is me," he whispered.

The drug was leaving him. They were leaving him. He stood up on his toes and then turned, swinging his arms lightly as he turned.

The disc vanished from the ceiling. Ligur suddenly crouched, and hissed, and looked down the hall to the door which had already opened. Two attendants stood there, smoking. One was inside the ward. The other was just outside, in the vestibule.

Ligur's hands flew up to his face. His face was getting small. He could feel his features shrinking. He could feel his toes and his fingers and his penis growing smaller. But all the other parts of his body grew larger and more powerful. His feet were transformed into great steel pistons.

One attendant turned around and laughed. Ligur was standing fifteen feet away, naked from the waist down.

"You got a visitor," said the attendant in the vestibule.

"Get back to bed," said the other one to Ligur.

Ligur cocked his head to one side, almost like a dog trying to comprehend a command.

"You heard me. Get back to bed."

Ligur held out his hands, palms up. He was pleading, but not for himself.

He leaped, explosively, covering the space between them in an instant, jamming his foot into the open doorway. The attendant in the vestibule tried to slam the door shut. Ligur's naked foot took the impact.

Ligur felt an arm around his neck. He brushed it aside, picked up the attendant by his jacket lapels and slammed him against the edge of the steel door. The skull shattered.

The attendant in the vestibule started to run. Ligur was after him, grabbing him from behind and bringing him down. He jumped high into the air and brought both feet down onto the man's windpipe. There was a gurgling sound and then silence. Ligur walked along the hall, occassionally placing his face against the wall. The wall was cool and felt nice. Seeing two large glass doors, darkness beyond, he stopped. A man in uniform stood beside the doors.

He stepped out in front of the man, in the light. The guard stared; he was unable to speak. Ligur placed his hands on either side of the man's face. The man screamed. Ligur threw him aside, like a doll. The guard rolled along the floor until stopped by a sofa.

Ligur opened the doors and walked outside. He stood absolutely still and stared up at the sky. There was part of a moon. He turned around and stared at the big building. Then he broke into a trot and went through the open stone gate, crossed the highway, and plunged into the woods beyond.

He ran for twenty minutes, oblivious to the branches that whipped him, oblivious to the wind that howled about his ears.

He stopped by a large pond. The edges were fringed with ice. Staring down at the murky water, he dropped a foot into it. Carefully he put his other foot in and then began to walk deeper into the pond. The water covered his ankles, his knees, his waist. It was up to his neck. Then he was completely submerged. He stayed submerged until his breath ran out. He walked out of the pond following the exact path he had used to enter it.

His body began to shake. His teeth chattered. His insides cramped up, then relaxed, then cramped again. He stood motionless for an hour, his senses straining to apprehend the visitor who was to come. He had bathed, he had cleansed himself, he was out in the night, and there would be a message. Soon.

There was a sound behind him. Ligur stiffened but did not move. Another sound. Then silence. He turned slowly. Something scattered in the underbrush. Had the message been brought by a child? No.

He looked at the moon. He squatted, picking up a clump of earth and moss. He smeared it over his face.

Another hour passed. And then Ligur understood. The message was that there was no message. Instructions had already been given.

He left the pond at a trot and ran steadily through the night.

His head remained level, his eyes open, his arms swinging in counterpoint to his feet. His brought his knees high, and the moment one foot touched ground it was drawn up quickly, as though his feet were powered by a force outside his thighs.

He thought of nothing as he ran. Not of colors or shapes or pain or persons. He felt nothing as he ran. He remembered nothing as he ran.

Suddenly there was no more shrubbery. It had vanished. In front of his feet was a paved road. Ligur stopped running and reached out with one naked foot to touch the foreign surface. He looked up then and across the road. He saw a small house. In front of the house was a car.

He stared at the house and the car. His right hand began to make its habitual journey from genitals to shoulder to forehead.

Emily was beginning to get fidgety. Her mother and father were having coffee in the kitchen. She ran past them frequently with spurious requests.

"When?" she finally asked.

"Soon," her mother answered.

She stomped out of the kitchen, this time through the side door, and stood on the gravel drive. It was a beautiful morning, cold and sunny, but without a wind.

"How do you feel?" asked Deirdre when Emily had left.

"Fine, fine," Paul said quickly.

"You weren't fine last night."

"I've had this dream rather frequently in the past few weeks. Actually, not the same dream, but the same figure shows up in various guises."

"It's too bad we don't know any psychoanalysts," she said. "You could see one of them—concerning this dream, I mean."

Stanislas grinned and sipped his coffee. Deirdre's cigarette smoke wreathed his face.

She stared at him through the smoke, wondering what Helene Roth would be saying to him now if she were sitting across the breakfast table from him.

"Your daughter wants her outing," he said.

"If you're not up to it, Paul, forget it."

"What's a little twenty-mile waterside jaunt among broken bottles and rocks covered with oil scum?"

His face was blank now, even as he spoke. No, "blank" is not the correct word, she thought. Nor is "mask." Nor is "calm." He was . . . she couldn't put together a descriptive phrase. Last night when he had screamed, standing in the center of the room and crushing a pillow, his face had changed—it was both more human and more grotesque. But now his familiar expression was back.

"No," he reiterated, "we'll have our outing."

They both heard the noise outside. Emily was flinging pebbles against the kitchen door.

What was the face he had shown Helene Roth? Deirdre had thrown the entire trip upstate out of her mind, except for that woman. She could visualize her now. She could recall every feature of her face, and the way she had folded her arms across that long white coat.

"You're thinking, Deirdre."

"It's a bit early to do that."

"What are you thinking about?"

"Coffee."

"You lie." The blankness of his face creased into a smile.

"I was thinking about you."

"Surely there are better things to think about."

It was his usual modest response.

"You know, Paul, I've always wondered if your modesty is authentic."

"In other words, you think I'm arrogant, and only talk like a modest man."

"Something like that."

"Why would I do it?"

"Perhaps because you think professionals should appear to be modest."

He reached across the table and touched her hand. She pulled her own hand away quickly.

"But Freud taught us all to be modest."

Deirdre was thinking that he couldn't be what that girl said he was. He couldn't be a rapist. Not possible.

"Anytime you're ready," he said.

"Not yet. I'm not ready yet," she said forcefully.

Stanislas shrugged his shoulders. Emily came back into the kitchen, ran the water, stared at them grimly, then walked out.

"Paul, what are you capable of?"

"I don't understand your question."

"Are you capable of violence?"

"I suppose I've been violent in the past. Hasn't everyone?"

"I mean true violence."

"You mean evil."

"All right, evil."

"Well, as a child, I once murdered a salamander."

"A salamander?"

"Yes, those small lizards you used to see in the country, orange all over with brown spots."

"You murdered one?"

"I stepped on it."

Deirdre laughed. In all these years she had never known that he had once murdered a salamander.

"Why did you kill it?"

"I don't know."

"You just stepped on it?"

"Yes."

"Alone, or with friends?"

"Alone."

"Paul Stanislas, the salamander killer."

"That was my last exploration into murder."

"And were you punished?"

"No."

"Because no one knew?"

"No one knew."

"You never told anyone?"

"I told someone."

She knew whom he had told—Helene Roth. Obviously he would tell his training analyst.

"And what did she say?"

"I don't remember."

He did remember. Helene Roth had asked him if he remembered the sound of the murder. The sound. The sound.

"That's all the evil you ever did?"

Stanislas pressed the palms of his hands down on the table. Evil was not a term he was conversant with. Evil was not for psychoanalysts—not for those who wanted to comprehend patterns. It did exist, he knew, but it had to be gone beyond.

"I never tore the wings off flies."

An overwhelming sense of a lie lay on him suddenly. And then fear of the lie. He straightened. No, he had never torn the wings off a fly. But he had torn something living. A chill seemed to center in his hands. His hands felt as if they were about to move. They slid across the table. The wood turned into flesh. He remembered Helene Roth's body; how it used to feel, how it used to rise and fall to his touch.

"You mean like Emily."

"I don't think Emily does that."

"Nor do I," Deirdre assented.

"Are you going to question me all morning?"

"Poor little Paul, he doesn't like to be questioned about his past. All day long he questions other people, but he doesn't like to be interrogated by his wife."

"What's bothering you?"

"Bothering me?"

"Yes. Interrogation is not one of your standard specialties."

"You're the one who was screaming in the middle of the bedroom last night."

"So I was."

"And that means nothing to you?"

"It means I had a bad dream."

"What else do you have?"

I have holes in my behavior, he thought, almost humorously, and an old and trivial act keeps trickling through, and a woman keeps meandering in and out.

But he said: "I have syphilis, pellagra, tuberculosis, and cancer of the prostate."

Deirdre stood, walked to the window, and looked out at Emily. The child was throwing stones at the trees. It was futile, she realized, to continue the conversation. She didn't know what she was searching for.

"You aren't telling me something," he said quietly.

"What are you talking about?"

"All these questions. This interrogation. These little asides. You're after something."

"I have long since given up trying to get anything from you."

Stanislas was quickly by her side. He put his hands on her shoulders.

"I realize you may have cause to say that."

"I have all the cause in the world."

"What? What, for God's sake?"

"The wreckage of a marriage for one."

"Nothing is wrecked."

She stepped back and laughed in his face.

"It was wreckage last night when you touched me and I felt nothing. Absolutely nothing."

"Nothing is wrecked," he repeated stubbornly.

"What do you want as proof? Bloodied bodies hanging from the walls? The wreck is here. All around us, Paul. Every hour. Every minute. The ship is shot full of holes."

"You've read too many books."

"And you've seen too many patients."

"Do you feel anything now?"

She looked down and saw his hand resting on her breast.

"We're getting pathetic."

He kept his hand there.

"Stop it, Paul."

When they heard the door open, they stepped apart. Emily stomped in, devoid of pretense and patience.

"Soon it's going to be dark out."

"It's not even noon yet," said her mother.

"Soon it'll be dark and we'll never get to the water. And then it'll be another week before Daddy comes. And then next week it will rain."

"Her logic is impeccable," Deirdre said to Paul.

"Let's go now," he said.

Deirdre opened the refrigerator and took out a paper bag containing three sandwiches she'd made the night before. They all left the house and headed down the path to the water.

"I forgot my hat," exclaimed Paul.

"You don't wear a hat."

He held up a hand, requesting patience, and jogged back to the house. Five minutes later he was jogging down the path, hatless.

"I couldn't find it."

"You don't have one."

"I have a small green woolen cap. Don't you remember?"

Deirdre shrugged. The point wasn't worth an argument.

"Are we going to the jetty?" asked Emily.

Deirdre had no idea where they were going.

"Oh no," said Paul, "we're going past the jetty. We're going to a place on the Sound that you've never been to."

Emily's eyes filled with excitement. She had no more questions. Her father's reply had been dramatic, suffused with promise. They were truly going on an adventure.

But Deirdre had been on too many of these outings. There was never any adventure—only wet feet, bad colds, and a twisted ankle while stumbling over the rocks.

"We may not even be home tonight," said Emily happily, hopping from one foot to the other.

"O Zeus, most glorious, most great dark cloud-collector, dwelling in the air, may not the sun set, nor darkness come on, before I have laid prostrate Priam's hall, blazing, and consumed its gates with the hostile fire; and cut away Hector's coat of mail around his breast, split asunder with the brass; and around him may many comrades, prone in the dust, seize the earth with their teeth."

Will Bunche stood next to the kitchen table and read the passage over and over. He had translated that sentence early Sunday morning. Now, a few hours later, he was returning to the Iliadic prayer. He realized that the translation was terrible. The wording was too literal, the sentence structure was messed up, the whole balance of the thought was off center. He picked up a pencil and was about to change "seize" to "bite" when he became aware of the futility of piecemeal corrections. Tomorrow morning he would do it all over. What did it matter? There were years ahead of him.

He looked around the house. There was little to do here. There was little to do at the hospital on Sundays. But it was better to do nothing there. He scribbled a note for his wife and left the house.

As soon as he drove through the hospital gates, he knew that something was wrong. There were too many people around for a Sunday noon. These were not visitors; they were staff, officials, and police. He parked the car and walked to the main entrance.

The director was standing at the entrance, without a topcoat, talking with a man in a brown hat. He looked abstracted. He listened to the man but let his eyes wander over the grounds. The moment he saw Bunche, he excused himself and took Will's arm, as though about to utter a great confidence.

"It's very bad," said the director.

"What's bad?"

The director applied a little more pressure to his arm and Bunche realized that he wanted to walk. He allowed himself to be led.

"An inmate broke out last night. Two attendants were hurt. One very badly. He's critical."

Bunche simply nodded. There had been many escapes over the years, but the inmates were quickly caught. Psychotics were easily confused, their sense of direction was distorted. The escapees were often found days later, just outside the grounds, having lived on the contents of hospital garbage pails. Violence during an escape was not common. The escapees usually just wandered off to take their walk in the sun.

"It's very bad," the director repeated.

"One of my patients?"

"No," the director replied thoughtfully, "he wasn't one of yours. He belonged to Dr. Roth."

Bunche thought the word "belonged" was peculiar.

"Who was it?" he asked.

"I doubt if you know him, though we've had trouble with John Ligur before."

"Ligur," Bunche said softly.

"Ligur," the director concluded emphatically.

"Have you contacted Dr. Roth?"

"She's not home. Or perhaps she's already here somewhere."

Bunche nodded and walked into the building. He made his

way to the coffee room and found it very crowded. Police min-
gled with doctors. Attendants chatted with the janitorial staff.
Someone had bought a box of doughnuts and they were laid out
on napkins next to the coffee machine.

He looked carefully through the crowd and ticked the faces off
one by one. The face he wanted to see was not present. He left
the coffee room and sought out the wounded attendants. She
was not there, either. He leaned against a wall, trying to imagine
another location where she might be. He tried the ward itself
and asked the attendant on duty if Dr. Roth had arrived. Nega-
tive.

A nurse greeted him. Bunche was unable to respond. Fear
made his body unresponsive, restricted the movement of his
lungs. He felt old suddenly, incredibly old.

If she was not in the hospital, she would be at home. He got
into his car and drove there. His hands were barely touching the
wheel.

Helene Roth's car was not in its usual place in front of the
house. Bunche parked there and walked to the door. He rang the
buzzer. No answer. He looked inside the front window. Nothing
was amiss.

He rang again, and again there was no answer. He tried the
door, but it was locked. Slowly, he walked around the house to
the rear door. He tried the rear door. It was open.

Walking inside, he flicked on the kitchen light. There appeared to be no one at home. Two coffee cups were on the table,
each one in its place.

"Helene!" he called out.

Thinking he heard her, he turned around. On the kitchen wall
was a drawing. He gazed at it, impressed by the sheer immense
size. The drawing was of a massive man's head, done in green
crayon. The man had a full beard and distorted features, though
there was something classical about the whole. Bunche sat
down at the table and put his head in his hands for a moment,
gently massaging his eyes.

Now he looked again. This time he perceived the wonder and
magnificence of the drawing. Where had it come from? Who had
done it? Had she commissioned it since their last meeting?

The more he looked the more sure he was of the drawing's

greatness. But it was of an indefinable genre. It was both sophisticated and primitive. The scale was done expertly, but the perspective was faulty. The features were too large and too cramped for the whole.

He reminded himself that he had other things to do. He went through the house, searching for a clue to her whereabouts, looking for a note, a letter, a train schedule. There was nothing. Nothing at all. When he walked into the study, he heard a faint whirring, as if the radio had been left on. But he saw no radio.

Could she have left for the weekend? Did she have family or friends elsewhere? He didn't know. The strain had exhausted him and made him thirsty.

Back in the kitchen he picked up a coffee cup and turned on the faucet at the kitchen sink. He screamed. The coffee cup fell from his hand and shattered into pieces on the floor. He himself was falling, and threw out his arms to break the fall. He rolled over on the floor, the horror of what he had seen contracting his gut. He began to dry heave.

She was in the sink. Her head.

He rolled onto his back, fighting for breath. From the far wall the green man regarded him. He had to breathe, sooner or later, or die. He managed to rise to his knees and pull some air into his lungs. He fought the dizziness and stood up on his feet. Stumbling to the far wall, he slammed his open hand into the drawing. As he fell to the floor again, his hand smeared the lines of the mouth. He blacked out.

When he came to, he cried. From fear, because he was afraid to look again. From hate, because the killer could no longer claim immunity. And from the sudden withering of his life, because he had loved her.

He thought that he had to get out of the kitchen. He had to get away from the sink. He crawled into the study and lay in a heap on the rug.

What he had seen came back to him and he cried out like a dog in pain. Then it passed. He thought that if it came again, he would slit his throat.

He heard the humming now. He fixed on it. He started to hum along with it, blotting out everything else. The sound was very close to him now. He crawled with his eyes shut.

The sound was right here. He sat up in front of the tape deck. There was the sound. A blinking red light and a sound. And a tape cassette, yet to be inserted. It was the tape she had chosen before . . . She loved music. Music was what he needed now.

Will Bunche got up and with shaking hands put the tape into the machine.

No music came to him. Her voice came to him. He listened to the only part of her left to him. He listened, and he pulled himself up on her chair, and remembered the way she had sat in it, and he folded his arms across his chest and continued to listen.

When the tape ended he looked for another. He found them all stacked in chronological order. He played the earliest.

Sitting in the chair for five hours, he heard all the tapes. He placed a call to the director. Then he called the police. Then he lay back in the chair. He wanted, most of all, to survive. After that, he wanted to understand.

"Let's stop here," Deirdre said, with an air of exhausted finality. It seemed they had been walking for hours, crawling over rocks, sinking into half-frozen sand, dodging sea spray, climbing, crawling. Even Emily was beginning to lose her enthusiasm. She was starting to pout. But Stanislas was still fresh, bending over to identify a mollusk, skipping stones into the water, pointing out the peculiarities of a gull's flight to Emily.

"Can we stop here?" said Deirdre again.

Stanislas gave her an aggrieved look. Emily was noncommittal.

"Why not?" he said finally.

Deirdre looked for a dry place to sit down. She chose a saddle-shaped rock devoid of slime. Holding the paper bag on her lap, she took out three sandwiches and three oranges.

"Two roast beef, one egg salad."

Paul and Emily took the roast beef. Deirdre returned the egg salad sandwich to the paper bag. She didn't want to eat; she wanted to smoke.

"Are we near the place?" asked Emily.

"What place?" said Deirdre.

"The place Daddy told us about."

"I don't know. Ask him."

"Close, we're close," said Paul. "It's right around the bend."

The sun was very strong now, but the air was colder; there had been a drop in the temperature. Deirdre smoked happily, thankful for the rest. When Emily and Paul had finished their sandwiches, she offered the oranges. Emily took one.

"Don't you want one?" she asked Paul when he made no move to take the fruit.

"What is it?" he said.

Deirdre laughed. "It's a new species of breadfruit, imported from Australia and grown by convict labor."

Stanislas didn't laugh. His hand shot out and knocked the orange from her grasp. Her hand hurt where his had struck.

"What the hell is the matter with you?"

Emily giggled. Paul looked at the orange on the ground. He got up and walked over to it, picked it up, cradled it in the palm of his hand, and then took three quick steps and threw it out toward the water.

They all watched the brightly colored sphere rise toward the sun and then begin to drop.

"Are you happy now?" said Deirdre.

"He threw the orange," said Emily.

"Yes, your father threw the orange."

"He threw it far," Emily exulted.

Stanislas was not listening. He had walked away from them and was standing on a rock, balancing himself first on one leg and then on the other.

Now Stanislas was hopping lightly from rock to rock. Deirdre was amazed at his activity; the man hadn't slept all night.

He was hopping back to them now, and finally stood before them smiling. "Are we ready for the final jaunt?"

"Where to?"

"Just around the bend."

"I'm ready!" Emily shouted.

"I think I'll just stay put," Deirdre remarked.

"But it's a beautiful place. It's a cove. The water cuts deep into the shore and the rocks are large, like at the ocean. Yes, the rocks are large like ocean rocks. You can hear the Sound—whoosh. You can hear it, Deirdre."

Stanislas rarely made poetic utterances. She smiled at his enthusiasm but shook her head.

"So, just Emily and I."

They were off. Deirdre gathered together the orange peels and
ends of sandwiches and buried them under the sandy soil. It was
getting even colder now.

They walked together along the shore. Emily was very happy,
even though she was tired, because her father had taken her
hand. They were holding hands and walking slowly.

"It's just around the curve," said Paul.

Their pace increased, and then he stopped and pointed.

"Do you see it? See how it falls back on itself, like a stage."

Emily couldn't understand what he was talking about. She
saw a spit of indented land with large rocks against the tree line.
The sand was much cleaner. It was real sand. And the water did
make a bigger noise.

"There, we'll sit by those large rocks."

He dropped her hand and they picked up speed.

"Look here," he said, stopping suddenly.

There was a thick plant jutting straight out of the rocky sand.
It was greenish blue in color.

"I'm going to give you a bouquet, Emily."

He reached into his pocket and pulled out a beautiful, long
pair of scissors. Emily remembered them.

"Do you want some flowers?"

She laughed, nodding her head.

"Look at it, Emily. See how strong and ugly it is. If you look at
it for a long time, however, it turns beautiful."

Stanislas cut the plant at its base and handed it to his daughter. She held the gift tightly.   ·

"Let's go to those big rocks," he said.

Emily followed along after her father. He carried the scissors
loosely in his hand. She carried the plant.

They reached the rocks. It was a natural chamber. One could
see all around, and see the water, but there was a sense of securi-
ty and aloneness.

Stanislas sat down and Emily followed. She carefully placed
her plant on the ground and groomed it. He put the scissors
point down into the sand, thrusting them deep.

"It's nice here," he said.

He put an arm around Emily and kissed her forehead.

Emily snuggled closer. Her father had never kissed her like that before, never so long, and so nice. He usually kissed her with little pecks.

"Are you comfortable?"

She nodded happily, moving her body closer to him. He kissed her again, on the bridge of her nose.

"Are you cold?"

"No."

"We can stay here as long as you like."

He picked her up and placed her on his lap. His hand was combing her hair. His fingers were separating the salt-blown strands. She liked the way his hands felt on her head. She felt very safe and she felt very good.

"Do you like it here?"

She nodded.

"Look at the scissors," he said.

He reached over and plucked them from the sand.

"They're very sharp."

He put the scissors down and stood her up in front of him. His hands went under her arms.

She giggled. It was a game. She laughed again and felt warm all over.

"Look," he said, picking up the scissors and making a single cutting motion at the bottom of her dress.

She leaned against him, watching.

"We should not cut anymore," he whispered.

Then he smiled and kissed her neck. His mouth tickled.

"Lay down for a while, you must be tired."

She lay down. She could see him hovering over her. She was glad they were playing.

"What am I doing?" he asked.

She didn't know, but she could feel something moving lightly on the inside of her thigh.

"I'm drawing a face," he whispered.

"Is it my face?" she asked excitedly.

"No, not your face."

"Then whose?"

"Guess."

She couldn't guess. She couldn't guess at all.

"I'm going to erase the face so you'll never know."

He kissed the image away. She squirmed in the sand.

"Daddy," she whispered, "I want to stand up."

He kissed her again and Emily blinked her eyes. The sun was strong, pouring down onto the large black rocks that surrounded them. She wanted her bear with her now. She wanted her father to kiss the bear, too.

A sharp, loud sound suddenly exploded. They both froze. Then her father ran to the highest point of the rocks. They heard men yelling.

"Come over here," said Stanislas.

She went to the rock and he pulled her up. They looked out toward the shore line. Small figures were moving in their direction, one figure out in front of the others. There were other men descending from the tree line. All were shouting and waving their arms.

"They're coming this way," said Stanislas.

John Ligur was running smoothly, undisturbed by the shouting. From time to time, without breaking stride, he reached down for a handful of water and threw it on his face.

He laughed into the sun as he ran. He was going home now.

"He has no pants on," said Emily, frightened, to her father.

Seeing the man perched on the rock with the small girl beside him, Ligur stopped. He turned and saw the men coming closer, calling out to him in a language he no longer understood.

Fifty feet separated him from the man on the high rock. He shook the water and sand from his eyes and looked directly into the sun. It was high above the water, but its green rays, its slivers of truth, would annihilate all the men behind him. He smiled and bowed to the round green face.

Ligur thought, I must bring him a gift, something beautiful and good for himself.

He dug a shell out of the sand with his toes. Holding it high above his head, tears streaming from his eyes, he trotted ceremoniously toward Stanislas.

Something burst inside his body. He fell down, rolled in the sand, then climbed to his feet. His leg exploded at the knee. He fell to his other knee. Something red was coming out of him. He fell on his back in it. He raised the shell high, toward the man on the rock. Green and black and yellow were dancing in front of his eyes. Ligur looked beyond them. The man was still so far away. He pushed the shell along the sand.

"William," he whispered—and died.

XII

Deirdre opened the door. Standing on the doorstep was a tall, heavily built man. He wore a crushed brown hat and carried a manila envelope in his hand. Looking past him, she saw his car. It blocked the driveway.

"Yes?" she said abruptly. She was not in the mood for visitors. The events of the preceding day had exhausted her. She had never before been in the proximity of violent death. Hearing the shots, she had run to the cove. Emily and Paul were safe. But on the ground lay a dead man, half clothed, surrounded by police, lying in blood-soaked sand. No, she had no use for visitors.

"May I speak to Paul Stanislas?"

She was about to say that Paul was in New York, in his office. Actually, he was in the house.

"It's quite important," the stranger added. He looked weary, and his eyes drifted off behind her.

"I'm his wife. Precisely what do you want to see him about?"

"About his goddamn life!" His anger made her step back.

She tried to shut the door, but he easily kept it open with the heel of his hand.

"Call your husband. I'll wait here," he said softly.

Even more softly, he said, "Call him. I didn't mean to frighten you. There's nothing to be frightened of."

"Deirdre?"

She turned around and saw Paul standing in the hall, his hands thrust into the pockets of his bathrobe.

"I'm a colleague of Helene Roth," the man said, and walked into the house, shutting the door behind him.

Stanislas stepped forward and extended his hand, but Will
Bunche made an almost imperceptible gesture that said he
would not shake hands.

"Well, chairs, chairs. I've come a long way," he said sardonically, "so why don't we all sit down."

He sat down graciously in the largest chair. Deirdre didn't
want to sit down: The man was a messenger and he stank of
something bad. She would rather hear it standing.

Stanislas sat down, keeping his hands in his pockets. She
finally followed suit.

"Look what we have come to," said Bunche. "The confrontation at the end of a bad detective novel. Here we all are, all the
protagonists. Well, not quite all." Suddenly his eyes filled up
with tears.

"What do you want?" said Stanislas.

"Helene Roth is dead."

Stanislas looked down at his feet, then at Deirdre. Deirdre was
staring at Bunche.

"She was beheaded," said Bunche.

Stanislas closed his eyes.

"By that gentleman whose death you witnessed yesterday."

Now Deirdre watched her husband. He seemed becalmed.
This man Bunche had a suffocating effect on the room. He was
drawing all the air out of it.

"That gentleman's name was John Ligur. He was psychotic.
He was also a thief. He was also a rapist. And other things."

Stanislas took his hands from his pockets and folded them.

"You are none of those things, are you, Dr. Stanislas?"

"Exactly what do you want?" said Deirdre.

"I mean, you have never stolen, or assaulted, or raped, Dr.
Stanislas, have you?"

Without waiting for an answer, he opened the manila envelope and withdrew a piece of crumpled paper. He smiled.

"I've brought along a friend of yours," he said and held out the
paper.

Stanislas didn't move from his chair.

"Just a well-executed drawing. An aesthetic interlude in our
conversation. Among civilized people the visual arts are to be
supported, don't you think?"

Deirdre thought, He's waiting for us to take it from him.

Will Bunche fluttered the piece of paper in his hand. He looked first at Deirdre, then at Stanislas.

Deirdre was wondering why Paul didn't take it. She wanted him to.

Stanislas got up, took the paper, and returned to his chair. He looked at it.

"Is it a good likeness?" said Bunche.

Stanislas was staring at the drawing. It was a picture of the face of a man. A green man. It was a face he had seen many times. It was the face of his dreams.

"Paul, what is it?"

She walked over to him and looked at the drawing. She tried to take it from him gently, but his hand resisted.

"Let your husband have it," said Bunche. "It's a very old friend."

"Where did you get this?" asked Stanislas finally.

"It was a present from patient Ligur to Dr. Roth."

"I don't understand why you've come here."

"Disclosure. Disclosure." And then Bunche laughed. He had to laugh or he would strike that calm, professional, bathrobed man.

"Well, thank you for your trip." Stanislas crumpled the paper, put it in his pocket, and stood up, signaling an end to the interview.

"The fifty-minute hour isn't up."

"Then perhaps you'd better get to the point of your visit. Or did you come here just to tell me of Helene Roth's death and to point out a coincidence?"

"A coincidence?"

"This picture."

"But if it is only a coincidence, how do I know that the picture reflects a recurrent dream?"

"I don't know."

"You don't know." Bunche mimicked the calm, professional voice.

Deirdre lit a cigarette, and, no longer able to sit, she circled the room in an arc, watching the men, weak from the sense of danger. Danger was in the room.

"But are you desolate over Helene Roth's death?"

"I am sorry she is dead."

"Ah, yes. You and she once . . . together . . . a long time ago. She loved you, didn't she? And you loved her, didn't you?" He laughed derisively.

Stanislas looked at Deirdre. She smiled reassuringly.

"I can't stand the sight of you, Stanislas. I'm here out of obligation. I'm here because I discovered what was left of Helene Roth, because I want you to know what you are, because I want you to know how much she hated you, and because I want to tell you about that thing that comes in the night, large and green and hideous. I want to tell you that you're not what you think you are. And perhaps I want to pay a debt to her."

"I am not what I think I am," Stanislas repeated, amused.

"What I am about to tell you, I will tell you only once. Do you understand? Only once. Helene Roth acquired a patient. His name was John Ligur. She sensed something in him, or about him. She began to feel that he was not just another psychotic. Eventually they slept together. Perhaps she loved him. I don't know. One day he made that drawing for her, the one you have. A few days later she had a dream about a green man."

Bunche paused and looked up at the ceiling. Deirdre saw that his large frame was trembling. He took several deep breaths before he continued.

"She began to have the dream frequently, and after each dream she committed a petty crime. First shoplifting, then forgery. Therefore a theory came to her. The drawing Ligur had made was a depiction of his dream. Whenever there was sexual contact with Ligur, afterward, she dreamed of the green man. And after the dream she committed a crime, unconsciously. Then the theory became more elaborate. She realized that each crime she committed was a copy of one of Ligur's own crimes that he had committed before his incarceration.

"So she realized she would have to abandon their sexual encounters or she would eventually recapitulate his most violent crimes."

Bunche folded the empty manila envelope first in half and then in quarters. Deirdre observed his powerful hands.

"She realized that Ligur could not only transfer the visual images of his dream to a sexual partner, but could also force that partner to recapitulate his crimes. She had come face to face with a man who, knowingly or unknowingly, could manipulate another human being like a puppet, with libidinous strings.

"She could have stopped there. She should have stopped there, and stepped back a little and made Ligur into an object of study. But Helene Roth was not interested in the academic side of her profession. You see, she hated a man. Not all men. Just one single, solitary man. We know who that was, don't we, Dr. Stanislas?"

Stanislas was trying to envision, to recall, Helene Roth. He could do nothing. The image wouldn't come. No face appeared. It was all so long ago, so many years ago. Salt. Had sewn salt on her love. A classical allusion. *Carthage nihilio est.* Carthage is no more, and the Romans sewed salt so it would not rise again, but rise it did. *Helene Roth nihilio est.*

The woman Bunche was describing was not the woman he knew. The woman he knew was warm and wise, wise and warm.

Stanislas turned to look at Deirdre. She was pale, so very pale. This man and his story were making her pale. She was moving her hands in the air, unconsciously. And smoking. She was always smoking.

He heard Bunche talking again and turned back to listen.

"She did not stop. She continued. With an alteration. Whenever they made love, she showed him a picture. You see, Ligur fantasized that he had a brother. Helene showed him this little snapshot and told him it was his brother. His brother, William. She theorized that the green-man dream would be transferred to this William. And William, rather than she, would pursue Ligur's criminal career."

Will Bunche unfolded the manila envelope and got up. He walked around the room slowly, picking up bric-a-brac, sliding his hand over tables and bookshelves. A vase took his fancy; he held it up with both hands and smiled.

"Breakable?" he wondered.

"Don't listen to him anymore!" Deirdre exploded.

"Ah, but he wants to listen, doesn't he?" Bunche put the vase back on the table. "Unfortunately, Helene Roth's theory proved correct. The dream was transferred to William. William, of course, does not exist. He was a fantasy in Ligur's mind."

Bunche reached into his back pocket and pulled out his wallet. From the wallet he extracted a photograph. He walked across the room to Stanislas.

"Would you like to see what William looks like?"

Paul Stanislas took the proffered photograph and turned it right side up. He stared at himself. He looked down upon his own image. That was him, Stanislas. It was a snapshot he had given her years ago.

"Then something happened. I don't know what. Something happened between the two of them. One cannot predict the behavior of psychotics. Isn't that so, Dr. Stanislas? Ligur escaped and went to her house. There she died. And then John Ligur came here, in her car, to see William. To see you, Dr. Stanislas."

Bunche crossed the room again and sat down. Smiling at Stanislas, he said, "Perhaps he wanted to enter psychoanalysis."

Stanislas was suddenly very tired. The snapshot in his hand seemed to weigh fifty pounds. He couldn't take his eyes away from his image.

"What does all this mean?" he said finally.

"What does it mean, Dr. Stanislas? Surely you understand."

"I understand this. A woman with whom I had an affair many years ago begins to develop bizarre dream theories, centering around a psychotic she's sleeping with. For some reason she shows him a photograph of me. For some reason both she and I dream the same dream. That's all I understand. That's all."

Bunche was smiling.

"You're missing the point, Dr. Stanislas. You see, if you were dreaming the green-man dream, you were also recapitulating Ligur's crimes."

"You can't be serious."

"Quite serious."

Stanislas looked over at Deirdre, as if for support against this absurdity. She was blowing smoke rings at the ceiling.

"And this is your proof? A snapshot and a napkin with a drawing?"

"Not much evidence for a court of law. Granted. Even less when you know that the green man drawn on the napkin is a fair representation of a figure on many medieval churches. A sort of combination devil and vegetative god. Very little proof for a court of law. But I am neither judge nor jury, Dr. Stanislas. I'm a tired man who loved Helene Roth."

"Then I'm sorry she's dead. Truly sorry. But that is all I'm sorry about."

"You're not sorry about the rape?"

"What rape?"

"The woman you raped. I believe she's a patient of yours."

"Are you crazy?" Stanislas barked the words, then crossed the room and threw the snapshot and the drawing on the lap of his antagonist.

"Am I crazy?" Will Bunche asked Deirdre.

Deirdre was sitting on the sofa with her legs crossed and her arms folded.

"Why do you ask her?" said Stanislas.

"Because she can tell you if I'm crazy or not. She really can."

Stanislas caught a ring of truth in his words. He went to his wife. "What's he talking about?"

She had no idea what to say. She said nothing.

"Dr. Stanislas, your wife paid Helene Roth a visit. Their discussion centered around rape. The rape of a woman patient. And the theft of a car. And the sudden discovery of unexplained money and trinkets."

Stanislas was waiting for Deirdre to say something.

"That was how Helene Roth knew for a fact that her theories were right. She wanted to destroy you, Dr. Stanislas, and she almost did."

"Rape," Stanislas whispered.

"And maybe more. Maybe much more. John Ligur had a remarkable life in crime. He particularly liked little girls. He raped and murdered one. Possibly others."

Stanislas begged Deirdre with his eyes. She longed to reassure him, to find a comforting truth.

"Yes, maybe you went after a child, Stanislas."

There was sweat on Deirdre's forehead. Looking at Paul, she could see the thought in his mind: Emily.

Stanislas seemed to be withering, his mind trying to grasp something it could not tolerate. His bathrobe fell open.

Bunche once again held the snapshot and drawing out to Stanislas. "Are you sure you don't want these for your professional files?" When there was no response, he opened the manila envelope and dropped them inside as though they were contaminated.

"For your information, I tried to dissuade her. I knew nothing about her plan for your destruction and nothing about Ligur's peculiarities. But I sensed it would end poorly. And it did. The wrong ones were destroyed. A woman. A psychotic. But the good analyst survives—healthy. You are healthy, aren't you, Stanislas?"

"And you're happy now, aren't you? You've told your little tale," said Deirdre.

"I told what had to be told, Mrs. Stanislas."

"You told what you wanted to tell."

Stanislas held up a hand. He wanted silence. He wanted to balance himself. He knew what the man had said, but the knowledge was not fully absorbed yet. The man had said that he, Stanislas, had stolen, assaulted, raped.

"Yes, think about it, Doctor," said Bunche, and walked toward the door.

"Wait," Stanislas whispered.

Bunche turned. "On second thought, you want your photograph, I presume."

"I want to know what I should do."

"Think."

"Think," Stanislas repeated, as if the word was impenetrable.

Then he clenched his fists and brought them slowly against the sides of his head.

"I deserved it," he said softly. "I deserved destruction. I betrayed her. I betrayed our analysis. I wanted her. I wanted to make love to my teacher. I wanted her and I broke down every barrier. I broke it down—until she was no longer a training analyst . . . until it was just a man and a woman in an office."

"You fool," Bunche replied, "you utter, arrogant fool. It was Helene Roth who seduced you. It was she who was in control. It was she who led you to that betrayal. She. I loved Helene Roth, but I absolve her of nothing. Confess all you want. Confess every day. But never think it has any bearing on reality. You were a presumptuous innocent. She was stronger than you, Dr. Stanislas, simply because she was evil."

He paused, then said, "What an odd word, evil."

Then he spat out, "The waste of it all." And he was gone.

The door was left wide open. Deirdre heard the engine start and followed the gradually receding sound of the car. She closed the door. Not wanting to look at her husband now, she walked past him into the kitchen. She lit a cigarette and set up the coffeepot.

Stanislas was in the doorway, hunched over. That last revelation had numbed him. That last charge of presumptuous innocence. Crime, loss of will, guilt, the inability to understand were all ultimately bearable. But this was more. This meant Paul Stanislas was a simple puppet. There had been strings on his arms and legs. She had pulled him forward and backward. She had revealed him as pathetic. Carefully, incredulously, he moved his arms just a bit.

"Is it true?"

"True, true, true," she muttered, making sure each spoonful of coffee was level.

"What should I do?"

"Forget it."

"Forget it?" He slumped down on a chair.

"What do you want me to say?"

"I don't know."

"Then don't ask me for something that can't be given. I can't give you absolution. I can't give you wisdom. I can't even tell you what to do for the next twelve hours."

"You knew."

"I didn't know for sure. There were hints. There were innuendos. There was a lot of strangeness."

"I feel nothing. Can you understand? I feel nothing."

"Do you *want* to feel something, Paul?"

He got up and left the kitchen. She could hear his slow, steady step on the stairs.

Deirdre sipped her coffee and smoked her cigarette. There was
no reason to go upstairs now; she would see him later. Everything that could happen, had happened. She felt safe, in an odd
way. And she felt that something good just might appear.

Margaret looked up and saw Lupica enter the bar. Would he
remember where they had sat that last, disastrous time? He did
remember; he was walking toward her. There must be no mis-
haps, she thought. She had asked him to meet her there after
work. He had been reluctant. She had, to her own astonishment,
pressed the matter—and finally he agreed. Aggressiveness, she
had mused, is the last refuge of a woman.

Now they were making small talk about her new project and
drinking. The bar was noisy—glasses sliding along the rail,
dishes clattering, men laughing and cursing.

Margaret continually stole glances at his profile. Did he know
he was the sacrificial sexual lamb? Amusing thought, but true.
Margaret had decided that she would never, never see Paul Stanislas again. Not just because he was crazy. And not just because
he had raped her. But because she had realized, after the rape,
that she would have to die alone. And perhaps she would have to
live alone.

Margaret is a cripple, she had decided. And cripples were best
advised to maximize their crutches. Bit by bit, she would have to
make the crutches more bearable.

She wondered if Lupica knew what he was here for. There was
no way for her to tell.

She ordered another drink. He ordered another drink. The last
time he drank only beer, but now he was drinking vodka,
straight, with a little soda on the side. He must know, she
thought.

Do it now, she persuaded herself. Do it now. She swung her
leg to the side and let it rest against his. She felt him stiffen for
just a moment, then accept her leg.

"Vodka is a strange drink," he said.

"How so?" she heard herself say.

"So clear. And so tasteless."

"Clear as a bell."

He sipped from the shot glass until the vodka was half gone, then drained the rest in a gulp and ordered another.

"One day," he said, "I'll do a thesis on the relationship between vodka and the city—between vodka and, say, Warsaw. Yes, vodka and Warsaw."

Lupica was getting high. That's good, she thought. That was very good. She rubbed her leg against him now. This was harder; it required an act of will; she had to command her leg to rub against his.

I'm going to be raped again tonight, only this time it's my choice. It is my activity. My acceptance. She knew there was something odd and very wrong in her formulation.

"And your thesis?" he asked.

"Cleaning stores."

"Cleaning stores?"

"Have you ever noticed that cleaning stores are the last places in the city that have large clocks on the walls?"

"I didn't notice," he replied politely, and then laughed.

"It's true. They keep the city aware of time. All over the city, cleaning stores are helping people know the time."

Lupica's face became sober. He picked up his shot glass. "To the conspiracy of cleaning stores and their efforts on behalf of time," he toasted, and downed the vodka.

"Why don't we go?" said Margaret.

"Where?"

"With me."

"With you?"

"Yes, with me." She had pulled her leg away from his.

He looked at her, then looked down the long line of drinkers, then looked at himself in the mirror across the bar. Finally he looked at her image in the mirror.

"With you," he repeated softly.

The fear was crawling back into her. She pushed it down by remembering the rape. *That* was the fate worse than death; this was nothing.

"Now," she said.

He nodded and left some bills on the bar. They walked out onto the street.

"Where do you live?"

"Uptown," she said.

"How do we get there?"

"We can walk a bit, then take a bus."

So they walked together, not touching. Forty-five minutes later Lupica stood in her small apartment.

"Would you like some tea, or coffee?"

"No, nothing," he replied.

She was standing by the window. How would they proceed? There was no place even to undress, unless they undressed in the kitchen. How does one proceed? She knew nothing.

"How long have you lived here?" he asked.

"Awhile."

She turned and looked out the window, thinking, I am going to go through with it. I am going to proceed. I am going to hone my crutches. I am going to make love with Lupica.

"I like your apartment."

"Thank you."

There was no other way. Lupica was the way to purge Stanislas, to purge those years of incessant struggle for something unobtainable—to wash those years out, and the rape.

Don't look at him, she thought. Don't look at him now. Just proceed.

Margaret left the window and went to the bed. She carefully turned the bedspread down, exposing the clean white sheets. How old-fashioned, she thought, how unsubtle. She turned off the light. Only the kitchen light remained, and cast a dull glow into the room.

Each on opposite sides of the room, they undressed. Margaret carefully folded her clothes.

"I feel strange," said Lupica.

She didn't want to speak anymore and said nothing. He sat down on the far side of the bed. The half light made his features indistinguishable.

"No, not strange," he corrected. "I feel good."

He won't see the bruises, she thought. They won't be visible in this light. But they were still there—yellowing.

She lay down on the bed and waited. She felt him move a little closer.

"You know," he said, "I don't understand you."

"There's nothing to understand. Nothing at all. My name is Margaret Olsen."

"Why are you lying so still?"

"Because I'm frightened."

"Of what?"

"Of you."

"Then why did you bring me here?"

She turned on her side, away from him. It must go quickly, she thought, or it won't go at all. She felt his hand on her back. When she stiffened, he lowered it to her bottom.

"Are you really frightened of me?"

He pulled his hand away and lay motionless. She desperately wanted him not to stop. She turned and faced him. Lupica was gazing at the darkened ceiling. He was looking at the ceiling the way she used to look at Stanislas.

She thought, There's no other way, I'm going to kiss him. She kissed him, gently, on the shoulder. There was no taste to his skin. Then she sat up and kneeled beside him on the bed. She was thinking that she would have to do it herself.

She put her hand between his legs and they moved apart. She kneeled between his legs. There it was. Large and erect. This was the thing that had made her life a hell. She couldn't tolerate it, but it was for some reason necessary. Absurd. She touched Lupica's erect penis. It's flesh and blood only. There's no danger in it. But fear was rolling right over her. She slipped her hands under his genitals, feeling the weight of the man.

If I am strong, she thought, the fear will become desire, and the desire will become need, and the need will become health. Why doesn't he make a sound? Why doesn't he move?

She sat back, her hands on her thighs. Her eyes had become accustomed to the dark and she could see his face.

"Are you still afraid of me?" he whispered.

He sat up and brushed his lips against her breasts. Then he buried his face between them. She was thinking that people shouldn't be that close and started to pull away, but there was nowhere to go.

His hands were between her legs. She draped her arms over his shoulders.

She felt an odd tremor, not fear. His hands were making her

move from side to side, making her quiet and then active, making her nervous and then calm.

I won't give myself to him, she thought. I'm not mine to give.

"Lay back," she whispered.

He stared, uncomprehending.

"Lay back," she repeated.

He lay back, his fingers lingering on her thigh. She pushed them away. Wrapping a hand around his penis, she raised herself and squatted over him. Her hand guided it into herself. Slowly, very slowly. She leaned forward and balanced herself with her hands. Her face was twisted and her breath was quick and irregular.

When she felt him raise his body, she pushed down. She didn't want him doing that. The thing was alive inside her. It was alive. She closed her eyes, not wanting to look at him or recognize him. Suddenly she hated him. She hated the impalement. She hated the intimacy. She was being sent back and forth and up and down, and she hated it.

I'm going to rape *him*, she thought. I'm raping him now! And she felt a terrific exuberance. The rhythm continued and deepened. Her body was flushed and sweating. She felt her own power. Repetitively she ground her body down, then loosened so he could drive upward. Her nails raked his chest. Let it grow inside of me, she thought. Let it grow. He was making noises. He was falling apart, jerking from side to side. Then he made a sound like a dog's bark and slipped out of her.

Twisted, excited, exhausted, Margaret lay back. The light hurt her eyes, but there was no light.

"That was nice," said Lupica.

"Was it nice?"

Lupica cursed and got up off the bed, searching for his clothes. Margaret watched him dress.

"Do you have any coffee?"

"No," she lied.

"You offered me coffee before."

"I suppose I did."

"You want me to leave, don't you?"

"Do what you want to do."

"Well, see you at work."

"Yes. See you at work."

He was about to say something else but caught himself and said nothing. He made a gesture of futility with his hands and left.

Margaret got out of bed and lit a cigarette. After making a cup of tea, she carried it into the bedroom and drank it standing by the window.

She had triumphed. She had done what she'd never been able to do before. But knowing that it was done at Lupica's expense did much to blunt the sense of triumph. She felt a bit edgy. She felt a bit tired. But, after all, she had worked very hard to get the job done.

When she finished the tea, she got dressed and went downstairs. In five minutes she was at the steps to the little park. Hesitating only a moment, she walked down them purposefully and strolled around the entire park. Finally, she stood beside the water fountain and watched the river.

"What do you think I should do?"

"The great Paul Stanislas is soliciting advice?"

"I'm soliciting my wife's advice."

"Then do nothing. Do what I have always done—nothing."

The morning had slipped into afternoon, and the afternoon into evening, and the evening into night. And there they were—husband and wife.

"Look," he said.

Deirdre sat up in bed and looked at his proffered arms. On the inside of each was a fading bruise.

"I don't know which of my crimes they're affiliated with. Rape? Theft? Assault? Murder?"

"It's over."

"Isn't that amusing? I don't know which of my crimes they reflect."

He wore a new face, one she had never seen before. It combined confusion and perplexity.

"Listen, Deirdre. Listen. I have absolutely no sense of having acted. I have absolutely no—no . . ."

His voice trailed off. This inability to articulate was also new.

"It's over," she repeated.

"Yes, you keep saying that."

"That's what has to be said. It's over."

"And the victims?"

She laughed bitterly. "Since when have you been an ethical animal?"

"Always."

"In your judgment, maybe, but not in mine."

She realized instantly that the words were a mistake. If it was over, the whole thing was over—*had* to be over.

Stanislas got up off the bed, went into the bathroom, and rinsed his mouth with water. Then he went back into the bedroom and stood in front of the bed. He was still wearing the bathrobe in which he had greeted Will Bunche that morning.

"I know what happened," said Stanislas, "but I don't know why it happened, or how. It's as if a man gave me a book and said, 'Here is a history of Paul Stanislas. Read it.' So I read the book and discover that I'm a criminal. But there's absolutely no point of contact between the reader Stanislas and the Stanislas being described in the book. Do you understand that?"

"It's over, Paul."

"Do I go to the police and say, "Here I am, the criminal, Paul Stanislas. But I can give you no details. I can point out no victims. I can tell you nothing."

Deirdre wanted to bury her head under the pillow and listen to the hum of his voice, not his words, the way she used to listen as a child to her parents when they fought.

"She took my body away from me."

Astonished by his own remark, he paused. He was astonished to find himself attributing so much power to Helene Roth.

"She took my body away from me. But she left me everything else. She gave me a dream. Somehow, using a madman, she sent me a dream. I dreamed the dream. And because it had nothing to do with what I know about dreams, because there were no associations I could make with it, the dream overwhelmed me. Do you know, Deirdre, what it did? It absconded with my body. It became the causal agent in my actions. Who knows why humans act? Who knows what determines behavior? Whatever it is, this dream bypassed it. And blithely constructed a map for me. And the map was crime. But listen, Deirdre, listen. At the same time I was acting normally. I was in my office practicing the art and craft of analysis. I was jogging around a track. I was coming home on a train to see you and Emily . . . I was doing everything."

He was short of breath. His bathrobe had opened and Deirdre could see he was naked beneath it.

She understood what he was saying, and understood his turmoil. But she had little sympathy. He had done the same thing to her. Absconded with her body. She envisioned sea nymphs and journeys and some sort of intelligible existence, but all she really had was a child, some cigarettes, and intermittent sessions of loveless lovemaking.

"Paul, lie down."

He ignored this. His eyes were darting around the room, seeing nothing. His hand chopped at the air, accentuating his words.

"I swear to you that I have no knowledge of what I've done, no inkling, no consciousness of these things whatsoever. I saw Margaret Olsen and didn't know, after. I did not know. I even questioned her about the rape. Told her to go to the police. I did not know. It wasn't me—not this Paul Stanislas."

He sat down on the edge of the bed and suddenly discovering his open robe, pulled it shut.

"You don't have to swear to me, Paul. Even when I thought you were acting strangely, when you pulled up in that stolen car in the village, I never thought you were aware of what you were doing."

He reached across the bed and grabbed her arm.

"You don't understand what I'm saying! I'm faced with something that couldn't happen."

"It did happen, Paul. It *did happen*."

She lit a cigarette. He leaned back on the bed, saying nothing for several minutes. Deirdre smoked and waited. There was nothing she could do.

"You know what this means," he said finally.

"No, I don't."

"I'm going to have to suspend my practice for a while."

"If you feel you must, certainly."

"I must."

"And what will you do?"

"Just lie here." He laughed. It seemed a funny answer. Paul Stanislas never lolled in bed. He moved methodically from activity to activity. He saw what he had to do on a given day and he did it.

"If you're almost destroyed by an event, then you're obligated to understand it."

"What event?"

"That dream."

"To whom are you obligated?"

"I don't know."

"You're a Freudian to the end, aren't you, Paul? Always looking for origins."

"And what would your suggestion be?"

"Leave it, as it has left you."

"I almost killed. I was almost killed. I'm afraid I can't leave it."

"Then don't leave it."

She knew what he was going to do. He would go back to all those books and periodicals written in English and German. He would do what he had done when they met. He would read and think.

Suddenly he reached over and brushed her hair back, his fingers touching her neck.

"And what are you going to do, Deirdre?"

"Grind out this cigarette." She did so.

"You know what I mean."

"No. What do you mean?"

He shook his head and moved closer to her, his hands on her breasts. She tried, without great force, to push him away.

"Why did she hate me so much?" he whispered, nuzzling her neck.

"Because you thought you could heal."

"Can't I?"

"Ask your patients, not me."

"I healed you once, Deirdre, a long time ago."

He had pushed her down and his face was pressed against her breasts.

He remembered the texture of Helene's breasts. I am lying to my wife, he thought. I am lying to myself. I cannot disclose to my own wife the real seduction of Helene Roth. It was a crime that only initiates would understand. The transference is the host. And the debasement of the former equals the debasement of the latter. It was an academic crime to himself and a profound betrayal to Helene Roth. He was now paying for that distinction, he knew. If she were alive and he could confront her, he would ask: Why after all these years? Why couldn't you forgive? "Faust," she had called him that last time. "A whore," she had called him, also—"whoring for wisdom," she had said.

But all that was past, she knew. Helene Roth was dead and her legacy was himself as Humpty Dumpty. Her triumph was Paul Stanislas in three pieces—the sober analyst, the rapist, and the fallen Faust. Perhaps Deirdre was the glue who kept the pieces together.

"You never healed me!"

He sat up abruptly and opened his mouth as if to speak. He said nothing.

"Never," she repeated. "You heard me, Paul, never."

"We used to make love differently."

"I suppose we did. I suppose we did."

What was the use, she thought, of going over that old ground. What was the use of bringing to light a passion that had dissipated a long time ago.

"You have no allegiance," he asked, "to what used to be?"

"Neither allegiance nor obligation. But, then, I have never presumed to heal, and therefore I was not visited by your large, strange, greenish man."

He dropped his hand between her thighs. It lay there, unmoving.

"I wonder why the world is round," he said in a singsong voice. Then he laughed. "I used to say that as a child."

"It's flat."

"Flat?"

"With four sharp edges."

They could hear the wind beginning to blow outside.

"Are you going to leave me, Deirdre?"

Now she knew what his hand wanted: the sex of desperation.

"I don't know."

"Don't," he said simply.

He was touching her now, instinctually trying to elicit a response.

"Not now, Paul."

He took his hand away.

"Go to sleep," she said.

"I can't sleep."

His face was so young, so sure. He looked exactly the way he had looked when she had met him. And exactly the way he must have looked when he made love to Helene Roth.

"We can talk more in the morning," she said.

"It's not talk we need."

Eros was what he needed, she realized, and that was something she could no longer give him. She could spread her legs for him and go through the motions—but eros? No. It was laughable that while all his theories were crumbling, while his life was being changed, he needed eros. He needed the entire panoply of intimacy and touch and language.

"What you need I can't supply."

"All you have to supply is yourself."

Then he turned away from her. She let the darkness surround her. When were they burying Helene Roth? Or was she already in the ground? Who, now, hated Paul Stanislas? Was there any reason to hate or not to hate? He would try to understand for a month or so, and then he would return to his patients and all else would be forgotten. Or perhaps not forgotten, but placed into the limbo of the irrational.

She grimaced. Was it possible that ten years from now she would hate Stanislas? Truly and irrevocably hate him? And could she send a dream to destroy him?

Deirdre felt a profound respect for the late Helene Roth. She felt she had lost someone.

Paul was asleep and she could hear him breathing regularly.

His robe had fallen open. As long as she stayed with him, there would always be a third person in the bed. If not Helene, then the green man. If not the green man, then a victim—Margaret Olsen.

She switched on the light and leafed through a pile of books. Nothing interested her and she switched the light off.

He was dreaming now. She saw the movement of his eyes and his hands clenching and unclenching. All his dreams from now on would be good dreams because the visitor would not be in them. She tried to remember the name of Helene Roth's patient. It was John Somebody. Maybe one day she would go to bed with a psychotic. That would give her something else in common with Helene Roth. And then, also, she might develop that look of wisdom.

What a mess we're in, she thought. She stared at Paul, her mess-mate. She felt a long absent tenderness for him, and an obligation to shelter the dreaming analyst.

We used to sleep back to back, she remembered, one back in the contour of the other. Turning her back next to his, she mimicked the past. If she mimicked long enough, the past would return.

The panic had come again. Margaret was sitting by the phone, Stanislas's number engraved on her mind. It was her only tattoo. She picked up the phone and put a finger in the dial. Then she replaced the receiver. She took it up and dropped it again and again. The petty triumph felt good.

She looked at the clock. Twenty minutes before Lupica. He had again accepted her invitation, and she knew he would come. The bed was already turned down. She was wearing only a robe.

What do I want with my rapist? Why? When will the struggle cease?

She dialed the first three numbers, then hung up. How many cigarettes had she had today? She couldn't remember. She lit one. If the struggle doesn't diminish, I will go back to him.

And then what? More years of nothing. Perhaps another night in the park.

She dialed the first four numbers and hesitated. The receiver was warm in her hand. Put it down, put it down. She put it down.

Opening her robe, she saw beads of perspiration between her breasts. Was that in anticipation of Lupica? Or was it from dialing the magic number?

If he had not helped her, why did she need him?

She dialed five of the seven numbers. Then she dropped the phone as though it were burning her hand. When it stumbled off the base, she replaced it.

Soon Lupica would be lying on the turned-down bed. Soon they would be making love. Soon she would have to run the entire gamut of choices, the maze that led to one simple little act.

If you struggle long enough, you get a boil. It was a Maryland folk saying and it used to make everyone laugh. There were no boils on her body, only bruises and sweat.

She had made a vow not to mimic rape again with Lupica. She was going to lie on her back and accept his embraces and let him enter her, without fighting it. That was the plan.

Perhaps it was the distance that was making her sweat. How many nights of lovemaking would it take to break into the light? Or at least into a mundane gray dawn. Perhaps it was the distance. Time she did not have. Time was moving so swiftly, descending on her like a hawk.

She wanted to dial. She touched herself between her legs. The cigarette was burning the bed. She cursed, knocked it to the floor, and picked up the butt. She tested the floor with her foot for sparks.

Lying down on her back, she shut her eyes. It would be nice, for a little while, to go back to Maryland. To be there at the end of summer. Yes. The end of summer. That was the best time. It would be hot, but suddenly a breeze would come up, bearing an intimation of fall. The trees were so heavy then!

If you struggle enough, you get a boil.

She crushed the nonsense out of her memory. God, she felt bad. She sat up. She dialed the numbers slowly. I will not make an appointment. I will just speak to him. That's all.

She dialed the seventh number. Silence. Then the first ring. Margaret slammed down the phone. No. No. No.

The clock read four minutes before Lupica. Four years for Stanislas.

She looked down at her breasts. She was struggling. Where was the boil?

Lupica was now at the door. She left the bed and let him in. He looked timid, tentative.

"Hello," he said.

What an odd greeting—hello—from a man who is about to make love to her. How did Stanislas greet her all those years?

"Did you finally get some coffee?"

She smiled. He followed her into the kitchen and sat on a chair, watching her set up the coffeepot.

"You know, Margaret . . . it occurred to me that I'm being used."

"Does that disturb you?" She was fumbling with the lid.

"Not really."

"Everybody is used." She finally got the lid on and sat down across the table from him.

"But what am I being used *for?*" he laughed.

She couldn't formulate an answer. He wouldn't understand. How could she tell him about the sweat that was drenching her? He'd tell her to get a towel. He was smiling at her now, a gentle smile. There was no salvation in a smile.

They sat in a long space of silence.

"I've seen you worse," he said.

His hand lay in the middle of the table. When she understood why, she let her hand drop into his.

"I think," he said, "that we're having an affair because we both believe that everything is as bad as it seems—or worse."

She was calm now. She would wait for the boils to rise, and then lance them.

His hand closed around hers. He was strong, she thought. The grip grew tighter. For a moment she felt fear—from the past, from that rain-swept park.

Then she felt a tremendous surge of strength. Could it be joy? It was as if every part of her body had shed its weight. She started to laugh and brought both joined hands swiftly against her face. God, she thought, how good it is to laugh.

Will Bunche was sipping his cold coffee as the man entered the conference room. It took him a few minutes to put together the face and the name—Paul Stanislas.

His first reaction was hate, and then the hate dissolved into just a massive weariness. He placed the cup on the table and sat down behind it.

"You've come a long way, Dr. Stanislas."

Stanislas unbuttoned his overcoat. His face was lined with fatigue and the cool professional manner with which he greeted Bunche in Cold Spring Harbor was nowhere evident. He stared at Bunche, then his eyes roamed the conference room.

"Do you think I should be in one of the wards, here, Dr. Bunche?"

"As staff or inmate?"

"Inmate."

"Either way, your eventual destination doesn't interest me in the least."

There was no response from Stanislas. He sat down at the table, facing the older man, one hand supporting his head.

"Why did you come? There's nothing here for you."

A slow, sad grin crept over Stanislas's face.

"Nothing at all," Stanislas intoned.

"Helene Roth is dead and John Ligur is dead. You're alive. So what you do with your life now is your problem."

"I got into the car and drove. The car pointed here and I arrived here."

"You seem to be bearing up poorly."

Stanislas's hand cracked down on the wooden table, furiously, sending a cannon volley of sound around the room.

"And losing control," Bunche noted, realizing that there was nothing in the world he would like better than to have Paul Stanislas disintegrate. Then the sentiment shamed him. Stanislas was just another poor fool, after all.

"Did you come to me for wisdom, like you once came to Helene Roth?"

Stanislas didn't answer.

"Because if you did, you came to the wrong place. I am surrounded by hundreds of lunatics and they have never imparted one iota of wisdom to me. I haven't the faintest idea how you should order your life in the future. I really don't care whether you survive this ordeal or not. I'm not even interested in the crimes you committed while under the influence of—how shall we say—the psychotic called Ligur."

"I wanted to be with someone who knew Helene," said Stanislas, quickly and quietly.

Bunche leaned back. The memories were still raw and salted. He could hear her steps in the conference room, always sure, always firm. He could hear the precise tone of her voice, that tiny, obscure accent breaking out of the modulated tone. The hate for Stanislas came back and almost choked him, then receded again.

"Well, I knew her," he said, "so here you are. What more?"

"What did she say about me?"

"Say?"

"What did she say?"

Bunche stood up and walked to the window. He felt an odd tightening in his neck and he rolled his head on his shoulders to alleviate it.

"Quite a lot," he lied.

"Tell me." The voice was ardent, almost desperate.

Bunche walked back to the table, emptied the cup, and then plucked his coat off the rack.

"Come with me," he said.

They left the hospital grounds in their own cars, one following the other, and drove until they reached a small house nestled off the highway.

Bunche entered the house. Stanislas followed. The two men walked swiftly and carefully past furniture that was draped with sheets. The house smelled musty, and the heat was turned off.

"Here, Dr. Stanislas, here is what Helene Roth thought of you."

Stanislas entered the kitchen and followed Bunche's pointing finger.

On the wall was his dream. It was there—on the wall, his dream.

Brilliant, focused, lucid, clear, as large and as powerful and as deviant as his actions. As evil as his actions.

He walked closer. The color made his head spin. He reached out with one hand as if to touch the figure—but then pulled back.

"The real thing, Dr. Stanislas, right? Not like that little drawing I showed you."

Stanislas stepped back.

"What do you feel, Dr. Stanislas? Like Schliemann finding the mask of Agamemnon at Troy?"

Bunche laughed, walked to the sink, wet a sponge, and splattered it again and again on the wall until the figure lost shape and potency and some brilliant green dropped to the kitchen floor a dull bronze.

"That is your only option, Dr. Stanislas. To squeeze yourself out and start again. I repeat. That is your only option."

"My only option," Stanislas whispered, his eyes on the brown stain now at the foot of the wall.

"Do you like my notion of treatment, Dr. Stanislas? Now, why don't you go home and practice psychoanalysis."

Stanislas stared at the older man for a long time. The advice was intelligent. Go home and practice psychoanalysis. What else was there? What else could be done? In what other area could redemption be found? He felt an absolute camaraderie with Bunche. He felt that they had both survived Helene Roth, and in that survival a friendship had been forged. But there was nothing that could be said.

Stanislas walked slowly out of the house. Will Bunche heard the car start and drive off.

He sat down on a kitchen chair, the dripping sponge in his hand. He squeezed it again and again until it was very dry. Then he drove back to the psychotics.

King, Frank
Night vision.